J.M. O'NEILL

J.M. O'Neill was born in Limerick, where his father was the city's postmaster, and educated at the Augustinian College, Dungarvan, Co. Waterford. In the early 1950s he worked as a bank official in Ireland, England, Nigeria and Ghana (the Gold Coast). After working in the building trade in London and the Home Counties for over ten years, in 1967 he became tenant landlord of the Duke of Wellington in the Ball's Pond Road in London. There he established the Sugawn Theatre and the Sugawn Kitchen, a well-known venue for folk music. In 1980 he retired from the licensed trade and settled in Hornsey, where he devoted himself to writing. His plays include *Now You See Him, Now You Don't, Diehards* and *God is Dead on the Ball's Pond Road*. But it is for his novels that he is best known: *Open Cut* (1986), *Duffy is Dead* (1987), *Canon Bang Bang* (1989), *Commissar Connell* (1992), *Bennett & Company* (1998) and *Rellighan, Undertaker* (1999). *Bennett & Company* won the Kerry Ingredients Book of the Year award in 1999. He lived in Kilkee, Co. Clare for several years until his death in May 1999.

RELLIGHAN, UNDERTAKER
A Winter's Tale

Also by J. M. O'Neill

Novels
Open Cut
Duffy Is Dead
Canon Bang Bang
Commissar Connell
Bennett & Company

Plays
God Is Dead on Ball's Pond Road
Diehards
Now You See Him, Now You Don't

J. M. O'NEILL

RELLIGHAN UNDERTAKER

BRANDON

A Brandon Paperback

This edition published in 1999 by
Brandon
an imprint of Mount Eagle Publications Ltd.
Dingle, Co. Kerry, Ireland

10 9 8 7 6 5 4 3 2 1

ISBN 0 86322 260 9
(original paperback)

This book is published with the assistance of
the Arts Council/An Chomhairle Ealaíonn

Cover design: id communications, Tralee
Printed by The Guernsey Press Ltd., Channel Islands

D r H. P. Sommerville had been born into reasonable wealth and property, and he accepted idleness as the privilege of his class.

He lived alone.

He had been born in this wilderness town, on a vast river estuary, a few miles from the sea. Demesne Street was select. From his surgery window he could look at the nearby cove and its protecting arm of stone pier. Half a dozen boats moved with the swell.

Sommerville was a Protestant – the only one in this town of perhaps six thousand Catholics. Once the town and its hinterland had nurtured more than a hundred. They had dwindled away, emigrated to the Colonies, been subsumed in mixed marriages, wasted in many wars for kings, queens and another country.

It was the fate of the conqueror, the implanted landlord, the conquistador and even accompanying men-at-arms, to pale, diminish, leave not a rack behind.

The Catholic church and its spire might dominate the town too, but only a single tottering priest manned it now. Sommerville could look across into the enclave that housed it and the huge empty convent. The funeral home where the dead were displayed was there too, and the imposing house of the sacristan, Simoney. Simoney was a big bitter man, devoted to God, the church and its furnishings.

In the early afternoon of this April day it was a quiet place where not a soul stirred. God was dead, Sommerville thought.

There was a Protestant church too but, in the entire parish, less than a dozen to support it. It sat in its churchyard by the river, dignified and surrounded by its dead.

It was a clean town. Four streets jutted out from a Square; three of them left the town behind and threaded a way through desolation to pockets of land and farmhouses or pushed through to scattered coastal settlements. The fourth, wider and with a fair surface, went inland to the importance of the county town.

The shops were good, well-maintained, attractive. New ventures thrived or failed. In the town there were two doctors, two pharmacies, an efficient cottage hospital, a relatively new housing estate of low-rental dwellings and the citadel of law and order, an impressive building, the Garda Station. Everything was catered for except the extremes of surgery or very haut couture.

Sommerville's house was a distinguished building of three storeys. Inside, more than a hundred years of care had accumulated a patina of near-luxury.

Sommerville was forty-eight.

He looked out at the town in the pale sickly light that sometimes comes with an April day. He was restless. April is the cruellest month, he thought; everything struggling to come to life and so much death. He was ageing, growing morbid, he felt.

Even in small lost towns nearing the Atlantic coast – hiding from it – in newsagents, side by side with national dailies, the imported London tabloids and even perhaps a broadsheet or two were on sale. The scandalous behaviour of people in high places, although far away, had humble counterparts here that faded them to indifference.

On Sommerville's desk was the local regional paper covering isolated communities, parishes, baronies and each small-town happening in its circulation area of eight hundred thousand acres. It was a weekly publication.

Sommerville's was a desultory scan, sometimes for the simplicity and gaucherie of its reportage, but there were occasions when he found something that caught his interest. Sommerville was a sensual man with an appetite not only for mischievous venery but for food, drink, the erotic and the arcane. Pleasure was very important.

He was reading now of a rural apparition, an epiphany of

the Virgin Mother of God, Queen of Heaven, out there some-where in the barren wilderness, forty miles or more north of him. He always followed these occasional hoaxes, near or very distant, to look at entranced faces in prayer, the fright-ening certainty and perhaps subconsciously the hope – burn-ing the congregation too – for some moment of magic. It was a game.

Sommerville's medical practice was for the chosen few, the Protestant survivors, aged, ageing, scattered far in the sur-rounding miles. Locals didn't come to him, he didn't encour-age them. And they were a little in awe of him.

Dressed in well-tailored casual wear, shirt, cravat, plain polished brogues, his hair only faintly grizzled, he was an attractive man. He could be pleasant or abrupt.

In the hallway he called out to his servants: "I'm out! Take messages. If you have to, ring Dr Keelehan."

Dr Keelehan was the dispensary doctor, a Catholic of course, a weak man, Sommerville judged him – with an out-wardly neglected surgery and house close to a clearance estate and its mixed bag of workers and idlers. But he had advised Keelehan of procedure in these absences, the dispositions and temper of his ageing, failing patients, and Keelehan was com-petent, could discern, communicate. A chore like that couldn't be left in the hands of servants; he repeated, "Dr Keelehan".

Sommerville went out into the cold but penetrating pale-ness of the day and drove through the town. Demesne Street was without movement; life seemed to begin at the Square and the streets that forked away from it. He saw the austere, shrouded premises of Rellighan, the undertaker, and Finegan's, one of two dozen pubs, important because Finegan had money and was chairman of the town council; he saw the deceptively slight figure of Coleman, Detective Inspector Coleman, who was thirty-five and ten years in the town. The streets were alive, the shops bright, the pale light enhanced them. The pavements were busy.

11

Sommerville didn't take the high road inland to civilization. He travelled Main Street that, incongruously, climbed a hill, unpeopled, of two hundred feet, before wandering through seemingly endless miles of scrub and rock, past occasional farms, deeper into loneliness. The school, a modern building, stood on the hill-top, surveying the town on one side and desolation on the other. Sommerville passed it, drove a performance car at good speed through narrow roads he had known since childhood.

He was of average height, strong, but a little weight was gathering on him. The rich food and drink and idleness didn't help. He found himself leaving the coarse acres of rushes and spiky grass, outcrops of rock, a sudden farm that came and went, and entering into a world of stone. The light fell on miles of exposed rock, gigantic paving that had a cold unpleasant fascination. Sweeping winds and the rain of millennia had scrubbed it clean. Sommerville parked his car and stood on the roadway. Rock stretched away to surrounding ridges that were bare and famished as flats and foothills. Vegetation was hidden and protected in crevices. He looked all about him. On the surface there was nothing, not even a single stunted tree. There was no sound except the wind, the road behind and ahead was empty. Loneliness imprisoned him. In darkness, in winter storm, it could be disquieting, fearful, perhaps even terrifying. People from afar, in summer sunshine, travelled to see this moonscape world, but Sommerville had always looked at it with distaste.

The light changed a little, darkened, and gave sharpness to edges and clefts. Nothing moved, it was a dead land of stone. An eddy of wind chilled him and passed on to scrape against a sweep of lime rock and waste itself. His father had brought him here often as a child to show him the dim world of dripping caves and long stalactite spears and, down in deep crevices, small rare plants that might have taken root when an ice-world had begun to melt.

He was forty miles from Demesne Street, the cove and

12

estuary now, and he turned towards the coast where, between jagged grotesque sculptures, moraines of clay and gravel, patches of arable soil had lodged. Farms were more plentiful, even elaborate, in some growing invisible prosperity. He felt the oppressiveness of the world of stone had been lifted.

He drove a few miles to his destination, a cross-roads village: a couple of dozen shops that carried the necessities of life and death, public houses, a post-office, a church for a great barren hinterland and few people. On the approach to it the caravans of travelling-people, new or neglected, were a grey blot: the debris of their presence soiled the roadway and the borders of grass. Sommerville and his father, long dead, would have called them tinkers. Once, in less prosperous days, they had repaired tinware and the worn-out bottoms of cooking pots. Now they had a catalogue of expensive minor services to offer and dole money to boot. They could afford not to plan their lives, to drink, procreate, move with the humour of a day or a month. They were a scab that never dried and fell away.

It was mid-week, past mid-afternoon. The intersecting ragged streets should have been quiet as the tundra of rock he had travelled. But middle-aged and ageing people, in best wear, moved towards the southern outskirt where a stone spire held aloft a crucifix in eternal repentance for the sinfulness of mankind.

The streets were narrow; people walked on the pavements and the carriageway. Where there was space, rusted weatherpocked cars were parked. The shuffling sound of feet was everywhere. But voices were hushed, scarcely heard; there was an air of great solemnity.

Sommerville found an alleyway between houses and plugged it with his car. He forced his heavy frame out to join the concourse. People walked with bowed heads, some had rosary beads and whispered their prayers. In shop windows he might see the statuettes of Christ and his Mother, even a candle burning here and there, coloured prints of the Pope, austere as in life, draped in papal colours, a great commander.

The churchyard had filled and was overflowing. A politician would have been glad to find such an audience gathered in a wilderness. A platform had been raised at the church door, wheelchairs and their occupants surrounded it. There was a stretcher case resting on trestles, people knelt on the stone steps. A great display of faith.

Strangely, at this hour of the afternoon, the Angelus bell was rung. Women draped veils on their heads, men removed caps and hats. A young cleric, with the fervour of an eastern avatar, mounted the dais with clasped hands. He recited the prayer and the congregation responded.

"The Angel of the Lord declared unto Mary."

"And she conceived of the Holy Ghost."

Sommerville watched the faces: mixtures of devotion, fear, curiosity, a few in tears. The prayer droned on with a kind of mesmeric humming sound. The travelling-people, he noted, had found strategic space to erect their stalls, to display a mountain of religious bric-a-brac. They, too, stood with bowed heads, perhaps in prayer, awaiting the end of devotion and the beginning of commerce.

The cleric, a young man in girdled alb and stole, held out his hands to them in a gesture of peace, or perhaps a command for silence.

Not only silence, but stillness, fell upon them.

"My Dear Brethren," he addressed them, "in a world made by God and desecrated by man, our parish has been blessed. God's name is not forgotten here. Look around the continents of the world and see the daily acts of massacre, mutilation, the ravaging of pious women who are in the image of God's Mother, the razing of places of worship that are sacred to God's name . . . and thank Him for giving us these sparse acres of peace and fertility.

He has chosen us. We must be worthy of that choice, cleanse ourselves, cast from our minds the pleasures and treasures of his world, clothe ourselves in humility, contemplate the paradise to come . . ."

Sommerville was thinking with humour behind his sobriety, 'Ah, take the cash in hand and waive the rest . . . the brave music of a distant drum.'

These primitive pustules of hysteria excited his curiosity. Somewhere in the course of each decade, near at hand or distant, there was a sighting, a confrontation with God's next of kin. God himself remained always hidden, that was his wisdom. Sommerville, although he felt moments of amusement, didn't travel to these haunted places solely to watch the emotion, the gaucherie that could be excited. He wondered what force stirred and fuelled these phenomena.

The face of the youthful apostle addressing them glowed with the fire of conviction; he flung words out into the clear air, let them wander into the desolation that encircled them.

'". . . Three of our innocent children, untouched, unspoiled, not yet at an age where the world can stain them, have on these ageing stone steps gazed at the Mother of God, that face of ineffable beauty, of smiling gentle compassion for the sins of the world. She raised her hand and blessed them. We know that blessing was to embrace all of our people, to strengthen us against evil, inspire us on our pilgrim's progress to eternal salvation. . ."

Sommerville pondered at what palace of magnificence beyond the universe and space did God reside. Or was he a wasted frame, a fakir, weak from prayer and fasting, hidden away in loneliness, beyond light years of light years, where nothing moved?

He closed his eyes and listened to the soft flow of wind that crept over the floor of melted rock to reach them. The young man of God poured out his clichés of the glory that awaited the righteous and the unspeakable pain that the loss of heaven could bring.

Sommerville was a handsome man; he knew that he had weight to lose. But beyond a first glance there was a weakness in his face. It would like pleasure, even pain, and the eyes had hardness. In his good casual clothing he would be

15

remarkable in this gathering if God's Mother had not upstaged him.

He envied this young anointed zealot in his singular belief, who had no doubts of his provenance, in the journey that was before him, the heavenly reward that was at the end of the rainbow. Life was a brief moment. Salvation, damnation. You had the choice. Heaven was ready to help, ignore it at your peril. Wasn't this visitation a hand held out from God, to brace you, to turn you towards him? He had sent his holy precious Mother to smile gentleness on this parish of stone.

The Sommervilles had brought their special religion with them so long ago: pay homage to God and to the incumbent of the Royal Throne. Prissy little Victoria was shapeless in swaddling clothes, a virtual generation then from her long grandeur of Queen and Empress, when the first of the Sommervilles were staking their claim to the land and its tenants in the rich alluvial soil of the river bank, the minuscule town, a sheltered cove. They had stripped their land of teeming tenants, exported them. They had prospered. Where land and opportunity was good, Protestants built their Manor Houses and marked the boundaries of their estates. Towns had begun as market places, and haphazard houses made winding streets. Churches were raised.

But the conquering people had wasted away, had been spent, and spent themselves. In Sommerville's parish there were ten survivors.

He was the last Protestant in the town.

He was aware of his isolation. But he was too hard for loneliness. Townspeople were a little afraid of him and his stock. They showed respect, that was sufficient. Sommerville accepted them, but they were his inferiors. He had all the amenities, the luxury; he travelled, enjoyed his indolence, his pleasures. He looked again at this holy young man calling out almost in tears of sincerity, a mere curate, an acolyte of the church. The founding Sommerville's prissy queen was Head of her Church, a randy little foreign charmer who had exhausted an imported husband to death and found solace with a stable-lad.

And who was God?

The crowd in the churchyard was singing now, the white-clothed figure of the curate pounding out a tempo, a rhythm, waving, ignored in a great blow of cacophony. The man of God was tiring.

In the crowd, Sommerville looked to left and right to find a route of departure, escape.

He saw Estel Machen.

She was thirty feet from him, clad in a long black penitential shawl. Black dominated: shoes, stockings, gloves, face veil. A nun, old, young, he wondered? They dressed in all the freaks of fashion in these modern times, from total conceal-ment of the body to bare faces, flowing hair and the fleshy gleam of legs in nylon tights. A dust of make-up even. He rushed to the fringe of the crowd and stepped away from it towards where his car was hidden.

He was never disappointed at the flat banality of these places of apparition; he arrived with just a gleam of hope and it faded. He didn't *believe*, of course. He wondered what brought the moment of hysteria, of illusion to these children. Some invisible dust of hallucinogens, present for a moment and gone? He had, of course, on occasion walked the roads and surrounding fields of other reported phantasms, search-ing the heavy grass and tangled ditches for some tiny prove-nance, but always without success. He had travelled to Mexico and seen peyote cactus, fungi, morning-glory. He had heard stories of disturbances of perception, visual dreams and nightmares, the sense of time disordered, and their closeness to the mystical, the transcendental . . .

He had left the crowd and walked the uneven broken pave-ments now. Shops and dwellings in neglected cross-roads vil-lages of wild country had a hang-dog timeless air. The dwelling house windows were blind eyes and, in shops, the window dressing a haphazard arrangement of items to fill a

17

void. Why did these shadows of afterlife, almost elementals, choose to manifest themselves to innocent, inchoate minds in such obscurity?

Few people moved on the streets, and only from public houses came the buzz of conversation, raised voices, laughter. Theosophists, theologists, ontologists had always made the bar-room their temple.

Sommerville thought again: ' "Myself when young did eagerly frequent, Doctor and saint and heard great argument about it and about, but evermore came out by the same door as in I went." '

He smiled and looked ahead and surprisingly he saw the shrouded woman draped in black standing at a bus-halt. It hadn't occurred to him that some form of public transport would route a vehicle through this countryside. Perhaps a couple of times a week, he would have thought, to accommodate the indigent and pensioners and the like. But this person in black was expensively clad. And he had passed from the churchyard, left her behind in the crowd. She was distinctive, unmistakable. He stopped and looked back to where she had stood. She hadn't passed him on this narrow street, that was certain, and here she was a little distance ahead. She might be waiting for him!

He moved towards her, suddenly seemed to have the need to speak and, as suddenly, became aware of impropriety. A strange person in a strange place where a few houses had huddled together against loneliness! To speak to her, to accost her? Hardly acceptable. He quickened his pace as he drew close. There must be some dust of unreality here. The sound of muddled, ragged singing arose and floated from the churchyard.

As he came abreast of her, she turned to him and said, "I noticed you at the prayers. Does it interest you?"

He was struck by the suddenness of it. "This?" he asked.

There might have been a trace of amusement in her voice, but her face, eyes, were hidden behind her veil. "These manifestations, phantasma?"

18

She had balanced it carefully between the sublime and the ridiculous.

He said, "Phantasmagoria," waited a few moments and said, "Are you waiting for a bus?"

"Yes."

"It might be a long time."

"Twenty minutes, a half an hour," she said; a little hint of humour again. "I'm never impatient."

Hardly a nun, he thought.

He warned, "They lease out these dirt-road backwoods journeys to local cowboys with twelve-seater rattling crumbling bone-shakers."

"I'm spending a few days on the coast," she said. "A pleasant little bleakness, a good hotel."

"This is an outing?"

"I saw a notice, 'Don't miss the Apparition'. I was curious, I suppose."

"Expensive?"

"Yes."

"And no sightings?"

"I thought there might have been a number of performances."

Sommerville laughed; this person had a pleasant voice but English wasn't her language. She spoke it perfectly with a trace of accent.

He said, "I took a day off to ramble about. My car is here. I'd enjoy a trip to the coast. We might get a decent meal at your hotel."

There was no hesitation; she said, "Wonderful."

They drove away from the church and the whistle-stop scene of spectral visitation.

Sommerville knew this jagged coast over many years; sand stone and rock-cliff that were a history of time since the melting of ice and the crawl of glaciers. It had great beauty when weather was kind but, in the frequent south-west rain laden gales, it could be bleak and unpeopled. Today a weak sun filtered through: all blues and greys, browns and greens caught the light and seemed to absorb it.

It had been a strange journey, almost in silence, through countryside without fertility or any wholesome growth; dark clusters of reed, tussocks like malignant clumps, wild briar and gorse, spongy ground of over-grown peat banks and trapped water black as ink.

The horizon, the sea, dark blue, came in sight first, and then headlands of cliff enclosing sand. They dropped down from high ground to a single street of a few houses. The hotel was more impressive than Sommerville could remember: lighted porch and windows against the first creep of darkness, the forecourt spacious, windswept and empty. The village houses might have been abandoned shells.

In the journey conversation had come only at odd moments. There hadn't been need for it. Silence wasn't disturbing. It had been the relaxed uneventful drive of persons accustomed to each other.

Estel Machen had not raised her veil, exposed her face. There had been no introductions. Sommerville pondered if perhaps she were hiding some hideous blemish, a scar, even a disfiguring port-wine stain growing with her since birth. He dismissed it. Even in silence she was good company. They would eat well and share a bottle of wine, he hoped. He would leave by nine-thirty, be home by eleven.

He parked in the forecourt and they went into the unexpected luxury of this small hotel. An impressive place. The manager, the receptionist smiled a greeting to Estel Machen, then included Sommerville.

It was almost seven o'clock; she said, "I'll take half an hour to freshen up and change. I could meet you in the bar perhaps?"

It was a hotel of great comfort. He had visited it on occasions before but now it had been transformed. A lounge steward came to him. He ordered a large measure of very old cognac and when it arrived he said, "I'll be staying for dinner. Would you reserve me a table for two?"

"Of course. Your name, sir?"

"Yes. Dr H. Sommerville."

He sipped his cognac and sunk into the luxury of his chair. He hadn't felt such contentment for a long time. He had set out this afternoon, a little empty, in search of some distraction. These sightings of rustic flying objects were usually depressing – exhibitions of vanished wonders. But always there was the urge to be there, perhaps to see something, even a shadow. He smiled. The luxury of the hotel surrounded, impressed him, had given some purpose to his journey.

Sommerville looked at his surroundings again; this was a little enclave of almost, wicked comfort, a piece of the most graceful past, pristine, untouched. He had been inside these walls before. It had always been reputed for its excellence of plain food, civility, warm tended bed-linen. Its lighted bar cabinet had been a high altar where, in the absence of a deity, spirits at least were there in abundance. Sommerville smiled at his own hackneyed bar-room wit that was old as time. He would remember this remarkable reconstructed place and visit it in the future.

He had taken his gaze, in politeness, from an exciting creature who had entered. Now he heard not her footsteps but the faint sensuous froufrou of delicate fabrics touching and in embrace.

She was facing him. He stood up at once.

"Out of my penitential black weeds and veil you don't recognise me?"

"Your voice I remember." He was a little breathless.

She sat. "Nothing for me," she said. "Please sit, take time over your cognac. My discarded costume of black? At esoteric religious raree-shows anonymity and a cloak of respect sets one apart, don't you agree?"

She laughed and Sommerville saw the fresh beauty of her eyes and lips; her hands were beautiful too, pale, unadorned. She wore no jewellery.

Sommerville joined in her amusement, drank a little cognac, felt a great warmth.

"Visitations of the Mother of God are not uncommon in rural parts. Even in towns and cities," he said. "Christ and his saints are less often on show. In fact, rarely."

"She represents all the beauty of womanhood of course. They call her the Blessed Virgin, don't they?"

For a moment Sommerville was in fear that he was being led into some wicked feminist tangle of bramble bushes: man's antagonism, a fear of weakness, seduction; the awful slash of emasculation.

He said, "I find it difficult to believe in anything."

"So we are always searching?"

"*You* are searching?" he asked.

"Searching is religion, very rewarding."

She was a beautiful woman, Sommerville thought again, and disciplined, pure, moral. Of that he was certain. He had looked into her eyes and felt comfort, reassurance to soothe his thoughts. He looked about him; she fitted into the perfection that surrounded them. Conversation was easy, an exchange of thoughts and convictions, amusement in everything. The awful human condition needed drenching, a great sluice of laughter.

Sommerville was a captive, besotted.

He had another cognac and they walked into dinner, silent as ghosts on the cushioned floor.

She said, "You engaged a table, I saw. You are a doctor?"

"Yes."

"Of divinity?"

Her laughter was a shiver of excitement in his body, and he wondered if he would ever forget her face. He laughed, inordinately, until he had to dab away moistness from his eyes. She was smiling at him.

"A physician," he said. "Herbert Sommerville. An hour's drive from here. Bigger than this but a small town." He named it. "One other doctor. He stands in, covers for me, from time to time."

She said, "I am Estel Machen. I would guess you are unfettered. Unmarried."

"Yes," he said.

"But you have house servants."

He nodded. "One getting on a bit. The other a young thing. I don't care very much for her. Perhaps I'm getting settled."

Estel Machen didn't take wine. She had poached salmon, ungarnished, untouched by the heavy Hollandaise blend of white sauce, stock, lemon juice, egg yolks, butter. A single dish was her meal.

Sommerville had to restrain his greed for food and drink, but he had a dish of filleted steak in cream sauce, surrounded by buttered mushrooms and pulses. He drank deep red fragrant claret. Then the matured cognac again.

The waiter came, very polite. "Will you be staying the night, sir? I could prepare a room."

Sommerville looked at his watch. "My God," he said, "It's turned eleven." A lot of wine and cognac, he thought, and pitch blackness out there. "Yes, yes, a room of course."

"It has been an enjoyable evening," Estel Machen said.

"Yes." He drank from his cognac, stood and held the chair for her to leave. "I'll see you in the morning perhaps."

She smiled. "Of course."

She crossed the dining-room, turned and stood for a moment, almost imperceptibly raised her hand to him and moved out of sight.

He spent an hour over this night-cap drink. He was filled with a great sense of happiness. He had been in boarding school and medical college of course, but he had grown up in this wild country with its sparse pockets of land and people. His Protestantism had isolated him throughout life, not by any form of bigotry, but by the lingering respect for his family provenance and the power they had brought with them even two hundred years past. He thought that he probably had pity for the acceptance of indigenous people.

Estel Machen had put brighter colours on his day. Times came when he was overcome with the drabness of people, their holdings, the watchful eyes on each other, greed, bitterness and, except for the very few, a token of religiosity that was renewable once a week. At a stroke she had banished gloom; she was indeed a blithe spirit. And the beauty of her body . . .

Sommerville was a person of carnality; desire too needed to be fed with great portions of sustenance. He had made a complicated life for himself. Abhorring the thought of marriage, he found excitement in paying for his women, men and boys. He was fond of boys. But all his desires now seemed to come at once in the shape of Estel Machen.

The waiter brought his key and he was directed to his room. The same restrained splendour everywhere: warm concealed bedside lamps, carpet of depth and colour, good furnishings, the luxurious en suite facilities. Even nightwear had been provided.

"In the morning, sir. Should I call you?"

"Eight-thirty," he said.

"Sleep well, sir."

Sommerville stood for minutes in the warm shower, washed away the film that food and drink could leave on the skin. He brushed teeth and rinsed his mouth. Everything was at hand, provided. He was refreshed. He sat for perhaps half an hour, almost in sloth, letting blood run slower, feeling the arrival of drowsiness.

The picture of Estel Machen was in his thoughts, pure thoughts they seemed, without desire, that would always clothe her. She was a sainted image.

Sommerville didn't wear night-clothes. Naked, he sunk into the embrace of the bed, pushed a button for darkness and was asleep.

He awoke without sense of time or place. The darkness was a warm twilight, the room took shape about him. The hotel, he remembered. Time didn't matter; he would drift off

24

again, and at eight-thirty he would be called. The sound of silence was like music, he thought; there seemed to be a wash of colours mixed in his crepuscular world.

He thought of Estel Machen. Then suddenly he *saw* her. In a white robe, spirit-like, standing beyond the end of his bed, looking down on him. He sat up in shock. She stood there, distanced from him on the carpeted floor. A dream? She stood motionless. She smiled on him. She was more beautiful than anything the heavens might release for appearance on stone-cold steps in a gravelled churchyard. He lay back, immersed himself in the pleasure of watching her. She let the robe slip from her shoulders and seemed to shine in glabrous magnificence before him. The bed clothes slid away from him until he was exposed.

Suddenly he was in her grip: hands on his shoulders, she sat astride him. She was a gentle ravenous vision. Her hands, her lips, explored him, caressed him until he thought his pleasure must be a kind of death. She knelt closer, drew him in, enveloped him. He remembered a last white flare and then the darkness of space . . .

The telephone at his bedside rang. A little morning light came through the curtains. The bed clothes were undisturbed, he had slept the sleep of the dead. He examined his body, looked at the perfect order of the room. Nothing out of place, nothing discarded.

He raised the telephone. "Yes?"

"Eight-thirty, Dr Sommerville."

"Thank you."

"Will you be taking breakfast?"

"Yes, in half an hour."

"Whenever it's convenient."

Sommerville found the dining room empty; at reception the clerk smiled his deference.

"I was in the company of a lady here last night."

The receptionist clerk said, "Madame Estel Machen."

Sommerville was relieved. "Yes," he said.

25

"She left an hour ago."

"How?"

"I assume she had a car, sir."

Sommerville cancelled breakfast, paid his bill and left. He turned his car towards home. He was remembering the evening, the night: a time of pleasure, a whirl of colour, the almost unbearable pain of it. Pleasure, pain were a mixture of colour. The early April day of cloud patches and a mild wash of sunlight swept by to clear his mind of fantasy; roadside ditches, flats of coarse grass and rushes returning to life. It wasn't the air and light to sustain the memory of last night's dream. He had been captivated by the beauty of that woman, and a little excess of wine and cognac could conjure images of the inaccessible. He turned on the radio, looked at the blue and white sky.

Her face, her body shone through it all, a magnificent succubus descending to take him in thrall.

It had been no dream; he could swear to it! He turned the radio to silence.

Had the hotel been a dream world? He had visited it before, drank in the bar, used its bedrooms. It was a comfortable commercial hotel that had survived the loss of overnight business travellers and was trading now on the tourist lure of desolation and endless acres of exposed timeless rock. Who would pour out money to give it such luxury?

For a moment he thought of turning back to inspect it. But the loss of Estel Machen clouded every decision. He was filled with impatience. He motored on to his hometown – a village he would call it – drove through Main Street and the Square to his residence in Demesne Street.

When he entered the hallway a matronly housekeeper said, "There's a patient in your waiting-room, Doctor."

"A regular patient. Who?"

"Not a regular patient."

He was angry. He said, "When I'm not here you send people away. Take an address. Ask them to call again. That's my arrangement. House calls, you refer them to Dr Keelehan. After years in a doctor's house you must know these things . . ."

"Yes, yes, of course. But a difficult person."

"Difficult?"

"Yes."

"I'm not in surgery for strays or itinerants."

"Yes, Doctor."

Sommerville said, "I am not in surgery now." He entered and closed the door behind him, sat restless, impatient, behind a polished hardwood desk, opened pieces of thrash-mail, crumpled them, dropped them in his waste-basket.

He was thinking of the hotel again. It had been empty, he suddenly remembered! Estel Machen and he had sat in an empty bar. The dining-room had been empty. Uniformed staff moved about – no arrivals, departures, residents? He tried to sharpen the image, bring it back again into focus, but it was an elusive memory . . .

The housekeeper's voice was in the hallway. Bloody stupid woman, he thought. There was a knock on his door and Estel Machen entered, the housekeeper in her wake. Her hair style had been changed, her clothes were good but plain and unflattering; she wore lisle stockings and flat shoes.

But it was Estel Machen.

Sommerville stared, felt a flood of relief and happiness. He said to his housekeeper, "You can leave us."

When she had gone they sat in silence for moments; the suddenness had confused Sommerville.

Estel Machen said, "It wasn't a dream."

"I thought you had gone."

"And left you? Oh no, you're much too special, important to me. I need you so much."

"It wasn't a dream?"

"Of course not. It was a night of pleasure. Do you remember every moment?"

"Yes."

"And I remember every moment." She held out her hands to him. "You must welcome me to your house."

Sommerville stood and came to her. She embraced him, walked him back and seated him again. She sat like a grateful patient in admiration of him.

"It's a beautiful house," she said. "But deserving of more care, I think."

"Yes."

"We must put things in order. You need a housekeeper. I'll deal with the servants. You can leave house matters to me."

He said, "I don't want you to work."

"I never work," she said. "I supervise. I need only cleaners. Every place must shine, be spotless. I will cook for us, of course."

Sommerville looked at her in these respectful working-class clothes and remembered the excitement that was hidden. She was smiling.

"You'll stay?" he asked.

"Yes."

"How did you get here?"

"My car is across the street."

It was an unremarkable car that could pass through the town without comment. They both looked at it. It stood at the short entrance to the holy ground of the church, the convent and environs.

They had tossed together last night in desire, he thought, until he had dropped away into forgetfulness. It had been real, she said. But wine and magnificent cognac could bring moments of illusion.

Suddenly she said, "I left you sleeping last night. I brushed your hair and dried your body, arranged the bed clothes for a gentle repose."

He held her hand, could feel his excitement. He said, "I wondered."

"This is a Catholic town, isn't it?"

"All Irish towns are Catholic."

28

"Then I must be a good Catholic. I must be humble, devotional, a credit to your household. Perhaps of some practical assistance to the church sacristan. And there's a school, isn't there?"

"On the hills above Main Street."

"A couple of hours on Saturday mornings. Speech and drama for the more senior students. No charge of course. It rounds them off."

He nodded; he was silent in his respect for her.

"There's a hospital?"

"Yes, there's a hospital, small but reasonable."

"I must call there from time to time. Leave little donations . . ."

Sommerville was in confusion, clasping his hands. "What can I do? How can I repay you? You're not a person who is employed, hired for work . . ."

She put her fingers on his cheeks. "I don't need money," she said. "I need pleasure, enchantment. My name, you know, is Estel Machen. I belong nowhere. I travel."

Sommerville had a sudden fear. "How long will you stay?"

"Until you ask me to leave."

Sommerville took her in his arms; embracing her was like another moment of intimacy.

"Don't ever go," he said.

She smiled, handed him her keys. "Ask the young servant whom you dislike to bring in my luggage. I'll visit the church and pray and perhaps catch the sacristan's eye. Later I might visit the school. I'll walk of course, see the town, let the town see me. Have I dressed like a housekeeper?"

"Yes."

Dr Daniel Keelehan's surgery and residence were in the less desirable end of the town. He was surrounded by huckster businesses or empty failed shops that were last desperate flings to avoid the unfriendliness of foreign roads and cities.

29

The flight of the entrepreneurs. It was a mean street with its quota of public houses and a fish and chip vendor who opened seven days a week and took money. Public houses balanced on the edge of prosperity.

Where the street straggled away to rubble and smear and opened on to reclaimed land, a cheap-rental housing scheme had been raised. It was five years old, still neat and maintained, but with the cold unwelcome of planned ghetto dwellings.

Keelehan used three rooms of a three storey house that had once, in Empire days, housed members of the Royal Irish Constabulary: a surgery, a waiting-room, a bedroom. A silent daily cleaning woman came and went. Before his arrival in town Keelehan had drunk his way through a childless marriage and, in his fifties now, had completed twenty years close enough to happiness in this wilderness.

It was nine o'clock. He sat up in bed. On a locker were a table lamp, a glass, a half-spent bottle of vodka. He swung his stockinged feet out on to the floor; he was wearing only underwear. The glass was a long-tom and he filled it one third from the bottle and drank it back as easily as water. He switched on a free-standing electric fire and changed his perpetual calendar. April 20th. In ten days it would be May and there was still a sting in the air, he thought. He pulled on trousers, socks, shoes, and went downstairs to his surgery. The street door was locked, the blinds drawn. There was hot water and a hand-basin. He shaved and went back to his bedroom, drank another third of vodka and felt that peace was not very distant. He was beginning to live.

His coat was hanging on a chair. He took an eight-ounce flask from each side pocket, opened a fresh bottle of vodka, filled the flasks and replaced them. Then he locked away all evidence of his drinking, unplugged the fire and went downstairs to draw the bolt on his front door, raise the blind. He picked his newspaper from the floor and sat at his table.

His cleaner arrived. "Good morning, Doctor."

"Morning."

She hoovered the surgery and waiting-room, dusted them, cleaned his toilet. Then she went upstairs to his bedroom. In half an hour she had finished. She turned the pendant notice on his street-door from 'closed' to 'open'.

"Good morning, Doctor."

"Morning."

She went; he heard patients arriving: one, two, three. He took a heavy mouthful from his flask and read his newspaper for fifteen minutes. Normality had returned, he could function. He pressed a bell-button on his table.

A past middle-age woman came in, dressed with great care, inexpensive rings and jewellery, even a hat. She carried an umbrella and a handbag. Visits to the doctor had not lost their due proprieties for her.

"Ah, Mrs Dignan, you're coming along fine, I see."

She brightened. "Yes, Doctor."

"Your medication?"

"Every day, Doctor."

"No little side effects? Headaches, tiredness?"

"Tired sometimes."

"That's normal. We'll keep you on it for a little while yet."

He went through the routine of blood pressure, listening to her and nodding; less than ten minutes would be lean time in the process of healing, restoration. He allowed her fifteen.

"Thank you, Doctor, thank you." Courtesy, a ceremonial leave-taking . . .

Nostrums for poor haunted healthy goats. He rested for four, five minutes, did his paperwork, was ready for the next. He rang.

"Mr Rohan."

"Yes, Doctor."

"Are you feeling better?"

"Yes and no." Rohan dropped his voice to a whisper of delicacy. "Still a touch of diarrhoea. A little pain too. My appetite is not good."

Keelehan looked at the great mass of his stomach. "Sea

31

food, Mr Rohan. Dangerous fare from public house kitchens. Patience is the thing."

"Nearly a week now, Doctor."

"Might take another fortnight. I'll renew your medication. Takes time, you know. Sea food can be poison."

"Yes."

"Come at the end of the week."

Keelehan watched him move away with a fat man's waddle. He thought of stinking mussels in garlic butter. Oh God! Obsession with drink would be kinder. He rested, went to his files. The next.

A pale, tired man came in; his eyes were sick, his skin a bad colour.

Keelehan smiled to him. "Mr Grimes."

Mr Grimes was failing.

Keelehan asked, "How long now?" He read his notes.

"Eight days, Doctor."

"Still bleeding?"

"Bleeding, yes."

"Weak, not eating?"

"Yes."

Keelehan was smiling, confident. "I'll give you a letter to the hospital. Then we can make you right as rain again. Tomorrow suit you?"

"Yes."

"Best to get these little upsets settled, out of the way, as soon as possible."

Keelehan watched him go; he didn't think he would see him again. Time came when you passed them on. Poor bastard. He felt in his pocket for a flask. A mouthful now of warm explosive life. A breather. Ready for the next.

Keelehan's morning surgery was from ten to midday. It dragged on at its usual pace. When he tired he drank a little. The drink lost its taste and some of its warmth, and its power was spent more quickly. But he knew the pace that would keep him on course.

The session was almost through, and this was his half-day. At ten minutes to twelve John Anthony, a council worker, arrived. He was a worried man, Keelehan could tell: searching eyes, restless hands, forehead a little damp.

"Sit down," Keelehan gestured to him.

A big man, he sat on the edge of the chair. "It's my son, James," he said.

"Yes?"

"He's too sick to walk. He's very sick, in pain. We need help, Doctor."

"Yes, of course. Since when?"

"Last night."

"Age?"

"Seventeen."

"At school?"

"Yes."

It was on the stroke of twelve; the waiting-room was empty.

Keelehan, out of sight, drank back two mouthfuls of liquor. He locked up and drove with John Anthony into the housing estate.

It was five past twelve.

At twelve forty five he was back in his surgery. He rang Sommerville.

"Herbert?"

"Yes?"

"Daniel Keelehan here. I need your opinion."

"Of course."

"A schoolboy from the housing estate, seventeen, curled up in a ball, paroxysms, headache, vomiting, stiff neck, rash."

"Could be anything from appendicitis to gastric flu."

Keelehan said, "You ask me the questions, Herbert."

"Rolled up in a ball, you said? Stiff neck, rash?"

"Yes. Head buried away from the light. Couldn't be touched, no communication. Headache, severe pain . . ."

"Temperature?"

33

"Rising."

"Did you get him to lie flat?"

"With help."

"And then?"

"His head was back, chin in the air. He cried out in pain, pleading for help. I won't forget that homeless moaning sound. Bloody frightening . . ."

"Wait," Sommerville said. "Did you get him to lie perfectly flat?"

"Except for one leg bent at the hip and the knee."

"You tried to straighten it?"

"Too much pain. And the other leg was coming up."

"Any illness in the family? Tuberculosis, something serious, wasting?"

"'Healthy as fishes, all of them."

"Wait," Sommerville said. "I must get back to my books. In this damn place our minds go to sleep."

Keelehan sat and drank. He had spent his life dealing with family illnesses and infections, sprains, breaks, rheumatism, arthritis, alcoholism. Even tuberculosis. And of course the terminals. Doctors led lonely lives. He topped up his glass and downed it.

Sommerville was back. "You still there?"

"Yes."

"Daniel, it has all the classic symptoms of meningitis. Could be from a nose or ear infection. But it's dangerous. Get rid of it," he said. "An ambulance, the hospital. There's a keen young houseman there, an Asian. Ring him, he'll be licking his lips."

"What can he do?"

"Fight against rising temperature, draw off spinal fluid which is pus. Send a specimen to Dublin. Get out his hypo and start making holes."

"How long for a result?"

"I don't know."

"Yes," Keelehan said.

He didn't delay; he made his telephone calls, sat and drank until he saw the ambulance passing his window to take away James Anthony, aged seventeen. He wished him well.

It was Keelehan's day to stock up his spirit store. An hour's drive to the county town and the supermarket: a half an hour to be loaded up with five cases of vodka. A tenner to a storeman covered the loading. He drove the round trip faultlessly: a stomach empty of vodka, a clean bloodstream, and he would have been a danger to himself and others.

His drinking was no secret but, discreetly, he would delay the off-loading until after midnight. He had a lightweight trolley and he locked away the cases beneath his hallway stairs. Vodka was his life, his confidence.

The following morning before opening his surgery he telephoned the hospital and talked to the Asian houseman. He sounded a dedicated pleasant young man. James Anthony's condition was critical. A good vague word, Keelehan thought. Fluid had been drawn off not only for analysis but to relieve the pressure on his brain. Everything possible was being done to ameliorate his condition, his suffering; he was slipping in and out of consciousness. The houseman had sought advice from the county hospital. He should await the result of the fluid analysis, he was told; the patient would probably reach a crisis point before improvement could be expected.

"Antibiotics?" Keelehan asked.

A long silence from the houseman. "Allergic to anything that might help him. The county is sending me on variants, even serum."

"Tuberculosis?"

"No trace."

Keelehan hung up; he drank from his flask and rang for his first patient. Another journey through the index of illnesses great or small, a litany of symptoms, real or imagined. Thank God for alcohol.

On the morning of the eighth day, James Anthony died.

Keelehan visited the hospital and his parents. These were little personal courtesies that Keelehan extended.

Death of an adult in a small town means the absence for ever more of a familiar frame and face, and general commiseration for the widow and perhaps a family. Death of an infant is accepted as a return to God, unspoiled by sin, of one of his creatures.

But the almost sudden demise of a schoolboy, seventeen years old, brings shock, and even anger.

Rellighan, the undertaker, prepared the body and placed it for viewing in his funeral home in the church enclave. Strangely, not a great number of people attended: they feared a young body that had been stricken by some nameless disease, malignancy, and in death they believed the corpse could be a raging mass of infection.

The church service with the coffin lid in place, and where the catafalque was distanced from the congregation, commenced. The attendance was scattered.

Estel Machen, Sommerville's custodian, scarcely a month in the town walked, veiled and in mourning, up the centre aisle carrying a memorial wreath to lay on the coffin. She was a distant person but even in her silence she had in a short time gained respect, if not affection, in the town. She was Dr Sommerville's housekeeper. She cared for the house of God. No task was too menial in her service to Simoney, the church sacristan. And, on Saturday mornings, she attended the town school to work with senior schoolchildren, teaching speech and verse and drama. James Anthony had attended her classes and now she came in mourning to pay her respects.

Simoney took the service and made the kind of thundering sermon that was expected, warning all of the slender thread of life and the gaping flames of eternity that could await the sinners. From behind the anonymity of her veil Estel Machen watched him.

Rellighan, the undertaker, stood aside in the shadows, awaiting the cessation of Simoney's noise. Coleman, Garda

Inspector, sat on the last seat of the church. He was uneasy. A little farther ahead sat Belle Cannon, proprietress of a small expensive boutique; she was also a school teacher and was accompanied by a dozen or more of her pupils.

The canon, who should have been the celebrant, sat huddled in the shadows of the sanctuary, the only anointed person in the congregation. He was a very old man who wanted to die while still working a little. He sat there, head bowed, in prayer. Except for the sacrifice of the Mass and the absolving of sins in the confessional, he had left the day-to-day offices and chores of the church to Simoney.

It was over. The crowd was filing out. Tomorrow in the parish cemetery, two miles from the town, the burial would take place.

In the empty church Simoney, in the sacristy, folded vestments and put them away with exaggerated piety. Estel Machen tidied the church. The cusped entrance doors, swinging on brass butts, had a great embellished lock: the doors were of heavy tropical hardwood. She pushed them closed, didn't secure them. She brought the key to Simoney in his domain of vestments and utensils. Tomorrow he would hand it to her again for opening.

Simoney said, "Thank you, Miss Machen, for your immense help. Until your arrival I must confess I found the job had become a little demanding. God must have sent you."

"It's a pleasure to be of assistance," she told him.

Simoney concluded his duties. They went out and parted in the churchyard, Simoney to his house at the fringes of the enclave, Estel Machen to where her car was parked close to Sommerville's house. She sat and waited.

The slow passage of time didn't bother her. Darkness had fallen now; the peace of the church environs had become loneliness. Sounds of people and traffic from the town Square and business streets seemed remote. In a little while she drove back to the churchyard and parked at the sacristy door, hidden behind the church. The sacred ground of trees, shrubs, shrines, buttresses, was a place of deep shadow. It was a desolate area now but she moved with great care.

She walked in gloom to the main doors, entered and pushed them shut. Only a speck of light from the sanctuary lamp glimmered in the blackness of space. She moved past the sacristy entrance to the catafalque and stood, like a forgotten mourner, keeping vigil by the coffin.

In a little while she unscrewed the lid and lifted out the body of James Anthony; she seemed to raise him up without effort. She laid him on the ground and screwed down the lid again, arranged all things: flowers, messages of sympathy, promises of a myriad prayers to be said for the repose of a soul.

Then she carried him out and covered him on the rear seat of her car. She pulled the sacristy door shut.

Not much more than an hour later she was standing in the blackness of the infinity of rock where Sommerville had stood and felt the coldness of the wind on a calm day of weeks past. It was the day he had met Estel Machen at the cross-roads village of the apparition.

She took the body now, stripped it naked, and carried it out to a flat tilt of rock. She watched it from her car. In a little while it stirred. Then, like an animal, on all fours. It moved away into the darkness.

She folded the clothes; she would return them to their coffin. She sat in silence for a long time. Then she turned back for the church and Herbert Sommerville's home.

Coleman, Inspector Coleman, had seen her car leave the town. He had wondered about it for moments only. An errand for Sommerville, he thought. Hardly a quest for fresh air with a wind gusting up from the estuary.

James Anthony died on the 28th of April and he was buried on the 30th. His empty coffin was buried on the 30th.

Scarcely two months later Dr Keelehan was found by his cleaner in his surgery chair, ice-cold, freed at last from the diurnal drudgery he had created.

Those Spring days were long gone. This was October 30th. Darkness falls early in the last days of October: an hour of darkness has been snatched from evening and given to sunrise. The winter solstice of Capricorn, with its greyness, is in the middle distance. Four o'clock and dusk is mixing with light.

From the cemetery gates the sodium lamps of the town – six thousand souls – would seem to gather power as daylight was spent.

Coleman looked back now across two miles of fading world at the deep yellow pinpoints of warmth, and pushed open the cemetery gate. It scraped in a long worn groove.

The wind was from the north-west, sweeping in from the Atlantic hardly fifteen miles distant, bitterly cold on flesh and marrow. A shiver of winter.

There was still light to look along the low dry-stone boundary walls of this cluster of sleeping citizens, across a perverse geometry of headstones, erect or tottering, or even the greater memorials – depicting a gentle Saviour – to mark the distinction of its incumbent and perhaps even a contribution to humanity.

There was a rough dirt circuit hugging the perimeter walls and a half dozen footworn tracks where bearers had carried their loads and mourners followed.

Coleman hadn't come to browse or nod sadly at impermanence. He wore a three-quarter length leather coat and tightened his belt against the wind, pulled a tweed cap down on his forehead. He had come to see a grave.

He stepped out across kerbs and high grass, neglected overgrown shrubs, a few containers of plastic flowers.

Here was his plot. A gravestone, a little weathered, discoloured. It chronicled sixty years. Forbears had been laid there since the late thirties and, in better times, the stone had been raised. Beneath fading names, fresh cut in the ageing tablet only in recent months, had been chiselled, *'James Anthony, Aged 17 years'*.

39

Coleman had been right; he had died in April. The recent wilted flowers marked lingering grief and loss. Six months dead, the ground had settled, the enclosing kerb had been wire brushed. He had been buried on the 30th April, Coleman remembered now. A lot of tears had been shed that day, Coleman recalled. People hadn't watched a coffin being lowered into its pit; they had seen a fair-haired schoolboy, a smiling face, a body that might have grown into strength and athleticism, being dropped out of sight forever.

Coleman attended funerals. Ten years in a small town and you knew the families, their fortunes and misfortunes. People feared death but respected it too. Coleman remembered James Anthony, his step, his swing, his style. He was six feet down, below him now but he still remembered.

A little illness and he had vanished. He had lasted seven days and a few hours.

Coleman had always been wary of Keelehan of course. But it wasn't police business, it wasn't a hushed sinister passing. Forget it. Keelehan was one of two practitioners dispensing to the town. A celibate by choice, he lived above his surgery and only a distant laconic cleaning woman had ever invaded its privacy: her voice she spread like warm butter, had measured words for shopkeepers, in her church pew made responses to prayers and litanies, sang songs of earnest praise to the Lord. She didn't cook for Keelehan. His sole meal of the day, at early evening time, was in a small seclusive hotel where he sat alone in an empty dining-room.

His surgery, his house, unimpressive, sat on the skirt-tails of the council estate of cheap housing. One could say that perhaps fortuitously he had become the poor man's practitioner: medicine for the less fortunate few, the idle, the unemployable, the indigent. It made little difference to Keelehan. Today, yesterday. Yesterday: 'that bloody awful day long ago, before this bloody awful day'. If the Judas rule of thirteen applied to medicine – the number on Keelehan's door – then the poor had a scrambled head to heal their wounds and blemishes.

But Keelehan, in his fifties, had sailed unscathed through twenty years of allopathy. Often, in the small drunken philosophic hours of the morning, he had been proclaimed in tavern toasts. A gifted man, a great healer, lost in a coastal wilderness! Toasted in his absence of course. Keelehan didn't frequent bar-rooms, and the fashionable healers for paying customers lived beyond the fringes of the town.

Keelehan was an alcoholic, a self-controlled alcoholic. He drank two bottles of vodka sunrise to sunrise. Unencumbered by marriage, after a night's broken stuporous sleep, breakfast was the finest drink of the day. It brought awareness, optimism. He dressed and groomed well and descended to his surgery. He was tall, thin, dignified. He knew his patients, he could smoothly manoeuvre them.

There were no secrets in a small town. Little scraps of information came your way and you stored them and connected them. Coleman knew of Keelehan's drives to the supermarket anonymity of the county town to leave behind cardboard cartons and load with provision for the future. He knew of the pocket flasks. But he had never seen him drink. He drove a car with the steadiness of a professional. Coleman shrugged: live and let live. He had died with a clean licence.

James Anthony, aged seventeen, had been Keelehan's patient, and Coleman had called on him.

"Talk to the family. It's best, wouldn't you agree?" The snub was almost lost in Keelehan's politeness.

"It's just routine," Coleman had said.

In the last days of April, six months past, James Anthony had died. He was seventeen. He died on the eighth day of his illness. The newspaper obituary, inserted by the family, had paid tribute to Dr Daniel Keelehan for the care and attention he had shown to their beloved son.

Keelehan had outlived him only by a few weeks. In his comfortable chair he had nodded off to death: alcoholics sometimes drifted effortlessly out of life as if they had suddenly tired of it. He had requested cremation in his legal will:

his ashes were scattered in some unstated place where once he might have had some moments of contentment . . .

Coleman took a trackless route across the graveyard, from plot to plot, across fresh and settled earth. Flowers that had been set in the summer had closed their doors against the weather. He walked away across the grass paths, pulled the rasping gateway closed. It was growing darker now, the gravestones stiff in wind and dusk, a glow on the village lights. Except where development had overtaken and surrounded them, graveyards were a little distant from villages and small towns. Not secreted. The privacy of the dead.

James Anthony had been a hardy schoolboy, full of gathering life, Coleman thought.

He walked along the rough unmade road, in darkness now, trees and the wild growth of hedges tangled like broken pieces of night time. He had walked out from the town – it was less obtrusive. Seeing the grave again, remembering graveside faces, the shape of bodies, tossed and sharpened his uneasiness. He joined the main road, felt the smoothness of tarmac beneath him, strode towards the yellow lights.

It was a small compact town: a market square and converging streets like odd spokes left in a hub. But it was clean and windswept. The shops had closed; their lighted windows shone on the pavements and roads, the yellow street-lamps filtered down like weak sunshine. Cars were moving, pedestrians hunched against the wind. Coleman nodded, here and there raised a hand in salutation. He crossed the Square. A towering Celtic cross with ornate iron railings was its centrepiece, a memorial to generations of glorious dead. A paper wrapper was blown across the open space, out of sight; a dog sniffed at the railings and marked his territory.

From the Square, Demesne Street was impressive, short and elegant, leading down to the miles of broad river estuary, a sheltered cove, a dozen or more pleasure boats still moored but soon to be wheeled up to dry ground and the shelter and security of boathouses. It was reserved and residential, quiet, no shops, not even a select tavern, polluted it. It was shielded from prevailing winds too, sweeping winter storms, and Coleman walked into its stillness.

A hundred yards and he stood before the door of Dr Herbert P. Sommerville, M.D., M.Ch., B.A.O., M.R.C.P. It was a handsome three storey dwelling where Sommerville's father had practised before him; and beyond *him*, Sommervilles, Protestant merchants, had amassed money to create a little dynasty. It was a black glistening door with brass furnishings worn by the years but shining in the pale yellow light. Coleman pressed the bell, heard it ringing and waited. He waited patiently a long time. It was a distant muted sound.

The door was suddenly opened. A woman in token bib and apron, a lace-trimmed head-dress perfect as a tiara, a face, eyes without movement, stood silent, gazing at him.

This was Sommerville's housekeeper. He had never been so close to her. In servile dress her face and eyes were bled, empty of emotion. Had he seen her before? Some haunting ghostly image slipped, re-gathered, tried to take shape. It seemed an infinite silence.

She said, "Dr Sommerville sees by appointment only."

Coleman nodded; he began, "My name is . . ."

"I know who you are."

Coleman continued, "My name is Inspector John Coleman."

"Don't you wear a uniform, policeman or garda or whatever your title?" Her voice was almost accentless, amused. She inspected him.

"Sometimes. I'm on leave."

"Sick leave?"

"A few days' winter leave," Coleman said; he smiled.

Sommerville wasn't a Catholic. Church of Ireland, Methodist, Presbyterian, something like that. To be in the employ of Protestant or Nonconformist brought to the indigenous worker a little robe of authority. There was cachet.

But this woman at the door, a comparative stranger, only

months settled in the town, was complete, not in need of reflected importance. Her name was Machen, Coleman knew.

Still the memory of an amorphous face from the past took shape and in an instant had dissolved again.

"I'll put your name in the book. He may or may not be able to see you. Call tomorrow, four-thirty."

Coleman wondered what fire might lie behind this practised austerity. She was still young. Thirty-five, hardly more than that.

"Now would be better," he said.

"Impossible, I'm afraid."

"Tell him it's official business."

"With Dr Sommerville?"

Coleman was tiring; he said, "Tell him."

She seemed to consider it for moments.

"Tell him."

She left Coleman in the hallway and drifted away into a carpeted world. Her uniform was below knee-length, the shoes flat-heeled.

There was a hallway table, a silver salver for calling cards, a great deal of old racing and hunting prints of air-borne splay-legged horses. There was a mirrored hallstand for hats, garments, umbrellas, canes. A glove-drawer. Everything shone.

Silently, Dr Sommerville appeared. He was Coleman's build, but more flesh than muscle. He seemed to walk from the hip with precise confident steps.

"Come in," he said in a special welcoming way. They went to his surgery and he sat behind his desk, at ease, and motioned Coleman to a chair.

"I'm not a patient," Coleman explained.

"I understand."

Coleman let silence return, settle; eventually he said, "I came regarding Dr Keelehan. He was never an easy man to reach . . ."

"Then or now, poor fellow," Sommerville said. "He wasn't very communicative."

Coleman paused for a moment or two. "This morning," he said, "I made a trip to the offices of the County Registrar. An unofficial visit."

"The county town. Not a short journey."

"No."

Sommerville considered it. "You needed information?"

"Yes."

"And now, more information?"

"There are ethics, you know."

Coleman gently ignored it; he said, "In the past six months a schoolboy died in the town. I wondered about the cause of death."

"No secret."

"Dr Keelehan, the late Dr Keelehan, consulted with you, I know," Coleman said.

"You mentioned cause of death."

"Yes."

"Meningitis," Sommerville said. "There are isolated cases from time to time. On national statistics of course. Then they vanish. Fluid was taken from the spine. Sent to Dublin. Meningitis."

Coleman paused. "Duration of illness," he said, "eight days approximately?"

"Yes."

"Is that normal?"

"'Normal' is a layman's word, old man."

"Inspector Coleman," Coleman introduced himself.

"Of course. Inspector. You'd like to conclude this conversation as soon as possible, I'm sure. Is there a complaint, a negligence charge or some such nonsense? Something I don't know?" Sommerville was smiling.

"Just one or two personal queries."

"I suggest that someone in authority write to the locum tenens at the late Dr Keelehan's surgery. That would be best, wouldn't it?"

Sommerville was being concerned now, helpful, anxious to

help and at once dismissive.

Coleman said eventually, "I learned that rapid death from meningitis . . ."

"Yes, yes. If the body is harbouring other forms of ill health, debilitating, the end can be accelerated." There was impatience now.

"That boy was healthy?"

"Healthy? Dangerous ground, Inspector." Sommerville had a forgiving humour. "Like telling criminals by rule of thumb. Judges need evidence."

Sommerville was smiling again.

Fingerprints crossed Coleman's mind; he said, "The death certificate, straight-forward. 'Cachexia . . . Meningitis . . . terminal'. Something like that."

"Yes."

"Cachexia, I'm told, means general ill health, perhaps wasting illness."

"Perhaps latent illness."

"You didn't see the death certificate, Doctor? Or the patient? Or the body?"

"Not my patient. The conditions were described to me on the telephone. Adequately. I agreed with the late Dr Keelehan's findings."

Coleman nodded. "Perhaps he was confused."

Sommerville walked with him to the door, stood and looked searchingly at him. "I should tell you," he said, although he seemed in no hurry with his words, "there's another case at the hospital. A young person."

"Yes, I know," Coleman said.

"The reason for your urgency, your call?"

"Yes."

"It's a schoolgirl," Sommerville said. "She's dead. A couple of hours now."

Coleman thought about it; he said, "Dead?"

"Yes."

"Symptoms?"

"As you probably know, identical with the young boy we buried so recently."

"You're worried, Dr Sommerville?"

"A little sad. Death is never pleasant to contemplate. A sense of failure. Our profession is sensitive."

Coleman thought the reins were in Sommerville's good hands: an easy unhurried pace, regrets.

"A schoolgirl," Coleman reiterated.

"Sixteen, seventeen years."

"Allergic to treatment, too. Strange."

"Not uncommon these days, Inspector. It's someone from the housing estate. Not my patient of course. The locum tenens telephoned me."

"A common practice?"

"Not uncommon. We all need reassurance from time to time."

Sommerville said, "The dead girl is Jennifer Anderson."

Coleman looked down the short distance to the blurred movements of boats in the wind, the great endless plane of darkness that swelled the estuary. The yellow street-lights ended at the jetty, threw two long turbulent pillars of reflection out across the water.

He said to Sommerville, "Thank you for your help."

"Keep me informed, will you, Inspector?"

Coleman walked up the slight gradient to the Square. Light from shop windows flooded the streets, people were in movement; voices, near and distant, were blown on the wind.

Every year death took its toll; that was part of small town life. Deaths and births. He thought about Sommerville. In the course of police business he had met him not more than three or four times. Doctors in small towns knew the exteriors and interiors of their patients, and a little of their minds. They moved in a small social group, a protective carapace where faults and excesses were hidden.

Only face to face with illnesses was public confidence and decision required.

And Sommerville was a Protestant, sharing with less than a dozen others in the surrounding miles a local church and a journeyman ageing pastor who came monthly to give praise with them or offer communion. Protestant burials were sad events, irreparable losses to a dying community.

Sommerville had changed of late, changed for the better, Coleman thought: he had a quick short-stepped springy walk, more youthful. He seemed a different man, eager, youthful. He gazed out through kindly unfocused eyes towards something fixed, distant. Not boredom. Some depth of tranquil thought. Even as he spoke he might be giving ear to the words of a prompter in the wings: a message of importance that compelled him to listen.

Coleman had thought at times that his own words had been squandered, unheard, but Sommerville's responses were always confident, to the point. And there seemed to be moments of quiet amusement.

In the hallway when he left, they had passed the motionless guardian figure of Estel Machen. From the doorstep, Coleman had watched her move away noiselessly out of sight. He took the memory of her face with him, searched in his mind for it.

Herbert Sommerville closed his door and stood, back to it, in contemplation of Coleman. Coleman would be reaching for his middle thirties, well-made, durable. A police inspector, young and with good rank, too intelligent to be wasted in this demographical wilderness, this vast bleak area, towns that were scarcely more than villages. He was here all of ten years. Well, he lived here, this was his base. A punishment perhaps for some error of thought or action not permitted to his station? Or perhaps Coleman's choice. Yes, Sommerville smiled for a moment and was sober again.

Coleman, if he were aware, was walking a perilous road. A youth had gone from the ranks of his peers; now a schoolgirl, attractive – beautiful one might say, but Sommerville preferred 'nubile' to describe what was desirable – and at the threshold of her life, had been swept away in what, medically, one would accept as an uncustomary visitation of fatal illness. Another corpse at the hospital now. The solution, if it were ever resolved, would shatter this little town. And Coleman, if he persisted on his chosen track, would perish.

Estel Machen was suddenly back with him in the hallway.

"I saw him off," Sommerville said. "He's nosing about."

"He is persistent, a persistent one," she said. "I'll deal with him."

"A policeman. He asked about James Anthony."

"I hope it didn't inconvenience you."

They were both amused.

Sommerville said, "No, he didn't inconvenience me."

She came and kissed him gently on the cheek. "You know I set James Anthony free," she said. "Now, *together*, we will release Jennifer Anderson to join him."

"Together?"

"Yes."

He felt excitement. He had taken sexual pleasure as it came. Male, female, it had been an act of release; young boys had been special. Estel Machen had changed him; she was all things to him.

He watched her penitent grey garb, coarse stockings, flat shoes, lightened only by the starched brilliance of bib, apron and headpiece. She seemed a cold efficient automaton. Sommerville thought of her nudity.

Sommerville's inversion had not been the clean genetic thing it should be; he was aware of his appetite. In world conurbations, he knew, closets had become obsolete, but in small rural patches they were still the refuge of hidden moral blemishes. Men lived a lifetime with inversion, and in ignorance of it. Perversion spread itself across apostles and apostates. For some, pleasure became a solitary act of guilt to be whispered in the darkness of confessional and perhaps shriven by an equally tormented soul.

Sommerville had wealth and property; he could arrange elaborate, complicated assignations, drive for an hour, two hours, to indulge himself. He liked pleasure to be a tangle of limbs, of soft young tender flesh. Sommerville had been an ageing pederast. That had been his preference. He had reached the age of forty-eight.

Estel Machen had changed him.

In medical school and in his time as a houseman he had always desired prurience. The human body, living or dead, dissected and examined, had always seemed to him a mere capsule of pulsing fleshy innards, from viscera to ganglia, of intelligence without provenance or destination. It excited him to abuse it, to ravish it, take it at his will.

He had always spent time in search of what was arcane, occult, forbidden. He had travelled and discovered the almost buried places of Chaldean and Persian sites, seen the first inscription, 'I am all that was, that is, that will be; no mortal can raise my veil'.

He had met mediums of sorcery who, their sacred books proclaimed '. . . gave life to phantoms, taught witchcraft, hovered among tombs, and haunted crossways and places accursed by the blood of the murdered or the suicide; they divined the message of the future, worshipped the dead, evoked the mystic ceremonies of darkness'.

Once, their words had brought excitement; he had written them in his diaries, memorised them.

Estel Machen had changed him.

Quietly she entered his surgery now and took her seat opposite him.

"I'm making a duty call," he explained. An obstinate tottering old featherhead who refuses to die."

"I'll leave out fresh clothes."

He thanked her.

"You'll be late."

"Yes, a little late perhaps."

"I have my prayers and duties at the church," she said.

He held out his hands and she took them.

"The schoolgirl in the hospital is dead," he reiterated. "A routine business. In the funeral home tomorrow. Tomorrow night she rests in the church."

"For a little while. The time is important to me."

"October 31st," he said.

"A very special night," she told him.

They embraced. He could feel her body beneath the dull housekeeper's uniform she wore. She helped him slowly loosen it and laid it on the floor. She gripped and held him there, the intensity hardly bearable it seemed. He watched her dress with such care, a cold mask placed on her face, her hair and uniform arranged. She was his housekeeper.

An hour later in her room she heard the street door close and the sound of Sommerville's car starting, moving away into silence. She bathed and dressed in modest outdoor clothes and walked to the church.

Since she had first stood on his threshold she had looked into Sommerville's thoughts: a cold unemotional perusal. She had given him appetite, passion, never sated desire, she knew, and he was changing.

Ostensibly, she was a zealous Catholic, seen daily, sometimes more often, in devout prayer. But she kept herself apart, held townspeople at a distance, had their respect. They were in awe of her. She had offered her services to the sacristan, a man of importance in the town, lofty, puritanical, but she had broken through his almost silent defence. He had given her menial work in the church, brush and duster work, but now she had access to the holiness of the sacristy itself. Her humility, her devotion, moved like an aura with her . . .

She looked at the town now and saw bare acres of coarse grass and bracken, the passage of time, and on the overlooking hill the remnants of fortified stone, shapes of defence or dwelling, crumbled by centuries. She saw conquests and ruins, lords of the land who came and went, the gathering here of serfs to barter and outwit, the slow painful growth from nothingness to nothingness. Time could in a moment wipe away this fringe of existence.

She walked into the holy ground where church and convent sat apart, keeping respectful distance from each other, on great open spaces of parterred plants and shrubs, gravelled stretches, asphalt approaches. The parochial house was a little distance away. The convent was apart where handmaids of the Lord had once renounced the world and toiled in weeping purity for the dubious reward of heaven.

The convent was empty now: a few ageing nuns. And the imposing parochial dwelling that had housed three, four priests was now a refuge for the canon, very old, living in a constant shadow of pain. The survivor of his breed.

Celibacy, mortification of the flesh, fasting, penance, the confession of sins, roads to the eternal bliss in the sight of God, or to the burning limitless flames of hell, these had lost place, had become fairy tales for the decrepit, the last shifting anchors of the fearful.

Estel Machen climbed the broad stone steps of the church and pushed open its door. She closed it carefully again. Simoney, the sacristan, would be watching, she knew. She walked up the centre aisle through the nave and knelt at the communion rail. The altar, the communion fabric close to her hand as she knelt, was immaculate. The nuns were tiring and Estel Machen had become laundress of sanctuary linen. For close on six months she had devoted her 'untutored' moments of free time to the care of God's house.

She knelt motionless now before the tabernacle, head bowed in devotion, in communion with heaven, the lamp of God's ever-presence above her head. She spent fifteen minutes in this posture of prayer. Then, in humbled measured steps, she made her way to the sacristy.

Simoney had been watching but, on her arrival, he was folding and storing vestments with careful precious hands. At one time Simoney would have been called the clerk of the church, a lay managerial job to deal with day-to-day routine of preparation for ceremony. He had farmed out a great deal of this work to volunteers and his tasks now were closer to holy orders. He administered the sacred host in the church and carried it to the bed-ridden, performed services for the dead, awaited impatiently the opportunities to preach of mankind's wickedness, his imminent damnation.

He was in his late forties, disciplined in countenance and carriage; thick greying hair sat on him like a judge's wig. His house, of good proportions, was a little way from the church. He lived there alone, offering his life in reparation of worldly folly and transgression.

Simoney said, "Good evening, Miss Machen."

"Mr Simoney."

"I heard your arrival, saw you praying."

"My poor distracted prayers," she disparaged herself.

"Nonsense," Simoney said; he ceased work for a moment. "I'm sure you have God's ear."

"Thank you."

He was deep in thought for a while, gazing as if in a vision.

"The altar and sanctuary linen are perfect," he said. "A credit to your industry."

She allowed her cold face to smile.

"Sister Catherine at the convent is growing old," he said. "She launders the *priestly* linen for the service of the holy Mass, you know."

"Yes."

He held up a vestment. "It leaves a lot to be desired, you'll agree."

He paused.

Estel Machen said, "Would she be offended if I did it?"

Simoney showed emotion. "My dear child," he said, "you would be relieving her of a great burden. But I am thinking of *you*. Am I asking too much?"

"Laborare est orare," Estel Machen said.

Simoney nodded devoutly. "You are a good labourer in the vineyard of salvation," he said. He took a small container of scented unction and anointed her hands and forehead with the sign of the cross.

"The *alb*," he said, "is a full-length linen gown, tied with a cord *girdle*. The *amice* is linen too, lies on the shoulders and the neck." He put them in a strapped black hold-all. "Give them your cleanliness. You will have God's blessings all your days." He joined his hands in conclusion.

Estel Machen was filled with humility. "Your knowledge of church liturgy is great," she said. "People spend life-times attending Mass and are in total ignorance of these things. Now I know the alb, the amice, the girdle."

Simoney was excited. "I will explain them to you," he said. "In time you will know all."

On a great polished dressing area he laid out the vestments: cloth of gold, brocade, patterned, embellished, embroidered, clasps of silver and precious alloys. "The alb, the amice, the girdle, the stole, the maniple, the tunic, the chasuble," he named them.

"Wonderful," she said; she watched him fold them and place them in long spacious drawers.

"One day perhaps I will permit you to lay them out for the celebrant. And perhaps teach you to read the liturgical diary and arrange the altar missal for the celebration of the Holy Sacrifice. One day soon."

She seemed overcome with gratitude.

"Wait," he said as she picked up the hold-all of soiled linen. "We have here a most precious vestment, touched by Papal hands, given with honour to our bishop-priest in dark tines of persecution and famine in the not so very distant past. Almost a hundred and fifty years past. A moment in the lim- itless mind of God. It is used rarely now, only by visiting high dignitaries of the church." He unlocked a small satin-lined receptacle, a precious thing. It held a circular woollen piece that would rest on the shoulders with pendants to the chest and back. It was marked with six black crosses. "It is called the Pallium," he said. "I never touch it. Only for truly anointed hands."

Estel Machen gazed at it, how it lay in its luxury, how it was arranged. She thanked him a little breathlessly and went out of the sacristy door, into the yellow twilight of the world, the churchyard and the town.

Simoney stood in thought. She was an inspiring person, dedicated to her work. He needed help and it had been sent to him. He knew she had beauty of face and limbs and hair but, in humility, she obscured, bemasked it. Humility was the mark of great holiness. Dr Sommerville had brought a person of great worth to the town.

Simoney was a Catholic, over-zealous, inordinate, but his blood was mixed. Protestant blood, too, flowed in his veins. He thought sometimes of its impurity and asked God to cleanse him. He drove himself on, as if hardship, drudgery, might be the remedy. He was unrelenting.

The Simoneys had been here on a riverside estate long before a Sommerville had arrived. They had tilled and manicured a thousand acres, created stately manor houses, surrounded by land, for their offspring. They had cleared and paved the area of the Square that had been the first market-pitch. They had fought and banished rebels, harassed and proselytised. They had been cruel people.

With forced labour, they had given depth to the cove and built the curving jetty with great slabs cut and dressed by imported masons. They had built towering five-storey mills and store-houses looking out on the estuary. Their sailing ships had travelled to far shores in pursuit of trade.

Then an ancestor had married a Catholic woman of rank and wealth. She was a person of unbending piety. But the mighty body of the family was split. Its factions lacked the driving force that had forged it. Some went westwards to new America, some to the easy foppish life of London. Some to France.

The town grew, the Simoneys diminished. The estates were squandered. The sailing ships rotted in the shallows of the cove or were lost in storms without the entrepreneur to replace them. The family died of indolence and sterility.

Simoney was the last, unmarried, priest-like. The Catholic blood ran strong in his veins as if that ancient ancestor had inhabited him. He had sufficient wealth and the glebe land of church and convent was his. His house he called 'the Sacristan's House'.

The Simoney estates were gone, the storehouses on the jetty were empty shells where winter winds tossed and tumbled for escape.

Coleman stood at the corner of Main Street and the Square. He stood, back to the wind, and in cupped hands lit a cigarette. In a little while he saw Sommerville's car moving out of town. Sommerville's patients were few, wealthy, scattered. And growing less.

Sommerville had been uneasy, he thought. If in conversation he had mentioned ethics and principles in defence, he had offered a little too. Scraps to show his concern, perhaps to confuse. Keep me informed, Inspector, will you?

There was another case in the hospital. Dead.

Sommerville's personal clientele could be numbered on two hands: scattered, substantial, of course, but also demanding. Sommerville didn't need to practise; he had wealth, property, a forty-foot cruiser in the cove, a car more costly than a town house. He had all the bright appendages and yet seemed a modest man who quietly enjoyed his privilege. It could be an outer shell.

And he was uneasy.

Coleman was uneasy. There was no confusion, but a slight distraction that came when he gathered information in scraps of fact, fiction, conjecture, and hadn't yet formed a pattern or plotted a course. And there was the face of Estel Machen.

Coleman, a garda inspector, lived here. His area was five hundred square miles of desolate country, small towns, villages, a long serrated coastal strip that bounded it. Holiday caravan sites and a couple of strung-out settlements blossomed by the sea, smeared the coast, for perhaps six, eight, weeks in a year – the 'season' – and then reverted to stasis. A wild famished country of far-spaced farms, outcrops of rock and scarce pockets of rich glacial soil.

The area of the town was small; it had spread in recent years, smartened, improved. The nucleus had what might eventually become 'style'. It was a good thriving market town, perhaps spurred towards excellence by such a vast featureless hinterland of solitude. Coleman liked the cleanliness that a day's rain could bring: scoured roadways, pavements, gutters, the estuary tossed and angry. And when sunshine came it seemed to colour the town with its warmth.

Secretiveness has its abode in rural places and parishes. Some things are locked away. There is always evasion, subterfuge. Coleman pondered it. Indispositions, inherited weaknesses, disorders however trivial, hidden blemishes, were all beyond a veil. Lunacy was unmentionable. Visible deformities of birth, God-given, were cruel acts of providence sent to test faith and fortitude.

The aged ones were villains of the piece, their unshakeable belief that the will of God created beauty and blemish, each with a purpose. God was thanked for everything. Rain or sunshine, storm or calm, it was a fine day, thank God. You admired a new-born child and, lest your stare carried evil with it, you appended a God Bless him or her. When monstrous tragedy fell, it was the will of God.

Tales were told and Coleman had heard them all. He watched cars move in and out of the town, glass and cellulose paintwork smeared in this land of rain and sand and corrosion. Machines wasted like lifetimes. In ten years of patrol he had glanced in more than a hundred farmyards, never to see a proud owner washing, polishing his car. It would have smacked of unmanliness. These were hard men, coarse-grained, playing their parts.

Foreign-owned cars passed too but their surfaces and wheels shone. There might be a liveried expressionless chauffeur. Strange people had come and settled along two hundred miles of Atlantic coast in recent times. They had built homes, spacious imposing residences, furnished in luxury. Their cars rested under cover and local labour washed and polished them, tended them like blood-stock. Who were they? They had high-speed launches and never the weather to loll on deck in the warmth of sunshine. At night-time Coleman carefully watched his stretch of coast and had never seen movement. But dope, he knew, could be left far out on small floating markers, the first wary step on its trip to a thousand places . . .

Now he had other worries.

There would be a body in Rellighan's funeral home tomorrow, and then a removal to the church for an evening service. The following day an open grave would be awaiting it in the cemetery he had visited.

This morning he had driven thirty odd miles to the county town to examine the death register. James Anthony, 17 years, died on the 28th April: cachexia, meningitis, terminal. April 28th, six months past.

And now another young corpse at the hospital. Jennifer Anderson. She had been alive when he had driven out of town this morning. Her illness had worried him and he had felt an urgency to enquire, to move. Coleman knew the schoolgirls of the town, by sight if not by name. From the housing estate, they crossed the Square morning and afternoon, and at lunch time. In ten years you saw them pass from childhood to maturity towards womanhood. The seven-year-olds unaware of their tossed hair, hanging socks; at seventeen, uniforms styled, shortened, tucked; hair, everything they could make of it. At weekends, out of uniform, a trace of eye-shadow and gaudiness of lips was their war-paint. The boys looked at legs, bums and breasts. Coleman had been ten years in the town;

he had seen a new generation sprout, grow, take shape, prepare for the battles ahead. They were a healthy crew, he thought.

He had grown himself, from twenty-five to thirty-five. He was angry. He liked this town in all its moods. He had known the remote Dr Keelehan, a failing man, an alcoholic; he had seen him, at night-time, carry in the paper-wrapped cases of spirits to his house. It was a colourless, odourless life-blood to him. Without alcohol he might have been a gibbering wreck, but he could expertly dose himself to a normality where he had peace and reasonable competence. Keelehan wouldn't gamble with his patients' lives.

Sommerville's practice was only a convenience for his diminishing peers; he wasn't a pleasant man but pleasure filled his mind, obsessed him. He had travelled near and far, Coleman knew, to find rough trade, male, female, catamite, and he paid for the best.

Times had changed. Since the arrival of this pious protective housekeeper, Machen, he had travelled less. Pious? Had she taught him to pray with her and to play with her? Coleman shrugged; private entertainments were Sommerville's business. Machen, her face, he thought again.

Six months past, the suddenness of James Anthony's death had left a doubt, a dissatisfaction. But now Keelehan was dead, his dust scattered. And there was another corpse.

Jennifer Anderson.

He looked out across this hub of the town; shop windows all alight, mingling with the fall of yellow glow from the street lamps, the flood-lit Celtic cross to honour patriots. He saw Colleran, a young person of twenty-five, at his corner, too thin, still as a sentry, a cigarette in his mouth. Ten years ago he had been a bright schoolboy and then was suddenly stricken with mental illness. Schizophrenia: listening to voices of his own private world, smiling. Coleman talked to him sometimes, gave him cigarettes. His madness skipped from moment to moment. He too was a dead child.

Coleman walked across the Square, turned down an alley-way to Rellighan's yard. The wicket gate was open and Rellighan, at the corner of the space, was seated in his light-ed office. Beside it was garage-parking for two hearses and a mourners' car. The opposing end was a storeroom for coffins and catalogues and furnishings, plastic flowers, sacred pic-tures. There was a wardrobe to house the black garments of Rellighan, the undertaker. And standing apart, a corpse room.

Rellighan's funeral home, where remains could be viewed, was a little more distant up town, close to the church. When he had packaged the merchandise he displayed it expertly in the pious image that was required.

He was a tall bony caricature of yellow face from where eyes could show a bare moment of commiseration. The yel-low skin might, down the years, have soaked up endless graveyard miseréres.

He had heard Coleman's footsteps in the alleyway, watched his shadow in the wicket and his progress across the yard. Rellighan was motionless, seemingly unaware as he studied his newspaper.

Rellighan waited for him to knock at his door. It had a plain glass panel; he nodded.

Coleman stepped in out of the wind. There was a scarce bleak feeling of heat in the office, no more: a board floor, two worn rugs, a few files, neat papers trapped beneath a paper-weight, a pen, a lead pencil, a newspaper on a bare table and, behind him, framed, a photograph of a thirties Vauxhall motor hearse, pride of a predecessor – a stirring of life in the death trade. Rellighan alone was remarkable.

He stared at Coleman.

Coleman saw the expensive free-standing gas heater; a sin-gle dull element made a fluttering noise. Rellighan seemed unaware.

The butane cylinder, too, was dying.

Coleman raised a hand. "Cold, isn't it?"

"Yes," Rellighan said and waited.

Rellighan was in his early seventies, and close on sixty years had passed since he had fled Europe for England, Ireland, Boston. He was twelve years of age then. He was a gypsy. In Europe the herding of itinerant people had begun even so early; they were gathered, driven, entrained, sent great distances, usefully to work out what remained of their lifespans. Europe was being changed, cleansed. People scattered.

In hard times in Boston you worked when and where you could, and Rellighan had become a corpse-washer, a dogsbody in a backstreet funeral parlour, hidden, occluded, but in what was an extensive property, busy. Corpses didn't worry Rellighan, they were useless dead meat. He had put in his time, learned his business well. And he had murdered. He lived with death; death followed him. He had sailed out of Boston.

In time he was in Ireland again with bundled ten dollar bills wrapped in dirty clothing, a battered suitcase. He was an accentless American citizen, celibate, unencumbered, uninterested. The thought of buggery was repulsive. He had stripped, washed, scrubbed and caulked too many pale cadavers for passion to survive . . .

"There's a school lassie in the hospital," Coleman said.

"She's dead."

"Yes."

"A couple of hours dead. They've gone to collect her."

Coleman paced to the window, looked out across the yard. "You mind if I smoke?" he said.

"I don't mind if you burn."

Coleman nodded. "Cause of death?"

"Look, Coleman, I'm an undertaker. I plug and wash them, restore a kind of peacefulness to their faces, put them underground, collect my money, lose it sometimes. Then I sit here and wait."

"Six months," Coleman said. "Two school pupils in six months. Good bodies, good lookers, healthy. Then a sudden temperature, blinding head pain, rigor, vomiting, hospital. A week and they're on your slab."

"It could be your turn next week."

"Or yours."

Rellighan might have been amused; he looked at the newspaper. "I know the town is whispering," he said.

"Talking," Coleman said. "They're talking now. Young corpses. Two in six months."

Rellighan shrugged. "They might even shout. Genital disease, someone said. A curse on us and our youth, clergy, doctors, politicians, tight-lipped. Morals, that'll be the cry. A curse on our wickedness."

Coleman said, "Genital disease wastes bodies away. A long time."

"I don't need instruction," Rellighan told him.

"Cause of death?" Coleman asked him. "Meningitis?"

Rellighan looked at him, nodded.

"Another one?"

"Yes."

"Two cases at once, a bit freakish but it happens. Ours, spaced out. Young bodies. Health today, death tomorrow. And the speed of departure. Seven, eight days. Weak ailing ones, yes. But these were the pick of the bunch."

Rellighan opened one finger from his tight fist and pointed at the town. "Tell *them* that. I have to work this corpse myself. Staff are absent, unenthusiastic."

Coleman ground out his cigarette in Rellighan's polished ashtray. "Tell me about it. The first one," he said.

Rellighan seemed to crouch behind his grey, almost achromic eyes.

"Just a death," he said, "that's all." He was angry to be involved even at the fringes of this small town witch-hunt. "That's my business here. Death. One, two, a dozen bodies, young, old, cold or growing cold, the same as everything we handle."

"There are silences out there too. Uneasiness. Who prepared the last corpse?"

"The last *young* corpse? James Anthony. That's six months

62

ago. *I* did. The staff thought he was corrupt. Wouldn't handle him!"

"Was he?"

"He was clean, untouched. I talked to the hospital. This one's the same, they say. A clean body."

Outside, the main gates were opened and a deep blue van pulled into the farthest corner of the yard.

Rellighan said, "If *I* drop down one of these days, who will touch me who has touched everything?" It was Rellighan's humour but he didn't smile.

Coleman nodded. "James Anthony was Keelehan's patient. Keelehan's four months dead."

"He poisoned himself. With alcohol. Twenty years of alcohol. He slipped away."

"But young deaths? The town is wondering."

"Small towns always wonder."

"I don't like it," Coleman said. "Somewhere there should be a pattern."

"Coincidence," Rellighan dismissed it.

"Same age, same infection, no resistance, allergic to drugs. A lot of coincidence."

"Undertakers bury the dead, Coleman." Rellighan nodded his vehemence. "I talked to that poor drunken bastard, Keelehan, when James Anthony died six months ago. Meningitis, he said. Two months hadn't passed and I had Keelehan on the table himself. He came from the hospital. His liver was a hobnailed boot. The staff decked him out but I could see fear in their eyes. I can smell fear. Keelehan's hands had touched the corrupt flesh of James Anthony too."

Coleman stopped him. "I came to see *you*," said Coleman. "You worked on the last body. You had no help?"

"No."

"You saw the body naked."

"You always see bodies naked."

"Marks? Were there marks on the flesh? Were there marks anywhere?"

"Needle marks where the spine was punctured. They took off fluid."

"Nose, ears? Signs of infection?"

Rellighan's voice was flat. "He was healthy," he said. "His face drawn from a week's illness, that's all. Decades ago I saw everything they had on Boston slabs. A big job or a little one, you think. I know my business, Coleman."

Coleman was silent for a few moments. "Tuberculosis, something that had begun to waste him? Nose or ear infection could trigger it off . . ."

"He was healthy. The family was healthy. That's Keelehan's opinion. Mine too."

Coleman paced about; a yellow crown of light sat on the town. "When this little dead one in the hospital is brought to you, you'll do the work yourself?"

"She's here now. The van brought her. She's Jennifer Anderson. You want to see her?"

They moved out across the yard. When leaving, the van men had locked the main gates; Rellighan pulled a heavy bolt across the wicket.

Beside the storeroom there was a heavy concrete cube, a building. Rellighan opened the door and locked it behind them. The light was brilliant, shining on the cold spotlessness of the room. There were two air extractors, no windows; stillness lived there, stainless steel hand basins and utensils, tiled floor and walls. A shining concave table with channels and draining vents was the centrepiece. On it a plastic body-bag lay where the van men had dropped it.

Rellighan and Coleman stood looking down at it.

Coleman said, "This could be a fuse-cord, a touch-paper."

"Another body."

"Keep a sharp eye on the town, Rellighan. Take care. There's something wrong."

Rellighan might not have been listening; he was empty, blank.

"If something comes to light . . ."

"People don't talk about family illnesses," Rellighan said.

"Other people do."

The body-bag was an opaque piece of plastic, zipped from top to toe.

"Now?" Rellighan asked.

"Yes."

He pulled open the zip, lifted out the shoulders, head, arms, exposed the torso, thighs, feet.

Coleman looked at her beauty, a little colour still left, the blood slowly draining away from the surface flesh. Illness had left traces of darkness beneath her eyes. He touched her hands. They were cold, moving on towards the total coldness of death. He took a flashlight from the pocket of his coat.

Rellighan watched him. He shone the light in her ears; her head was hanging back and he could look down into the cavities of nose and throat. Her skin was unblemished.

"The back," he told Rellighan.

Rellighan turned her. The skin was a little darker, less cold perhaps. There were only the tiny spinal punctures where fluid had been drawn.

"The same symptoms?" he asked again.

"There's a locum for Keelehan. His verdict."

"The locum consulted Sommerville."

Coleman thanked him. Rellighan walked with him across the yard and along the cobbled alleyway to the street.

Down behind the farthest end the ground rose gently to the still new housing estate: rows of terraced dwellings, fresh, reasonably tended, less than a few years old.

"People are getting restless over there, aren't they?"

Rellighan closed his eyes, was corpse-like. "There are stories in the air. The land is a fairy fort, they left their poison there to protect it. All that folklore crap." Rellighan looked towards the estate. "Where would they go? People in the town are pulling away from them, don't want them in their kitchens, or behind their counters. Anywhere. Even labouring men in the fields."

"And Keelehan is dead," Coleman said. "What about you? You handled the corpse."

"James Anthony. And this one here in the morning."

"No staff, you said?"

"Small town undertakers lead quiet lives. Killer flu, diphtheria, consumption, the black plague, the pox. I bury them all."

Coleman looked at the worn creviced face. "They respect you, Rellighan," he said.

"They fear me. I'm the raven, the black dog, the headless coachman."

Coleman said, "They're not in love with squad cars either." He looked at Rellighan's pale grey eyes as if a life with death had soaked away all colour.

"You're going to stay with it?" Rellighan asked.

"Unofficially."

Rellighan nodded. "You know where to find me," he said and turned away.

Coleman walked to the housing estate and through its empty streets. Lights shone in windows, not a soul abroad.

Small towns had taken root where there was proximity to water and pasture, squares of arable land. Animals grazed and gave milk and meat, vegetation gave fruit and root crops. But water, without taste colour smell, was life itself.

A great river flowed past the cove at the dip of the town, widening into an estuary miles wide, moving on to mingle with an ocean.

Old towns, like Coleman's, once had crooked streets where mismatched houses had clung to each other. The shopkeeper arranged his counter, laid out stock in the window, another supplied him. The carpenter, the farrier, the smithy, the publican, the coffin makers, the clothier, the shoemaker, the baker, the farmer, made work for each other and for the labouring man. The roads were dirt roads without pavements. Peat burned on open hearths and pots and kettles hung from iron cranes.

When times were good there was life and warmth; in bad times, diseases, starvation, death.

Priests and schoolmasters came. Churches and schools were made to accommodate them. Thou shall, thou shalt not was preached. The pedagogue chanted his text. Minds were set free or strangulated. The pattern was laid. Healers healed the sick or killed them. They learned their trades.

Very old people could remember a time when there was a pump in Main Street with a hook to hang a bucket, and an iron handle to draw up ice-cold water from deep down. It was a gathering place for women. The news of the town was exchanged there. Musicians stopped, played for farthings, moved on.

And there was a workhouse where the housing estate stood now. A two storey stone building, small windows, tall chimneys. A sad place. There was a wing for dying and a wing for existing. The sexes were segregated, aged husbands and wives divorced after lifetimes of hardship shared. A lonely place. If you had strength they worked you for your keep.

A transformed town now. Plastic and shining windows, a small supermarket, pavements and tarmacadamed roads, shops of dash and style. A hotel, flash pubs, piped music. Motor cars were parked nose to tail; pleasure boats moored in the cove; doctors, a hospital, an imposing school, a towering church and convent. Coleman walked on.

Every village, small town, big town, made its own ghettoes. Segregation wasn't imposed, people found their own levels: up-town, down-town, east end, west end. It was an opening stage only. From there you climbed or fell. And every ghetto has its ghetto.

Coleman walked the entire estate, passed the house where death had visited, and looked for some variance, some incongruity. He saw polished door furniture, name-plates, clean curtains, patches of garden, every house the house next door.

He looked for some random pattern, the uncommon factor, a linkage, and could find only uniformity. They were neat, decent, maintained houses.

The streets were empty.

Coleman walked back again to the town centre, the Square. The north-west wind pierced his face and eyes and it was stronger now, but there was a false warmth, a security, in bright shop windows, street lights. People too, their voices, profanity, laughter, distanced the housing estate and Rellighan's workaday dealings with bereavements and grief.

In Main Street he stood at a shop window, small, dressed and lighted with simplicity: only a half dozen items were on display, suspended by thread-fine wire so that they seemed like graceful grotesqueries on the wing. It was called, 'Night Out', stylish, exclusive, expensive. The soft lighting spilt across the pavement. The shop was locked. There was a private door, a lighted bell and the legend, 'Annabelle Cannon'. Coleman pressed on it: one long ring.

Annabelle Cannon was five feet eight inches tall, with dark auburn hair. Her face, not beautiful – although you didn't forget it – had sense and humour. She fitted neatly into her black slacks and a deep red polo-neck. In the expanding town school she gave classes to students in the science and economy of housecraft. She was thirty-one and didn't look it, smart, agile, dedicated to the single life and, like Coleman, she was an outsider, also ten years in the town and busy.

She opened the door to the hallway; her face had warmth for Coleman.

He acknowledged with the careful smile she liked; he followed her up the carpeted stairs, water-colours, prints, all the way, could feel the warmth of heating, smell good food from her kitchen.

"You didn't phone," she said. "I didn't expect you. But there's plenty of food."

"I need it," Coleman said. He hadn't eaten since a cup-in-hand breakfast.

68

She went to her kitchen: clean, bright, everything there, material, mechanical, to sustain the good life. Plain foods for Annabelle Cannon: a little to chew on morning and midday, but at seven-thirty each evening she dined. No starters or puddings. But a real main course, a glass of wine or two, and coffee. She thought of Coleman out in the lounge and gave him a deep plate. Coleman's face had a lot of placidity behind it. He could be cross of course. She had seen him once disperse a crew of street fighters, and it was frightening. But when he had met her again and smiled, she thought he was so handsome she could have hugged him.

She could hear him now sluicing down in the bathroom.

She called out, "You still there, Coleman?"

"Still here."

"Any minute now."

"Good."

She arrived. Coleman stood in her lounge-diner, looking down from the window along a lively Main Street at people, shop-displays, passing cars. He could see in the near distance the silhouetted school on the hill, lighted windows of houses on the fringe like yellow posters against a black bulk of sky. The quiet rhythm of the town should be reassuring. At once it was an impenetrable shield, he thought; and in an instant it could be shattered. Life was a fragile passage from where to where?

Belle Cannon brought a meal of brittle casseroled beef, vegetables, herbs, moist in deep brown dressing: a large brimming oval dish for Coleman. She poured wine.

He turned. She came to the window, pulled the curtains, shut out the world. Coleman saw her here two, three, times a week. They each had other lives to live but they had been in love for a long time. They never talked marriage.

"Give love a chance," Coleman would say. "Live at opposite sides of the park."

He took her in his arms now, held her, let her calmness unwind him a little.

"You kiss better every year," he said.

"I get in a little practice when you're not looking, Coleman."

They sat and ate, hardly talking; an occasional glance, a raised glass. She cleared the table, brought coffee.

"I want to talk," Coleman said.

"You didn't come to see me. You came to quiz me."

"I always want to see you."

"I'll get you a drink," she said. "I know when something's burning you." She brought a measure of whiskey.

"I'd like to smoke."

She nodded. "It must be bad."

Coleman drank a little, felt the warmth, put his glass on the coffee table, paced slowly about, looking absently at paintings, line drawings, brass, crystal, a lot of books on white shelves, scarcely seeing them, forgetting them. She watched him, waited. You couldn't hurry Coleman; he would talk when he was ready.

"There's something I want to discuss."

"Yes, I know."

"You know?"

"I know what you want to discuss."

"Yes?"

"Death."

"Yes," he said.

She was sitting at the far end of a great floral couch; he leant against the arm-rest and looked across at her. "Deaths of school-leavers, you could call it. From your school."

She was silent for a little while. "It's under wraps, Coleman. For teachers, it's under wraps."

Coleman nodded, he understood. "The wraps will be off now. There's another one in Rellighan's make-up parlour."

"I know. She's been ill for days."

"Seven days. And fear is moving on the street out there. They'll want a quarantine on the housing estate, blood tests, witch-hunts, Christ!"

"We have threats in classrooms," Belle Cannon said. No estate children, no disease."

Coleman had known. "What will you do?" he asked.

"Wait."

He finished his drink, went on pacing again. The same symptoms, Sommerville knew. Rellighan knew. That much was right. Two cases, strung out, isolated, haphazard. But still a pattern of infection. And a six month gap, almost to the day. Young deaths stirred emotion, fear. The tests had said *meningitis*. The same bug. Coleman puzzled over it. What was unusual about two deaths, even three? Sommerville in his surgery had said, "'normal' is a layman's word, old man."

"What are you looking for, Coleman?" Belle Cannon asked him. "Tell me."

"Something to string them together."

"James Anthony, Jennifer Anderson."

"That's right."

"They had meningitis."

"Yes," he said "They were healthy. But they're dead. Six months, almost to the day. Allergic to what could have saved them too. Both of them."

"Ages, sixteen, seventeen."

"Well-made, good lookers."

Belle Cannon watched him.

"No fight in them!" he said. "They lasted seven, eight days. No strength."

"Estate children aren't weak, Coleman," she said. "Stronger than the rest, maybe. You came to quiz me about their school life, didn't you?"

Coleman said, "If you don't want to talk about it, I'll understand."

"I don't mind talking to you."

Coleman nodded.

"There was no bond between them. Different groups, friends, different subjects. Jennifer Anderson came to me for domestic classes. Not James Anthony."

71

Outside the wind had risen again and brought rain with it. It gusted and hammered against the windows, made a kind of crying sound as it swept between houses. This was a marshalling yard of winds and rains and mists, from where the curving arrows of the weather-men took route and isobars pulled close together for the erratic sudden storms of winter.

Belle Cannon came to Coleman. It was warm and comfortable here. He put his hands on her shoulders.

"Cold?" he said.

"A shiver. Someone walked on my grave, that's the saying, isn't it?"

"All our graves are walked on."

He sat on the edge of the sofa. He liked the countryside in sunshine, wind or rain; he liked to walk on fallen leaves or wet grass; to sit by the estuary, push out a dinghy; in soft fading autumn light to 'flight' for mallard until darkness fell. This was his place, he wanted to stay here, he needed to stay here, to keep it intact. And there was Belle Cannon, of course. He smiled at her.

"You're in deep," she said.

He nodded.

"You think there's a stalking horse somewhere?"

"I don't know."

"A freak?"

"I don't believe in freaks. Meningitis kills. Kills sickly people in a few days."

"They were strong."

"Should they have died in days?" Coleman asked. "Or battled on for longer? I talked with Sommerville."

"Nothing?"

"Not his patients. He's very calm, reassuring." Coleman stood and she brought him his coat. "Thanks for the drink, the meal, for being here, I'll move about, talk, listen."

Belle Cannon kissed him. "When you get home, ring me."

"Yes," he said.

Coleman had a bachelor house at the fringes of the town.

The wind met him on the pavement, cold, piercing. He tightened the jacket about him, pulled on a cap. The street was clear of people, even the roads clear of traffic, but shop windows illuminated the blowing rain. As he passed along Main Street to Finegan's he saw again the suspended mats of light, the distant windows, the sky black behind them.

He entered the comfort of Finegan's bar; it embraced him. He settled himself on a stool at the counter. The usual groups were ensconced. The wind and rain were out there in another world.

Finegan brought him a drink. "Another one dead," he said. "The town is poxed. I told you."

"Yes."

"What do you think, Inspector?" someone called out.

"No idea," Coleman said.

"Sex," a voice said from the shadows. "A good school we have here. Teaches them to poke and smoke."

Coleman saw it wasn't a time for discussion; he paid Finegan and nursed his drink.

Softly Finegan asked, "Is anyone, anywhere, doing anything. You should know."

"There's a doctor."

"There *isn't* a doctor."

"When he's appointed. There's a locum now," Coleman said.

"Jesus, locums are like part-time staff."

Background talk was controlled, predictable. "Two factories in the town. Shit, waste, pollution."

Finegan closed it down; factories were money. "Work for forty people!" he said, "We've had them here for fifteen years now."

"Waste in the river."

"No waste in the river."

When there was silence, Coleman said "Meningitis."

"That's fancy name for something."

"It affects the brain and spine."

73

"Bollocks!"

"Maybe your bollocks too."

Finegan murmured in his confidential tone to Coleman. "What's different, is that a worry? In this town what's different in six months? Nothing."

Coleman nodded. "A few new people. A pharmacist, a bank clerk, a hair-dresser . . ."

"People come and go."

Coleman sat and drank. Conversation had dwindled. Fear was an enemy, dangerous, it could crawl over a town, disturb its slumber, its peace. When this young one on Rellighan's table was taken away to the funeral home and to the church, how many would attend the mourning, the burial.

The town was in dread. The housing estate was a plague spot. Family, relatives would carry the coffin, backfill the grave. He, Coleman would be there. A small crowd, a handful of people, children, Rellighan.

He thought of Sommerville. Sommerville had been cool, defensive, confident. He had said his piece. Coleman had felt that, close at hand, ready to be floated, were all the complications of germs, serums, mutations.

Nothing was moving out there; only whispers of disquiet were abroad.

Finegan, inside the counter, opposite him, listened in silence to wind and rain, occasional gusts against the window. The sound of winter, he knew.

He said to Coleman, "The market days will be thinner. They're thin already. Soon country people won't set foot in a poisoned town. They'll turn away. There's marts and markets everywhere now. They'll change direction. Another five or ten miles is a small price to pay for safety."

Coleman thought about it for a long time; he said eventually, "What about Sommerville's housekeeper?"

"*Dr* Sommerville's housekeeper. What about her?"

"What's different in six months," Coleman said.

Finegan forced a smile of regret for the town. "If all our Catholics had her virtue."

"I just wondered," Coleman said. "New people, little changes we hardly notice."

Finegan dismissed it. "Foreigners have been settling along this coast since the war. Dutch, Germans, Poles, Greeks, Italians. Asians like flies, they never sleep. You name it, they have it. They bring money."

Coleman nodded.

Finegan was in full flow. "The Sommerville family has given distinction to this town for a hundred and fifty years, more than that. Dr Herbert Sommerville is the last. His housekeeper is an example to us."

"Yes."

"A silent woman," someone said.

"Modesty," Finegan told him. "A short time here and she's part of the town."

"Charitable."

"Finds time to visit the sick too, lays her gifted hands on them. A quiet graceful woman."

Coleman was thinking, studying the bar-room faces. "Heals them, does she?" he asked.

"Comforts them is how she puts it. She visits the hospital, supports it. That's what charity is. She prays at bedsides and in the dying-rooms."

"God rest the dead," someone said.

"And at the school," Finegan spat out his sermon, "she helps the school, Saturday mornings, gives lessons, no charge. Speech and drama or something."

Coleman said, "She's English, I suppose."

"English, what else? The English aristocracy left us a legacy of graceful living."

"Yes," Coleman agreed; he was remembering Estel Machen's trace of accent.

Finegan stared at him for a moment, and moved down the counter to tend his customers.

Coleman sat on until after midnight, stayed on the fringe of the conversation, listened. Time and alcohol brought a kind of softness, peace. Approbation flowed for the lady of the doctor's house: she had healing hands.

Finegan moved about. A farming woman, he told, from the surrounding acres, had touched her sleeve in the hospital wards one day and said that her eyes were failing, a darkness growing on her. That night she was blind and in the morning awoke restored. She could see blades of grass in a distant field. Finegan shook his head in wonder.

Coleman said, "She died within a month."

"An old woman," Finegan said.

"One sunrise she was found lifeless on a stretch of road," Coleman said.

"Struck by something, torn, lacerated. A car, a truck, drunken drivers."

"An open case," Coleman said.

He lapsed to silence, kept his own company. Talk was the life blood of small places. Wherever people met to sit and face each other there was something to be spoken or whispered; but the absorbing exchanges were those of conjecture, a jig-saw, the piecing together of improbable ends for unfinished incidents. Old histories could be raked and examined, the dead disturbed in their rest, the final conclusions unspoken, hinted at by tight lips and nodding heads.

The 'torn, lacerated' woman somewhere in the hospital wards or grounds, who had touched the sleeve of Estel Machen in months past had some irreversible disease of the retina. The loss and restoration of sight overnight – if it had credence – was some freak of blood, some twitch of muscle, an ictus. Or it had never happened. Coleman, in his patrols about the twisted skein of coastal roads in the weeks that followed, had looked often in her farmyard. She lived alone, widowed, an emigrated family that might be dead or alive. He had seen her tapping and poking, groping her way from house to outhouse, through pools of gathering water, wasting away her days, waiting for a darkness that was total. Distant neighbours shopped in town for her, with kindness supplemented her needs. When they said she 'rambled' they meant the occasional incoherent thoughts she expressed. But she rambled on the roadway too and in fading evening light she had been stricken and breathed her last there. Thrombosis was the medical verdict, the cuts and abrasions inflicted after death. Her dead body had been run over – perhaps another bump on a stony road – but no culprit had ever been found. She had been dead for hours; the lacerations to her legs and thighs showed only an ooze of blood.

An unsatisfactory ending to a story with all the dark whispers of foul play. And the miracle of sight too lost out there in that lonely world.

Deaths, superstitions, misdeeds were the stuff of conversation. Nothing should be begun on a Friday, birds flying this way or that were portents; dreams had meanings, the spilling of salt might herald disaster, six magpies made a wake, watch the animals that cross your path. Lunar changes had strange influence; marriage was fenced about with superstition. If the moon in full so is the bride's cup full of happiness. But more important than the moon's age is the day of the week for matrimony.

'Monday for wealth, Tuesday for health,
Wednesday the best day of all;
Thursday for crosses, Friday for losses,
Saturday no luck at all.'
Superstition died hard. An open case.

When Coleman left he walked in the interminable wind and rain to the town fringes and his home. The shrouded stone school on the hill was a smudge of blackness smeared over night-time. The town windows were darkening for sleep. The houses, the people, in peace, he wondered? It was a short walk to his home; it was a small town. Rain had streaked across his jacket.

Coleman's place had been a blacksmith's forge; transformed now. The outer shell of unfinished pointed stone had stood unmoved, impenetrable, for more than a hundred years. With his own hands Coleman had fitted his rooms and amenities, re-roofed it, left an open stairway to a half-loft that was his bedroom. It was a comfortable place of bright coloured walls, cold now except for the warmth of lighting. But with a fire in the open hearth it was a place to laze, to squander time.

There was no hallway, only a small lobby, a tiny vestibule where he left his 'defence' of outer garments. He crossed the lounge, took the plug-in telephone with him up the stairs and put it beside his bed.

He rang Belle Cannon.

"Yes," she said, almost at once. "You're late. Are you all right?"

"It was a quiet night," he said.

"Nothing to tell?"

"Something to ask."

"Yes?"

"Estel Machen," he said, "Sommerville's housekeeper. She gives classes at the school."

"Saturday mornings," Belle Cannon said. "Voluntary pupils. No charge. Drama and speech. It's good, takes the corners off them. They'll have lots of interviews and orals ahead."

"Good of her too."

"Yes."

"How long?"

She thought about it. "Almost since she arrived. All of seven months, I suppose."

"Girls and boys?"

"Yes."

Coleman said, slowly turning it over. "This young corpse in the cemetery? And the one who is lying in Rellighan's?"

"Yes?"

"They were drama pupils?"

There was silence for a few moments. "Yes," she said.

"They were drama pupils." Silence settled again. "Coleman," she said eventually.

"Yes."

"You don't think . . ."

Coleman said, "It's just a venue where all these drama pupils met once a week. A link maybe. They talked, they touched. A big class."

He lit a cigarette. She could hear the snap of the lighter. Leave Coleman to his ponderings for a few moments. She held her phone, listened to his stirrings. Coleman, in the chilliness of his home, took hold of something and, sleepless, chased it down the hours and days . . .

Belle Cannon had met Estel Machen, talked to her. She hadn't told Coleman. Estel Machen, she had felt, could smile a great warmth of friendliness and leave behind a feeling of chill. It seemed a kind of ghoulish dream, looking back. Estel Machen had left her in fear.

Belle Cannon had sat in her class one evening, sat apart from her pupils, an observer. Estel Machen was in black: black slacks, turtle-neck top, leather shoes soft as fabric. The perfection of body, poise, movement, captured the imagination; it might have been a composition in balance and harmony. If she paused, stopped, gestured, she was a frozen beautiful image, her features, her hair, caught in deep stillness. Pupils gazed at her, motionless, encapsulated in thought. She held them with every movement, every word.

Belle Cannon might have been unseen, sitting alone, a vapour, a ghost.

Estel Machen was saying ". . . improvisation can help you in social and emotional development. In psychiatric hospitals, improvisation in used in the treatment of neurotics and delinquents. You become a force. In it you are no longer alone, isolated. You drive out unhappiness, you create. You create *with others*. Life is something we do with one another, the road to create, to be spontaneous together."

She paused, smiled, brought her class to life. The faces of

pupils were bright, animated. They were smitten.

"In a few moments," she said, "I will break you into groups of twos and threes. Stand apart, take an idea, a word, whisper your thoughts to each other. You will have five minutes. Then you will enact your dramas for me."

She smiled again: excitement, laughter, rippled along their faces.

"Yes," she said, "love, hate, life, death, whatever rises up in your minds. Now form yourself into groups."

In the noise, the sudden confusion, she turned her gaze on Belle Cannon. She came to her, her face calm, in humiliation. A saint.

She said, "I deeply appreciate your interest in my work. I am flattered."

Belle Cannon suddenly had to fight back a nausea that was rising inside her, a bitterness, a sourness of bile. She was cold, trembling a little. She looked at Estel Machen's eyes, the empty depths of them.

"I've watched your classes from outside before now," she said. "Tonight I thought I might sit quietly in a corner and not intrude." She felt illness.

"You look unwell," Estel Machen said. "We should stand in the coolness of the corridors for some air. Come."

Belle Cannon might have been a lifeless figure she had animated; she followed her slowly from the classroom into the cold terrazzo passage. Through the glass she could see the pupils posing, waving, rehearsing.

"School children are so sensitive," Estel Machen said.

"You think so?"

"Oh yes."

"You like schoolchildren to work with?"

"Yes."

"Am I intruding?"

"Perhaps you inhibit them," Estel Machen said.

The sourness seemed to have soaked into her mind; Belle Cannon stood powerless there. Estel Machen's face was close to hers. She thought it had crumpled into an ageing mass of skin and almost sightless distant eyes; the flowing hair had gone, even the scalp was creased and mottled.

"Oh God!" she said.

"You're not well," Estel Machen told her. "I could get someone to walk you home."

"I have a car."

She closed her eyes. Sweetness, mild at first, seemed to creep about her; then suddenly it was smothering.

Estel Machen's unspoken words were reiterated in her mind. "Go now. In future never come."

For a moment she wondered if it had been a voice, a thought? Had there ever been a voice, a thought?

She looked and saw the beautiful Estel Machen before her again. Her eyes were soft, sympathetic.

"Forgive me," she said. "They work better unwatched by others. Thank you for coming."

Belle Cannon looked from the gentle face before her to the classroom beyond the glass partition and saw Estel Machen *there too* in all her poise and perfection! She looked at the smiling doppelganger figure before her. Estel Machen bowed to her. She was left standing alone in the empty corridor. The improvisation class, the spate of noisy applause, Estel Machen urging it on, swallowed up the illusion of a minute past.

She drove home. Had it been real or a moment of fantasy? She was shaken, angry. She had hidden it, pushed it out of her mind . . .

She looked at the telephone in her hand. She felt fear. "Coleman," she said.

"I'm here," he said.

"Good, but you were miles away."

"Yes."

"You're going out again. At this hour?"

"Yes."

"Be careful, Coleman."

81

"I'll be careful," he told her.

"Estel Machen seems good in every young mind she shapes," she said, "but there's something wrong, Coleman."

Silence for a few moments.

"Something rotten?" he asked.

"Come and have dinner with me every night until it's over. Seven o'clock. Whenever you come. Promise, Coleman."

"Yes," he said. "I'll come."

It was after midnight. In Coleman's house there was a small gable-end window high in the apex; a wooden handrail at the edge of this loft bedroom. The bare floor was honey-stained. His bed jutted out from a side wall. There was a bedside locker, a reading lamp, his telephone.

He put the telephone carefully in its cradle, walked to the handrail and leant on it like a day-tripper looking down at the ebb and flow of the tide, listening to the hoarse sound of gravel. The lounge below with its comfort and neatness, always surprised him. These days of late autumn chill there should be a fire burning, a chair pulled close, comfort, peace.

His mind was a cluttered space of undertaker's rooms, chrome, cold flesh, the cemetery beyond the town, the surrounding drystone wall, the blown-high grass, the wind jigging between desolate graves.

He turned and walked back to the gable window and stood erect. There had been rain but the sweeping wind had dried it. Chill and darkness. It wasn't a night for walking.

The rise that climbed out of the town and took the road to the wilderness was called the 'hill'. In local lore the scattered embedded stone was the remnant of some fort, a safehold, perhaps a dwelling. It didn't matter much to the town. Nothing was left. Stone was sometimes prised loose from it to fill potholes or gaps. Coleman walked there often, past the school, along sheep-tracks and barren ground. The surviving spikes of rock were markers of timelessness.

He thought of Demesne Street again. For all of seven months the Machen woman had been in residence now, arranging Sommerville's lifestyle, an unfailing worker in the care of the church, brushing with the town, yet keeping it at a distance. Finegan might have spoken for all: she was a good person, charitable; privacy was her affair. Children were captivated. She managed the Sommerville house, brought to it her own spotless purity. Passing through the town streets she had a changeless unseeing smile for everyone, a smile that was unassessable, a shield. At intervals she would walk to the hospital to leave an envelope of charitable donation; not large amounts, it was said. What she could afford. She sacrificed her comforts for others. She walked through the wards, the dying rooms, prayed in the mortuary even if it were empty, reached out to the infirm and the dead.

"She sounds English, says a few words only. She's a silent woman. Oh, a good person certainly." That was the Matron's brief appraisal.

Estel Machen took the schoolchildren for lessons in drama and speech. That was no secret. The town and Coleman were aware of it. Coleman had heard all the words of praise for her. The pupils would be in love with Estel Machen, her looks, her grace, flowing hair, a voice of expression and resonance, her gentleness. And her hands were beautiful. In her quiet dedicated life she had won the hearts and minds of the people.

"How old?" he had asked Belle Cannon once.

She had to think about it. "Oh, not old."

"Forty?"

"Less. Hard to say."

As Coleman raised his eyes the last visible light from his window had been extinguished; it had been a yellow blot on the night and it had vanished. He looked at his bed and out at the blackness. Only the sodium street lights of the town seemed awake.

The dimmed headlamps of some late bibbler passed outside and faded into the darkness and silence. Beyond the yellow glare of the town, beyond the hill, you were suddenly wrapped in the depth of blackness. Isolated farmhouses had quenched their lamps and vanished. Only lonely sounds remained: crying wind or dogs distantly answering each other's calls.

Coleman looked down at his bed and knew that sleep was a distant hope. He went out into the night. He would visit the cemetery again, see the grave of James Anthony and the open pit awaiting the corpse of Jennifer Anderson within a few hours. A graveyard was a place of rest for the dead. Coleman was angry, confused.

He followed the road that he had so recently walked to the cemetery. Jennifer Anderson's death was passing in shock and grief. The will of God; a spotless child of innocence taken into the glory of heaven. Doctors would scribble the finality of death certificates. Coleman stopped and listened.

The rain came and passed and the wind suddenly had a piercing edge. In moments he felt the chill of it reaching, spiking, into his body.

He stood again and listened. The sound of wind.

It was two miles from the town to the cemetery. Coleman was no stranger to pit black nights. He could hear his own footsteps on the tarmac; he flinched before the sharpness of the wind. Were there other footsteps?

He listened in the perishing cold for minutes. His eyes were streaming. Something had breathed an almost unbearable cold into the windrush.

Was he being followed?

He walked, scarcely visible in the darkness, found himself listening, even from moment to moment; listening to the howl of the wind that was scattered, sent astray, against outcrops of rising ground and stone.

He peered back the winding road he had travelled. Nothing. Blackness. A yellow corona sitting on the distant town.

Except for the wind, silence.

He walked again and, instantly, from somewhere the noise

was recalled, invoked. It wasn't a stealthy sound. It was a heavy deliberate step. He spun round. Silence. Only the wind blowing out of this impenetrable darkness. He stood on the crown of the road and waited. A long time. A minute, two minutes, three minutes. Numbness was creeping along his body. There was a sweet overpowering smell. In the gale it clung like an aura to his flesh. He tensed, awaiting an arrival. Nothing. He turned and moved away at a quickened pace on the stiff gradient and heard the clear footfalls in his wake. He reached the cemetery gates, stopped and spun. Sweetness all about him.

Suddenly he was slapped by what might have been a great open palm that knocked him to his knees. Pain, cold bitter pain burned into his body. He was in confusion, his eyes streaming from the unseen blow that had felled him. He fought his weakness, was staggering to his feet when it struck again. Jesus, the pain!

He was helpless, hands and knees on the road, surrounded by darkness.

There was nothing but black night and blades of cutting wind. In five minutes he was upright again, tightening his grip on the gate, cold almost as the dead, facing downhill. When you were losing a battle you retreated, saved what you could. But he was powerless. His legs could take his bodyweight but the power of moving them had gone.

He was a helpless target. He would be left to perish in the unbearable wind. Who? Even thought seemed to be perishing, crumbling. He gathered what power he had to shout, stored it up in his lungs, released it.

Not even the sound of his breath emerged.

Tears were blown across his cheeks by the wind. They should be frozen stiff bands of ice; his eyes, his mouth should be sealed. Tears? Fear or anger?

Suddenly his coat was cleft open, his clothing ripped apart, neck to groin. From each stripped shoulder he could feel the entry of a blade that cut deep into the flesh, sliced across his chest, his ribs. He was gripped tight in a dreadful ictus, agape, helpless. He could see blood teeming from his wounds and his screaming was a terrifying silence. Was this fear? Then the blade was in his nose, each side slit open, his lips left hanging. The blood flowed, poured, dripped down on the mutilation below.

When did pain push beyond endurance, and would consciousness slip away? If only he could hear his own silent screams there might be a split second of respite. But he was in a searing deathless grip of agony.

Then he felt the blade on his stomach. Whatever power guided it would disembowel him. Twice he felt the razor edge cutting through the flesh, torment bursting through a wall of motionless suffering. Blood was draining from him. Gut and the mass of viscera pushed against the intersecting wounds.

"Jesus, Jesus!" his silent screams were calling.

He stood in timelessness, struck as if by seizure, a bleeding pile of flesh, a whole world of pain without a voice to shout, cry, weep. He held the leather coat about him, his hands against his stomach. The wind rocked him. His feet stirred, he had motion again.

The town was a distant speck.

The hospital should be twenty minutes but weakness was a load bearing down on him. The raising of each foot, the groping with it for substantial ground, was a battle against pain. It took him two hours, stumbling, groping through darkness, never leaving it. When he reached the lighted streets, windswept, unpeopled, he inched his way along, scraping, bleeding, holding his stomach intact, leaving bloodied palm marks on painted walls when he rested along Main Street. It was desolate. The time? His watch-face caked in blood. The town was silent. Not a soul abroad. He passed Belle Cannon's. The shop windows were all in darkness now. Crossing the Square he looked back and saw the trail of blood behind him; weakness was deeper than pain. He was dying, the hospital beyond his reach. He turned down Demesne

Street. At Sommerville's door he paused, laid a bloody palm against the bell and held it there.

How long? Minutes or an hour? His hand slid from the bell, leaving a track of drying blood. It was the end. Like an animal he must find somewhere to hide. He edged down the gradient of Demesne Street to the waterfront, found an empty boathouse. The wind slammed the door behind him but, in darkness, he found a wall, lay against it, let his body slide down to the rough cobbled ground.

Consciousness was slipping away and then suddenly wrenched back. A choking rancidness gripped him. He was silently retching, convulsing, shaking in agony, feeling his stomach wounds open, and his ejected vomit spewing out in a torrent. He died.

The morning was almost still; the wind and rain belt had swept inland. The sky changed colour and light. Atlantic weather was a fickle hour to hour prediction. The wind came in small gusts but there were moments of quiet.

The town slept late.

Light filtered through corrugated opaque panels on the roof of the boathouse, lost its brightness. It gave shelter but it was a cold open space except for an empty boat-cradle mounted on wheels, discarded oddments of tackle, a light anchor with a straightened arm and a fluke that had been dragged out of shape.

Coleman, eyes closed in his own private darkness, became aware, heard sounds of water lapping in the cove, heard the little whispering wind that blew. He remembered each moment of his death, his mutilation and terror, sliding into weakness down this wall, the revolting stench, the eruction from his stomach. And earlier, the beating, the precise cutting of the scalpel; his chest, his open viscera, his shredded nose, his lips; the blood trail he had left behind from the cemetery road to the town.

He remained motionless, afraid to stir.

87

The wind gusted slightly and the door rattled. He was cold. He could feel the cold but there was no pain. Was he still alive, feeling the cold, but no pain? Would it all begin again? Had there been rain in the night and the blood trail washed away? Memory? Date of birth, height, weight; the events of yesterday, of a week, a month, a year past? He could put everything in place. No pain, only cold.

He retraced the journey on the black tarmac cemetery road, the Main Street, the sleeping town, remembered the dripping blood, the smear of his hand on Sommerville's door. Then his legs could still move, his hands. He remembered the boathouse and death.

Eyes closed, he stayed in his own black security now and listened. Up in the Square a car was starting, cold, struggling; it laboured endlessly, then the engine fired and raced; he listened to it driving away out of earshot. He heard the wind again. He moved a finger, a foot. No pain. He raised a hand slowly from where it was clasped across his stomach and brushed his lips, his nose. Nothing. There were no mounds of what could be wounds or dried blood.

He lowered his hands, drew in a deep breath and opened his eyes. His hands were clean, unmarked; his watch-face shone. The time. It had turned eight o'clock. His leather coat was buttoned, belted. He felt the firmness of his chest, his stomach. He moved with great care. He stood up and moved about; he took off his coat, looked at the back. There should be scrape marks on the leather. It was untouched. He exposed his chest and stomach. Clear, not a mark. His clothes, his shoes were intact, unstained.

But it had happened, he knew.

He tidied his clothing, stood out on the jetty and lit a cigarette.

The miles of estuary spread out before him, the small turbulence giving it life; the far shore, distant hills and mountains were clear as charcoal sketches in the morning air. He felt the comfort and security of it.

He walked back along the footpath he had travelled during the night. It was dry and windswept. There had been no rain.

There was no blood. Sommerville's door was pristine, unsmudged, shining brass and paint. At a shop window in the Square he stood and looked at his reflection; even his cap sat as he had always worn it, the merest tilt. There was slight movement on the streets now: pedestrians, the occasional car. He raised a hand, nodded.

On the hill, dignified, the school caught the morning light. Ghosts from the distant graveyard could be watching his progress. He walked the bloodless Main Street and rang Belle Cannon's doorbell. In a few moments she came, wearing a housecoat and slippers, her hair tied back. She was reality. It was scarcely eight-thirty.

"Coleman!" she said.

"I didn't mean to catch you on the hop. I thought you'd be up and moving."

"Friday," she said. "No classes on Friday. And the school is closed in mourning. I was house-cleaning."

He was in the hallway and she closed the door, put her arms on his shoulders and kissed him. She could feel him trembling. He held her there. She had locked out a world of nightmare, fantasy: the cemetery gate, Rellighan's strange yellowing face, the young naked body, Jennifer Anderson's grave. The black roads. The awful punishment.

On the staircase she took his hand. "My God, you're cold," she said.

"It was a cold night."

She was silent; when they reached the lounge she studied him; she said, "Your feet?"

"Cold."

She knew that he had spent hours somewhere in the night's darkness. She thought of Estel Machen, the awful face, the school, the classes. Was Coleman trespassing close to danger and had suffered for it?

"I'll get you some food," she said. "Take off your coat, sit by the radiator."

"Very little," he said. "Very little food." The rancid fumes of last night's 'death' rose up for a moment. "I need a shower," he said.

She looked hard at him; his face was firm, set, but greyness, paleness, tinged it. He seemed distant from her, unreachable. She took his coat and said, "You know where everything is. Undress in the bedroom."

As he left the lounge he paused and turned back to her; he said, "Belle?"

"Yes?"

"I'm glad you're here."

He undressed and walked across the corridor to the comfort of the shower. He was remembering scars and blood and silent screams; and now running his hands over taut unmarked flesh. The warm water flooded down; he soaped and let it flow. He was feeling warm, could even feel a trace of anger growing in his mind. He dried off, ran his fingers through clean hair, wrapped a towel about his waist. He went back to the bedroom.

Belle Cannon was standing there, waiting. She said, "Come to bed with me, Coleman."

She let the robe fall away, slid between the sheets, held back the bedclothes for him.

He lay naked beside her and she wrapped him close to her. Embracing her, the soft smoothness of open lips held them tight together. She leant forward, put her lips on his forehead. Her eyes were drowsy. Coleman drifted away into the softness of her body . . .

They lay side by side for a long time, hands clasped, calm returning, peace.

She said, "Coleman?"

"Yes?"

"In the hallway you were trembling."

"Yes."

"Estel Machen? I saw her once and, for an instant, her ugliness could bring terror. Then suddenly she was beautiful again. I pushed her out of my mind. But it was real, Coleman, wasn't it?"

Coleman looked at her. "I was trembling," he said "but I feel good now."

She knew Coleman and his tactics well; she was out of bed, putting on a robe. "I'll cook you a real meal, Coleman. You need it."

"No," he said. "A small meal . . ."

In the shower again, suddenly, the warmth vanished, coldness of fear returned, all the moments of love were distant, premonition cramped about him.

He dressed and sat in the lounge, in warmth, listening to the growing traffic in the town. Friday, he thought; market day: long hours of trading for shops and street stalls. From his chair he could see the town streets walking, trotting into another day. Coleman could be cool, dispassionate. That was how he worked: listen to hearsay, gossip, fairy tale, the harmless, the vindictive, but carefully sift the jumble, gather in the facts. Last night had been a wind of malignance, he knew; a gory visitation had been made. He had suffered it alone and it had left him unblemished. But traces of fear were alive. To retail it now could only lessen him, shatter his credibility. Knife wounds, entrails, blood, a stumbling journey, silent, screaming pain. Had he disturbed some forbidden bones, some entity, and had been turned away? There was cause and effect. He glanced again at the town, thought of the schoolchildren and Estel Machen's long flowing hair, her smiling largesse to the sick and dying. To give credence, even for a moment, to his thoughts was an act of defeat, he thought.

It *was* real, wasn't it? Belle Cannon had asked.

She was calling now from the table. "Come on, everything's ready, Coleman."

He took his place. She had grilled a small round of gammon bacon and given him a little spinach and wholemeal bread. She poured tea. She looked at his eyes, his face, remembered it softened in love-making.

"This is fine," he said.

"It's just a scrap. Eat it, Coleman. You look deprived."

"You take holding down," he said.

She kissed him, took a cup of tea and sat in an easy chair. He was giving a good performance, she thought.

"No breakfast?" he asked.

She raised the cup of tea. "We girls must watch our bums and thighs and other places to keep men hungry for us."

"You're doing a fine job."

"Coleman?" she said and paused.

"Yes?"

"Estel Machen, the schoolchildren . . ."

"The *school*," Coleman said. "A place where the dead ones met. A venue. Something in common."

Belle Cannon watched him. He left his meal unfinished. She said, "Where they all met Estel Machen."

Coleman came across to her and she stood to meet him. "Don't become involved," he said. "It could be dangerous. It could be dangerous knowing *me*."

She nodded. "But you're in danger."

Coleman let it pass. "I'd like to see one of her classes. To spy," he said.

"I'll bring you."

"No," Coleman said. "Tell me where I can spy. Tomorrow is Saturday. That's her day, isn't it?"

"No class tomorrow. Respect for the dead. There's a pupil dead, remember?"

Coleman remembered. "I'm not thinking," he said.

"The body will be in the funeral home today. Resting in the church tonight. The march to the cemetery and the burial tomorrow. The end of Jennifer Anderson."

"Yes," Coleman said.

He held up a pack of cigarettes. She nodded. He stood at the window and smoked. If he had drowned in the terror of hallucination – beating, cutting, blood, viscera – somewhere there was a cause. You went on searching for a cause. That was the rule book. Was there a rule book for every twist of emotion, passion, madness? Was there cause too, deadly, sinister, for the incurable illness of the young?

Belle Cannon watched him. She knew he had been wounded; there were no visible marks but Coleman had been wounded. His face was tight and hard. In the hallway, when he had arrived and she had kissed him, she had felt the trembling of his body. In his coldness of hands and feet, it had been there too.

For a moment, in the warmth and colour of the room, she felt chilled. Coleman in fear? Who, what could frighten Coleman? Estel Machen?

She said, "I've sat and watched Estel Machen's classes at the school."

"They were just classes?" Coleman asked.

"They were good," Belle Cannon told him. "She got them to shout and scream, dance with each other, swing their arms. Amazing, they loved it. They were breathless, laughing, relaxed. She taught them the gracefulness of walking, boys and girls, shoulders loose, heads high. Even the worst of them improved. Some were impressive. They read Goldsmith, Sheridan, Wilde, enacted pieces. She gave them confidence to speak." Belle Cannon held out open hands in puzzlement. "Yes, Coleman, she's good." She was remembering the awful rotting face.

"The impressive ones?" Coleman said.

"Yes?"

"Are two of them dead?"

Belle Cannon looked at him, thought about it for what seemed a long time; she said eventually "Yes, Coleman, they were impressive."

"Good looking, smart, weren't they?"

"Yes."

"Did she touch them, straighten, relax their shoulders with her hands? Tilt their heads?"

"For everyone," she said.

93

"Did she touch their hair?"

"She would bring up a pupil, put boy or girl facing the class, stand behind, with her hands toss and shape the hair, let them see the difference it might make."

"And the dead ones?"

She said, "I saw only random classes. She used different models every week. A lot of people."

She brought Coleman his coat and cap. His hands were warm, almost steady now.

"It was good," he said.

She smiled. "The breakfast?"

"That too."

"Take this," she said. She handed him a spare door-key.

Belle Cannon listened to Coleman's footsteps in the hallway and the hollow sound as he shut the door behind him. Coleman was never defeated but now he was close to it. She was glad she had taken him to bed; she felt loving him had healed him. But pain had been creeping back into his eyes. Or the memory of pain.

Downstairs she heard the door of her shop being opened, her staff of one arriving. Another day. It was holiday weekend. Halloween. Friday and Saturday would be busy. A little style, a little colour to celebrate. The funeral would steal from it of course.

Saturday night she and Coleman should be miles away, dining by candle-light, drinking red house-wine, in love. But this evening there would be a body in the church and tomorrow a burial. This evening Jennifer Anderson's remains would be moved from Rellighan's funeral home to the church and Simoney would rage through the death service. There was anxiety in the town and it would steal the ghostly magic, the masks and treats, in celebration of All Saints and All Souls.

Seven years ago Belle Cannon had been twenty-four, settled in the school-teaching routine, in love with Coleman, looking in shop windows and dressing them with her own flair of colour and light. Belle Cannon had style and needed to share it.

She had said to Coleman, "I'm going to open a shop."

"Fashion."

"Yes."

"I think you'd be good."

"You always think I'm good, don't you, Coleman?"

"I think you're great."

Seven years! That had been a summer of sunshine and fresh breeze on the estuary, the water paved with countless impressionist shreds of light. There were minuscule islands in the deep sweeping channels that were once the refuge of beleaguered groups who fished and farmed. She was remembering it.

They had been empty places for more than a century.

Coleman knew the winds and races; he sailed cross-current, loosed the rigging and let the single lug-sail flop. She watched him swing down the outboard and jerk it to life. He steered in against a stone jetty and moored tight on cast-iron rings against the rising tide.

"Will days always be like this?" she had asked.

"If we don't crowd them."

"Yes."

She spread the rug on the stones above them and they lay in the sun. Belle Cannon's food-stock was stored in the shade, a wet sopping towel lying across it; the water evaporated in the heat of the day, left coolness behind. Would sun evaporate love and leave coolness too?

"How long have we known each other, Coleman?"

"Forever."

"I know."

"Years and years, give or take."

"Yes," she had said, "years and years."

In the warm sunshine, surrounded by miles of flashing water, silence except for the lap of the tide, he was feeling uneasy.

She might be awakening from a long sleep, a tranquil dream, and asking where time had gone. Were these the slow dragging steps to an ending, he wondered. He felt emptiness. Years, years, he thought. Was there a question to be asked? He didn't want to ask. He had built about him his life. There was satisfaction in everything, big or small, that he did. And he loved Belle Cannon. He didn't want knots tied by working-men or men of God. He didn't want progeny in a crowded starving world. He didn't want to bring age to her before her time. He wanted freedom for both of them.

He had stood up and walked to the end of the jetty and looked into the breeze. He thought of her face that was always beautiful to him, her lips, the softness of her eyes. He looked at the profile of her tall slender body. The beauty of the day was vanishing.

She had said, "yes, years and years."

Belle Cannon feeling the warmth of the sun, the soft push of the wind against her body; she looked out beyond the estuary to the sea and then followed the river bank, distant now, from the tiny matchstick of lighthouse on the bare point, along the craggy shore to the cove. The town was a mere bundle of haphazard buildings, the church steeple pointing to God. The peak of the town hill rose behind it.

Unhappiness had taken her like a sudden illness. She had been laughing, without a care, as they travelled through the town, the Square, Demesne Street; Coleman was driving a blue mini-estate. Behind them was food; rugs, waterproofs, fishing tackle. She was wearing grey linen shorts and a loose buttoned shirt. Her skin was tanned.

Seven years ago! It seemed only a moment.

"I always feel useless in this boat," she had said.

She was sitting forward in the sun, legs and arms stretched, watching Coleman at work with tiller and mainsheet, tacking upriver.

He nodded his humour. He held an upriver course for two hours, standing, sitting, sliding on bare feet. He wore only heavy shorts buttoned tight on his waist. Then he swung round and let the boat swing downriver with the current. She had cans of beer dragging in a net. She opened one and brought it to him. He put her sitting beside him at the helm. She wound an arm round him; he was hard and smooth.

"Now your hand on mine on the tiller."

She could feel the drags and pushes of wind and current; the boat was a sensitive speck in the immense setting of river and ocean.

It was like steering through life together, she had suddenly thought! It was a moment of disquiet, fear. The day seemed colder, less bright.

It brought a memory of moments in the journey through childhood, tugs and heartbreak at leaving the safety of home, to move into a world of new days and people. She was the youngest of four. After a life-time, parents, then ageing figures in a ten-year-old car, driving her to the coach-stop, returning to an empty house where they had started it all. Pushing through life to reach loneliness. She thought of the silence that could be there.

She had smiled at Coleman and gripped his hand. They had driven a hundred miles to see them once a month while they still survived. She had telephoned each week. Coleman's parents had been laid to rest long since and his family scattered on prosperous perches, happy to follow old reliable patterns. He didn't have much to say about them. Her own siblings were happy too, she supposed: erratic letters, a phone call perhaps, a card at Christmas were reassurances . . .

Yes, she had been happy driving down to the cove with Coleman, loading the paraphernalia for a day on the water, stretched lazing on the sun, sitting with him beside the helm when, without even the passing shadow of cloud, the day seemed to have grown cold.

It would happen like this, she had always imagined. A day of great colours and magic, warmth, a stir of breeze, dazzling small turbulences of tide and river-flow. A few words and all the closeness, the happiness that had been gathered would in an instant be squandered. Coleman would turn and say the words she didn't want to hear. But she loved Coleman; there never would be another one.

She had turned and saw him walking towards her. They sat on the jetty-end, looked down through the shining water at the weed plants like magnificent ribbons tangled in the wind. Shell-fish stirred, moved a little, there was a glitter that might be a rush of salmon.

"Coleman," she said, "we've had a lot of good times together."

Coleman said, "We have good times now."

"Yes."

"People make good times."

"Coleman, I'm afraid. Afraid of you. I couldn't live with contracts, solemn vows, signed agreements. Thinking always for two. Or three or four. You see me now. I'm free. All that would vanish."

"Yes?" Coleman waited.

"I don't want marriage ever." She was in tears. "But I want you. I love you, Coleman."

Coleman stood and helped her to her feet. They walked back to the rug and sat facing each other.

Coleman said, "In the boat you asked, will days always be like this? and how long have we known each other? You were reminding me of time. Years, years. Was it a time for bended knee and a speech, the end of courtship?" Coleman paused. "I want courtship forever. I want us free in good times and bad. At opposite sides of the park."

"Did you feel my unhappiness, Coleman?" she had asked.

"I felt a chill."

They took the rug into the grassy slopes. They undressed and made love in the warm sunshine; drowsed and made love again. Then they walked, arms about waists, to the shore line, into the cool sharp water.

Back, dried, dressed, sitting on the jetty again, she had said,

"I feel good now, Coleman."

He smiled.

"The food is good, the wine is good."

Coleman said, "We had reached a crossroads, that's all. There will always be crossroads."

"No more crossroads, Coleman."

Coleman laughed . . .

Years had passed, Belle Cannon thought, with the good and over-cast weather of living, had drawn them closer together. She remembered always the excitement of loving. It had grown strong with them. They had passed a lot of crossroads.

From her window she watched Coleman leave her doorstep and step out on the pavement. Yes, she loved Coleman.

Lunchtime had passed when Coleman pulled Belle Cannon's door closed behind him. Morning air was clear and dry, restoring, the streets blown clean; traffic of people and vehicles, intimate noises of small town streets, the babble of voices above traffic, were real.

He walked.

Finegan was at his pub doorway and he stopped to bid him the time of day.

"Fine fresh weather if it lasts," Finegan said. "Too fine and fresh to have a schoolgirl's young body in Rellighan's deadhouse."

Coleman listened.

"Look around you. Japanese cars. Expensive clothes. Overalls and twilled bloody coarse cotton that tradesmen and skivvies might have worn when I was a boy. Fashion!"

"Sixty years ago," Coleman said.

"Fifty years. Look at their faces, their gleaming teeth. Bloody sharks. Coffee-shops and shop-abouts. Where have all the old ones gone, Coleman? They're not in the cemetery yet. Sitting at home before a fire or remembering, looking out across wet fields."

"The young build houses for parents now. A hundred yards up or down the road. They live apart. Better."

"Puts them in quarantine," Finegan said.

Coleman thought: 'Today Finegan is angry with the world, and there's a little fear growing inside him every day for his children's children.'

"There was a time when a death like this would bring silence to the town. Now look at them."

Coleman said, "The town is restless."

"The town is damned."

"The world is damned."

Finegan looked at him. "For grown people this town is coming to the boil, Coleman."

Coleman nodded. "I'll call in and have a drink later," he said.

At the Square he looked back to where he had seen his own trail of blood marking his passage of a few hours ago. There was nothing. It was dry clean ground now, dotted with the tents of market stalls. A foreign market. A few indigenous fruit and vegetable displays, but mostly Asians, a creeping army, patient, impassive, beside endless racks of cheap clothing and tables of gaudy accessories and gewgaws. They had reached the Atlantic. The sea, the sea!

Coleman walked on to Rellighan's and pushed open the wicket gate. Time might have stood still. Rellighan sat motionless at the table with his newspaper; he didn't look, stir, move a finger, when Coleman rapped on his door. The past night of fear and cutting and blood might never have been. Had there been a young dead body in the concrete cube? Had Rellighan shown him the pale remains? Had he inspected it?

"Rellighan," he said.

Only Rellighan's eyes moved. "Yes?"

"You're alive."

"Did you want something?"

It was a big office and Coleman sat at an extremity and

100

looked at the crouched Munchlike gauntness of Rellighan, clad in deep clerical grey, a white shirt, a black tie, his face more shrunken and pitted in the poor daylight that reached him. He had strong useful hands.

"Did I come to see you yesterday?"

"The evening time." Rellighan's eyes fixed him for a moment. "It was late when you came."

"And the body was on your table out there?"

"It's still there now but it's coffined."

"I wanted to be sure."

Rellighan raised his head and studied Coleman; he remained silent behind pale unemotional eyes.

Coleman said, "You've been in this business a few years and more?"

"A lifetime."

Coleman sat a while in silence. "Have you ever felt, Rellighan, that you're being watched?"

"Yes."

The suddenness of it took Coleman by surprise. "I mean by the dead. When they're on your table, without dignity, naked, and you're working on them?"

"Even the naked have dignity. I respect them."

"You feel you're watched?"

"Yes. And in the funeral home, in the church, at the grave-side too. Watched all the time. Sometimes they are slow to leave, that's all."

"Spirits?"

"Spirit, soul, whatever leaves the body at death."

"Yesterday you opened that plastic sack and exposed Jennifer Anderson?"

"I felt she was in attendance."

"A spirit?"

"Yes."

Rellighan was no longer the gaunt yellowing figure walking beside the hearse, erect, a slow even pace. Abiding with death had brought him closer to life. He lived alone in this

101

great empty house that presided over his mortuary. He stared sightlessly at Coleman.

Coleman said, "You *know*, don't you?"

"You were punished?" Rellighan asked. "That's what I feel. Punishment."

"An awful rancid death, Rellighan."

"Yes. Your punishment. It will fade. For me death has no longer a smell of decay."

"But you knew?"

"Only that."

Coleman was on his feet. "I was slapped to the ground, Rellighan, beaten, slashed, my gut hanging out. I left a trail of blood behind, across the town. I had no voice to scream. In an empty boathouse on the jetty, I died. I awoke untouched, healed."

"A punishment, a warning. You were trespassing on someone's ground," Rellighan said.

"The cemetery gate. Who?"

"A lot of sleeping corpses there. I buried most of them."

"Who? Flesh and blood?" Coleman asked, but Rellighan was silent.

Coleman sat and smoked, looked out beyond the yard at the roof-tops and gables, listened to the faint traffic sounds from the Square and Main Street. He felt reality was slipping away from him. He was waiting for uncertainty to fade.

Rellighan held his silence.

Coleman was angry.

"Spirits standing guard in your mortuary by their own coffins? At gravesides? For Christ's sake, Rellighan!"

"*Some* spirits," Rellighan said. "Others, substantial or vaporous, can strike you down and kill."

"The schoolchildren?" Coleman asked.

"They're dead."

"Why?"

"Meddling won't solve it."

From the table drawer Rellighan took a flat half-bottle of

liquor. It was full. He broke the seal of the screw-cap and held it out

"It's Scotch," he said.

Coleman took a mouthful and let it burn inside him. "I didn't know you drank, Rellighan."

"At times," Rellighan said.

Coleman went back to his chair. Rellighan took three short sips from the bottle and put it back in its place.

"At times."

"Yes."

Rellighan was remembering days in Boston, fifty, sixty years past, when he had met death in the narrow hilly slum-land not far from ships and the bustle of docks.

"Rellighan," Coleman was calling.

"Yes."

"The deaths. There was a six month gap between deaths."

"Yes."

Rellighan, beneath his newspaper, had spread out two single-sheet twelve month calendars. He had marked his funeral schedule on them.

"The last days of April and October," he said.

"Does it mean anything?"

"For some people."

Coleman was silent now, remembering, somehow face to face with the bane he had envisaged. "A drink?" he asked.

Rellighan gave him the bottle and he drank just a little. "They want bodies, don't they, Rellighan?"

"*She* wants bodies."

"Who?"

"The beautiful woman," Rellighan said.

"The beautiful woman?"

"I call her *the beautiful woman*."

"Yes," Coleman said. "She's here."

"Sommerville's woman. She's in the church, the hospital, she's everywhere."

"Young bodies?"

"Virgin bodies."

Coleman sat in silence, let time pass, collected himself. "The last days of October?" he said. "The time of All Souls' Night?"

"All spirits night, if you want to believe it. Good and evil. In the past they gathered, made sacrilege, lit fires to catch a glimpse of the future. If you want to believe it."

"The beautiful woman is evil?"

"Yes."

"When did you know?"

"A long time ago. And at James Anthony's funeral. I've met evil before."

"The last days of April?" Coleman said.

"A festival, a time of celebration for them." Rellighan spoke without emotion: pale eyes, yellowing face. "The church burns charcoal and incense, makes sacrifice in the Mass. Timeless traditions of sacrifice for every aeon. The beautiful woman is a messenger. She brings evil."

"You don't believe that, Rellighan."

"Yes, I believe it."

Coleman looked at this almost grotesque man, clean, well dressed, seeing himself in every corpse, a deaf man for words of sorrow at gravesides, more approachable now than Coleman would have thought possible.

"You kept your silence, Rellighan."

It angered Rellighan. "Would you have believed it?"

"No."

"You would have said I was mad."

"You've seen her before?"

"Death is my business. Spirits are close to it."

"But in this town?"

Rellighan said, "I went to see James Anthony's grave months ago."

Coleman waited.

"I felt it was empty."

The morning freshness was clouding over now; the light

was grey. There would be sharpness in the wind and sudden gusts of rain. That was the changeless pattern of the west coast. Coleman thought of all the barren windswept moorland, the stripped naked rock, heather and tussocks of coarse grass, black pools, reaching across fifteen miles to cliff-edges and relentless hammering seas. A desert of loneliness. Suddenly he thought of Belle Cannon and her warmth.

"Are we in danger?" he asked.

"Yes."

"Others too? Friends?"

"Yours maybe. I don't have friends."

Coleman looked at the still dispassion of Rellighan.

"Can we drive her out?" he asked.

"When she's ready to go."

Rellighan opened his drawer; it was deep and neatly packed. He took out a slender green book from it. He opened it and laid it on the table. "October," he said and turned over the pages. "Jennifer Anderson died last evening." He spoke quietly, monotonously. "This is an important day for them. The last day of October."

"Oh, for Christ's sake," Coleman said.

Rellighan looked at him. "For *them*," he said.

"Who are they?

"You were killed and resurrected last night."

Coleman was silent.

"Tonight will Jennifer Anderson rest alone in the church? The festival of all spirits. Tomorrow is the burial. Will it be an empty coffin?"

Out there the little town was bright, a place of movement, living another day. This shadow was creeping over it, poisoning confidence. People had less certainty. It was physical illness they feared. Schoolchildren had pills and condoms, other people's children. Everyone was sure of that. There was a poisoned one at large too, some felt. But leave problems to God.

The town preferred simple stories.

105

Coleman said, "Estel Machen meets the town's schoolchildren on Saturdays."

Rellighan said, "The beautiful one."

Coleman paused. "She touches their faces, their hair. Is she
the poisoner?"

"She kills," Rellighan said. "She doesn't leave traces."

"You don't know, do you, Rellighan?"

Rellighan said, "I don't know."

"When Jennifer Anderson's body is buried tomorrow.
When they are filling in the grave . . ."

"They will bury an empty coffin."

"She will have taken the body?"

"Yes."

"An empty coffin, the weight, Rellighan, the weight?"

Rellighan looked at him; silence was his answer.

Coleman lit a cigarette, stood at the window and smoked.
"Can we stop it?"

"The girl is dead. You can be found lifeless too."

Coleman thought of Belle Cannon, her confidence, her helplessness; she had seen a beautiful face changing to a death's-
head, stood before the ghostly dualism of Estel Machen and in
a moment wondered about madness, possession.

He said, "What is she, Rellighan? Flesh and blood?"

"Was she flesh and blood last night when she beat and
slashed you? Left you screaming without a voice. Left you
dead and restored you?"

"A hand struck in pitch blackness. Twice. Was the rest hallucination?"

Rellighan was silent again.

"Is she flesh and blood?" Coleman called out.

"She is a spirit," Rellighan said. "She can send you into a
world of horror. She can kill."

"A ghost of substance?"

"When she needs to be."

Coleman came across and stared into the paleness of
Rellighan's eyes. "Can we banish her?" he asked.

Rellighan opened out the newspaper, covered the calendars again. It was the regional weekly broadsheet: a front page of farming or small town interest, parish tittle-tattle, bizarre personality features, scattered items, space fillers, a prominence given to death, columns of inserted memorials to those already passed over, pages of sports reportage, a poets' corner of faceless Clares and Kavanaghs, a catalogue of entertainment, photographs of pot-bellied important men, and girls arranging their smiles, their beauty or lack of it.

He opened the paper fully, seemingly without choice of page. Parish news columns were enclosed in dark frames, council meetings were reported verbatim. Desultory items of news were fitted like stop-gaps.

Coleman noted lines ringed by Rellighan's pencil: a small headline, a couple of paragraphs to give it importance.

ANIMALS SAVAGED

Mysterious reports have been reaching the Gardaí in this area over a number of weeks and there is growing concern among the isolated and scattered farmers. Lacerated animals, sheep, young calves, even a bloodstock foal have been found dead in remote places. Deep wounds and torn flesh were in evidence as if these unfortunate animals had been preyed upon by wild beasts. Veterinary surgeons have refused to confirm or deny that it might be the work of abandoned dogs living in the wild. Meanwhile a close watch should be kept until the matter is resolved.

Coleman remembered his own death and restoration: the cutting knives, bulging entrails, the mess of flowing blood, the silent screams. He put his finger on the headline, watched Rellighan turn and focus him.

He said, "That's forty miles north of here."

"Yes," Rellighan said. "A desert of stone. Strange country, you know it, when darkness falls."

"There's something there? We should find it?"

107

Rellighan nodded.

"What?"

Rellighan was cautious; he raised his voice. "I don't know," he said.

"Today."

"*Tonight* when the church service is ended. Be here. Bring your car."

At the door he handed Coleman a heavy embellished key, old as the door lock it fitted. "A key to the church," he said. "Tell her to watch in the church tonight."

"Belle Cannon?"

"Whatever she's called."

"There's danger, Rellighan."

"We are all in danger . . ."

Coleman stood for minutes in the darkness of Rellighan's alleyway; it was a cobbled surface, a hundred years old. Rellighan had spent close on fifty-five years here. Like so many names of older ones, his would die with him. In towns and countryside men and women died, unattached, alone. The pattern of money marrying money, even a very small share of money, set the style, created a hierarchy. And earners married earners and the poor were left with the poor. But every town had its celibates who had chosen their own paths.

Rellighan had chosen his own path.

Preparation and burial of the dead had changed its style in fifty years. When Rellighan had returned from Boston, it was still a time when people died in their own dwellings. They were nursed through short or protracted illnesses, infrequent calls from a doctor, until the sound of their last breath left almost unbearable silence.

Every townland had its own corpse-woman. She would wash and prepare the body, sometimes imperfectly, leave the sick-room heavy with disinfectant losing its battle against malodour. The remains would be shrouded in its habit of death.

Habits were brown, covering the naked body from neck to toe, sometimes a garish oleograph of a bleeding heart of Jesus sewn on the breast below the white face, ropy neck and chin propped up, held in position with a prayer-book until it had set in rigor. A last head-erect dignity.

People came, mourners perhaps to drink and eat in other rooms and briefly visit the corpse chamber to stare at it, even to pray.

Only on funeral day, and removal of remains to the church, did the undertaker make his appearance. He brought the coffin, arranged its occupant. The black hearse of figured glass drawn by plumed horses made the last journey. The undertaker, in comic-opera clothes, walked in sorrow before the cortege.

Now you died in hospital privacy or were removed to its morgue. Or removed to the undertaker's care. People could afford flowers and Mass offerings.

Another world, Coleman thought.

After the gloom of Rellighan's office, the low compressing confines of walls and ceiling, the town's brightness was intense. The wind was changing, the weather.

Coleman felt as if a skin of grime had vacuum-wrapped his body.

Substantial ghosts, savaged animals! He thought of the warm water at Belle Cannon's flowing over him; he thought of danger. Belle Cannon. Punishment would be meted out to her now, some visitation of creeping defilement until terror had crept over her. Silent terror.

Estel Machen. He wondered if she could bleed like her victims. But he knew she was beyond the reach of all of them. In a few hours the body of Jennifer Anderson would leave the funeral home and be left to rest in the church for prayers and incantations, the asperges of holy-water on the coffin. Tomorrow in daylight the burial. Tonight the journey north with Rellighan to the world of stone and silence, in search of something. Rellighan's Halloween of spirit festivals, good and

109

evil, empty graves, stolen corpses had the ring of fortune-teller lingo, fairground-speak. But you looked at him and saw his hardness.

Belle Cannon would be in danger.

Coleman thought again of the cutting knife, hands holding his bursting entrails from falling on the pavement, death in the boathouse.

He walked quickly away from the Square; Demesne Street opened out before him. He looked along its precious houses down to the cove and the spread of estuary. He rang the door-bell of Dr H. Sommerville M.D. The pure pale untouchable woman in starched tiara and token bib and apron held her chin high, beheld him as if in fortitude. It was after three o'clock, a hint of early darkness falling.

Expressionless, Coleman said, "Inspector Coleman."

"Yes?"

"To see Dr Sommerville."

She took her book. "An appointment?"

"A personal appointment. Now."

Silently over heavy carpets Herbert Sommerville came in view; he was smiling. "It's quite all right," he said. "If the Inspector calls, I'll see him at any time."

"Yes, Doctor." She made an almost pious obeisance and seemed to drift out of sight.

Coleman noticed the street door: a single slab of hard-wood, two and a half inches in thickness, hung on four brass hinges; a brass runner bolt, a safety chain, a spring lock and a heavy mortice. The brass was gleaming, even in fading day-light. Impregnable, Coleman thought.

Sommerville brought him to his surgery and sat facing him. "A sad business," he said.

"Indeed."

The surgery was at street level, heavy curtains drawn back. Coleman was looking at the window behind Sommerville: woodwork smooth as silk, panelled embrasures that would open across to form heavy shutters and there would be an ornate swivel-bar to seal them. There was a half-size wardrobe for starched gowns and coats and oddments; or perhaps some impedimenta of country practice and emergency.

It was a room of fine dimensions, polished, tended with care. But it seemed an undisturbed place, perfect, hardly used. There was a combination safe with dial and numbers, small, not more than two feet high, painted in spotless cream gloss, its brass-work shining and raised on a carpeted plinth – a tribute to his housekeeper's industry. At the end wall there stood a scales and a Victorian cheval mirror. Sommerville was a Mason, Coleman knew; perhaps this was a dressing-room, a meeting-room. Behind his desk he would be a figure of dignity.

"I take it there wasn't anything unusual?" Sommerville smiled his friendliness.

"No," Coleman reassured him. "Just a straightforward illness. Tragic of course. Rumours are spun and get about and are doctored as they go. A small town. People worry. Young things now, not long in their teens, will lift their bibs for hash or a sniff of solvent."

"Solvents too?" Sommerville might be surprised.

"An occasional one."

"But Jennifer Anderson will rest in peace."

"The town thinks someone is carrying a bug."

"Plenty of those."

"I thought I'd take a few moments of your time. A personal matter," Coleman said.

Sommerville looked at his watch. "Of course. I have an hour. What can I do?"

"A few minutes only," Coleman said.

"Yes, yes."

Coleman stared past him at the window, through the curtains to the restfulness of Demesne Street; to Sommerville he appeared a man in doubt.

"I don't take drugs," he said eventually. "I'm a moderate drinker."

"Yes."

"I'm talking about hallucination."

There was no movement of face or eyes; Sommerville was patient, impassive. But his hands stirred for an instant and then relaxed, were in control again. Sommerville was in thought, perhaps plotting a course.

"Hallucination?"

"Yes."

"You?"

"Yes."

Sommerville was silent, looking at his blotter. "You're not the type. But who can tell? How often?"

"Once," Coleman said. "Last night, I was walking late, very late. It's something I do from time to time. I was beaten, slashed, disembowelled. I staggered bleeding across the town. I died in a boathouse down there."

Sommerville said, "You awoke. Not a mark?"

"Yes."

"Do you want to talk about it?"

"I thought you might explain it to me."

Sommerville nodded. He was in charge, relaxed again, reassuring. Coleman could see his quiet hands, his face settling into its mould of confidence.

He was a man of some importance in the town, without need to work. Unmarried. His formidable Estel Machen was the chatelaine of his house. Hardly a live-in housekeeper, Coleman thought. She spent her spare minutes of every day in a rota of prayer and good works at the church: high altar, side altars, flickering candelabra, dying with the Saviour on the Way of the Cross. Appearances were important in small towns. Coleman thought of Rellighan's *beautiful woman*.

She knew that Sommerville was a degenerate; most of the town didn't, the few didn't care. The Sommerville who, at regular intervals, had driven to his passionate liaisons, when distance and time didn't matter, to meet chosen discreet lovers and pay them handsomely, had become a home-lover. A settled man. He was drowning in pleasure.

Estel Machen had consumed him. She had taken his house in control, banished his staff. Cleaners and scullions in his house now were the common run, from the surrounding countryside; she kept them at a distance, commanded them.

"Live-in?" she had said once in astonishment. "People of that calibre living in Dr Sommerville's house?" She had been talking in her humble tones to Simoney. "They attend to their chores and leave. Much better."

Simoney agreed; she was considered Sommerville's protectress, a person of manners, beyond reproach . . .

Sommerville had paused, glancing about his surgery as if examining with exaggerated care the quality of its essential changeless furnishings.

He sat back, folded his arms, pondered a little, looked at Coleman. "Not exactly my line of work," he said. "I'd have to ask you some questions. Personal questions."

"Yes."

"Is there a family history?"

"No."

"Thinking of it now, do you feel afraid?"

Coleman considered it. "I remember it in detail," he said. "The cutting, the blood."

"You remember dying?"

"In the boathouse. Frightening at the end."

"Frightening?"

"Yes."

Coleman was patiently manoeuvring, displaying for Sommerville little chinks of weakness, confusion. Sommerville still had questions to ask.

Coleman held his silence, let him wait. He could see, beyond the rooftops, the eroding pinnacle of the hill. On bright days he would walk to the summit, lean against the outcrops of decaying stone, look across the town at the sweep of the glistening estuary, watch distant coasters from upriver running with the tide into the open sea. Good days would come again, he told himself. He stared through the polished glass of the window. Sommerville was watching him, he knew.

Sommerville said, "You were remembering it again?"

"Yes."

"A day or two and it will fade."

"Yes."

"You were walking late," Sommerville said eventually. "Very late. You staggered across the town to the cove, a boathouse. A long journey, was it?"

It had come at last.

"From the cemetery," Coleman said. "I came from the gates of the cemetery."

"Not a usual time for visiting."

"I was passing. I stopped to light a cigarette. I must have awakened a wicked spirit."

Sommerville shook with laughter; he said, "Next time . . ."

"There won't be a next time."

Sommerville slowly recovered his sobriety, thought about it, very confident, convincing. He began to write, made a diary entry. "I'll prescribe you a mild sedative," he said. "Just a strange nightmare, I would say, except the boathouse doesn't fit. That upsets it. Fully clothed?"

"Yes."

"Have you ever sleep-walked?"

"No," Coleman said.

"Somnambulism, sleep-walking, even once in a life-time has been recorded. And cases go unrecorded. A great number, I would say. People afraid of being branded unstable. Even mentally disturbed. Nonsense of course. It is only a minor passing disorder." Sommerville pushed across the prescription and laughed. The laughter seemed to linger as if the room were hungry for sounds of merriment. "Hallucination would put you in good company. Luther, Walter Scott, Earl Grey. Luther was troubled by Satan, Earl Grey saw a gory dripping head from time to time." Sommerville clasped his hands, was in high humour.

114

Coleman thought of the label, *even mentally disturbed.* That was the affirmation he needed. A joking remark by Sommerville. But it wasn't the disconnected phrase it seemed in context; it was a threat. It could be used. It was constructed with care. Sommerville was an accomplice, played some walk-on acolyte role in the ceremony.

Coleman stood. "I'm grateful," he said; he took the prescription, was reaching for money.

"No, no," Sommerville swept it aside. "Payment is out of the question. I'm glad you came to discuss it. That's often half the cure."

Coleman nodded his thanks. "The ghost of this meningitis bug has been laid to rest, I think."

Sommerville walked with him to the door. "Good," he said. "Small town fears and phobias can be alarming. In my father's time someone saw a church statue move. The town was crowded for months. Extraordinary. Even cures were effected, they say. Such is faith."

Coleman raised a hand. As he turned towards the Square he heard the closing noise of Sommerville's door. He crumpled the prescription in his pocket.

He went to his untenanted house and sat before the empty grate, remembering. Estel Machen had punished him with fear and the shadows of it still remained. The faces of shadow and substance spun and mixed in his mind.

Coleman was angry. He sat before the cold grey peat-ash of a dead fire. Thirty-five, Coleman was thinking. When he had been twenty-one, thirty-five was a distant point. Now it was good to be thirty-five . . .

He couldn't banish the Machen woman from his mind.

Coleman was a graduate. He had qualified early; a Master's at twenty-one. Economics. He had a good degree in the first year of the rapacious eighties decade. His course seemed to be set. Correspondence came, interviews were there for the taking. The financial world was sloughing its old skin and taking on the role of turf-accountant. There was no hurry.

But a choice had been made for Coleman, aged twenty-one.

Looking back, he knew he had been watched, vetted, assessed over a period. He had disliked student politics, the boredom, all the hard-men trendy left-wing splinters, revolutionaries, anarchists, die-hards who would move gently into the smash and grab of greed, of normal living, of respectability. He was strong, fit, made for playing-fields, athletics tracks. He enjoyed his lifestyle. He dallied with the girls, liked their impermanence: he could laugh with them, say the right things, slept with a few. Some of them might even have loved him.

Moments of decision arrive suddenly and at odd venues. Not all enterprises have premises or titles, brass plates or headed notepaper. Coleman was at a rugby match, applauding at half-time the teams huddling for tactics and hype and the magic of glucose. A man beside him, strong, perhaps twice his age, had turned and smiled. He wore spectacles which gave him a special kind of academic friendliness.

There was no preamble; he said, "I have a job you might like to do."

Coleman was saying, "Economics? I'm not long qualified . . ."

"I know. It's more difficult than that. You might find it interesting."

"Not outside the law?"

"No."

Coleman was looking at the eyes; without a smile they were careful, observant.

"After the game we could have a drink. No obligation of course. You're in charge."

Coleman nodded.

Later they sat anonymously in the crowded exclusiveness of a five-star buttery. This would be no piece of cake, he was told. There would be weeks of slog, grind, hard work to reach peak: independence, survival, fitness, intelligence, work in sweat until you drop . . .

The job?

The training first. Success in that and details could be discussed. Good money, even in training. There was a challenge about it. A secrecy. Coleman felt he was entering a dark tunnel. But he was curious.

He was trained alone; he was a class of one. There were three instructors. He was driven in a closed van to the working area, featureless mountain terrain, harsh, dangerous, unpeopled. It was a murderous course, relentless. He was fed like a prizefighter, ran thirty miles a day, lost ten pounds weight. With a compass and a scrap of ordnance paper he would be cowelled and dumped. He had learned how to move in secrecy, outwit, surprise. Coleman was good.

After ten weeks he emerged.

"The job, Mr Coleman," he was told, "is vigilance."

"Watching?"

"Yes."

Coleman thought about it. "Killing?" he asked.

"People may want to kill *you*. You would defend yourself of course. As you know, we have an international frontier existing in our country which must be honoured. But all frontiers are infiltrated. From both sides. Dangerous work at times. Very expert operators. Assassins, if needs be."

"Terrorists?"

"Terrorists are just little people tumbling in a brawl. We are vigilant, that is our job. We watch the frontier, the coastline, what passes over and back. Special contraband."

"Arms?"

"We have lost personnel in recent months. The work of two special people, we think."

"You want me to find them?"

"Remove them."

"Kill them?" Coleman asked.

117

"We would train you in the use of firearms and other weapons, if you agree. If you have any doubts, refuse. We can drive you back to civilization in the morning."

"Who are *we*?"

"When you finish your training in weaponry you will be a loner. You cannot reach us. You are a non-person, no I.D., nothing. Money will be sent, poste restante, to a specified office. From this moment your name will be *Kearns*. There is a reasonable bounty, of course."

"When the job is finished, what then?"

"You may be killed in the line of duty, you realise?"

"Yes."

"When the work is complete you will contact us. Poste restante. An empty envelope to Kearns . . ."

In two weeks Coleman drove an Opel Kadett into a bustling frontier town. Counting its quota of thieves, terrorists, druggies, swagmen, an assortment of criminals, there was a population of several thousand. Coleman dressed for his part. He found a bed and breakfast. People didn't ask for provenance or profession.

He was just south of the fortified frontier and twenty minutes away, in foreign territory, was an enemy army garrison, walled, netted, a stronghold.

Kearns's town was a crucible, almost a no-man's-land.

It was growing place, impersonal, coastal. Illicit trading, varying with the winds of change and rates of exchange, at a whim, brought prosperity north and then south.

It was a wealthy town of thriving businesses, sufficiently big and busy to give anonymity. Coleman, a twenty-one-year-old, slipped easily into the ways of nightlife, met peers and scum, male and female, and in a small unobtrusive way he dealt a little in hemp.

He always carried a hand gun, a spare clip, and in a jacket pocket a screw-on silencer.

It was late in the Autumn season. In daylight he drove into the surrounding hills and glens, lonely neglected roads, and parked. He climbed to vantage points from where he could look down on a stretch of seawater prodding inland and, on its opposite shore, foreign towns that had once been places of summertime resort; and, strangely, the Mountains of Mourne, foreign too. He could see troop patrols, armed vehicles passing along the coastal road. A scene of peace. Mountains sprung up on each side of the lough, little towns faced each other; it was a piece of another man's land.

At intervals, bodies had been found floating in the shallows. Floating. They had been shot and dumped.

Coleman walked his territory, learnt his geography: the open roads where armed police were restless, searching, always in motion; the blocked unauthorised roads where danger might be a shadow.

At night-time a lone pedestrian with a keen ear and a wary eye, could slip out of sight, survive. Coleman walked and spent nights watching creeping blobs of headlights, their will-o-the-wisp routes and destinations, passing so close he could almost touch them. It was a mixed bag of army, police, militia, landrovers and transports.

And he was a non-person, a target.

In four weeks he was without progress. Nothing stirred. He had become part of a small group; he bought dope and sold it to them, secretly drove to collect wages when they fell due. He fitted. Football-wise, they called him Kearnsie. He was patient. He waited. something would move. He spent time with hard-liners, drop-outs, pushers, talked, listened, drank. And there was a woman called Cassland.

She told him, "I'm hooked, Kearnsie." She pulled back her sleeves to expose a pox of needle-marks.

"Not from grass," he said.

"Grass is just for while you're waiting."

"For a fix?"

"'Yes."

"I don't carry it."

"I know who does."

119

"You need money?"

"Yes," she said. "Come with me, Kearnsie. If you're with me, you're okay. He's a good guy."

Cassland talked a lot, didn't say very much. She could be stoned on crack or grass or booze. Or was she? She needed fixes too? Her flesh hadn't wasted. Needles shaped faces, consumed bodies, made eyes bright or dull. Coleman felt time was gathering pace. He was looking for danger but was living with it. He waited.

"Okay?" she asked again.

He nodded.

"It's round the corner. A few steps. He's a final Med, should be gone back, his term is started. Jesus, without him I'm lost, I'll die."

She pushed the doorbell. Beneath his loose jacket, Coleman's gun was tight in his waistband. He felt it, rested his elbow against it. It was a first floor flat furnished with a comfortable permanence. Carpeted stairway. Too comfortable for a passing student, Coleman thought.

"This is Kearnsie," Cassland said and held her thumb up. "He's kosher. Deals a bit. I need a fix."

Coleman looked and saw a fairly seasoned medical student. There was a woman sitting apart, striking in style and features.

"Yes," this smiling student said; he was looking at Coleman. He saw a hard face, a hard body. Interesting.

"Oh," Cassland came to life. "This is Mike Broder." A momentary pause. "And Mike's friend."

A bleak smile of welcome from this friend.

A nameless friend, Coleman thought.

Broder said with convincing warmth, "Park yourself somewhere." He told Cassland, "The stuff's in the back. Take a fix."

Cassland hurried away.

His accent was good, very pure, inherited. "You're English," Coleman said.

"Born there," Broder nodded. "Irish parents want their children to be English gentlemen. It opens the gate to Trinity too. I'm a medical, final year," he reinforced her story. "You want a fix? Be my guest."

"Never touch it."

"Grass?"

"Sometimes. Not now."

Broder brought a bottle of ten-year-old Talisker malt from his sideboard, two squat crystal glasses. They shimmered. He smiled at Coleman, filled them.

'Friend' was not included; she was a beautiful woman, silent.

"Sláinte," Broder said; he drained his glass.

Almost a party trick, Coleman thought. He slowly drank back the beautiful smoky whisky of Skye. Broder was filling the glasses again. They drank.

Coleman smiled; he might seem a little drunk. Cassland arrived, empty-handed, revived, her eyes glittering with contentment. She played her part well.

"I'll pay you now," Coleman said.

"My guests," Broder repeated, "there's a party at The Point on Saturday. A very fair Club there. Looking across at enemy territory. You must come. I'll pick you up. Nine o'clock. A good night guaranteed."

Coleman was at the window, looking out at the evening traffic; he said, "There's a hotel across the street here. I'll be there. Nine o'clock."

"Fine."

Cassland said, "Then you can both collect me. I'm on your way." She smiled to Coleman.

Broder would be an MI man, public school, England his heritage, a Catholic perhaps, Coleman would guess. The English carried Catholicism like Puritan hats. Cassland's hide-out was to be the place of execution. Broder would hate to have blood spilt on his precious carpet.

Coleman said, "Thanks for the invitation."

121

"Delighted to have met you." Broder smiled his friendly smile. "There'll be good malt out there."

His friend was remarkable too for her silence.

Cassland led him down the carpeted stairs and, on the pavement, took his arm. She should be a little unsteady yet, jiggy, but she was a rock.

"That fix saved my life," she said.

"Good . . ."

Saturday was a bright day into evening time. Darkness came and street lights. The east coast wind was sharp with night-time. At nine o'clock the town was stirring, rigged and polished for the weekend fling. A few pedestrians, but cars moving everywhere. Coleman drove his Kadett and found parking space. He walked a short distance to the rendezvous.

It wasn't a small town and it wasn't big. Its hotels were good. The bar, with its concealed amber lighting spilling into the colours of spirits and liqueurs, reflected behind it another crowded place of noise and talk and tobacco fumes: a welcome home to the tippler.

He saw Broder at the end of a long counter, waving. At a distance he had a clear view of him now. He was big and strong, handsome. He would be armed. He was alone.

Beneath a jacket and a light mackintosh Coleman could feel the bulk of his own weapon.

"Malt?"

"Yes."

"Good, but it's not Talisker.'

Coleman drank a little. "It's good," he said.

"Are you staying long in town?"

"So long as business lasts and the climate's right."

Broder smiled his admiration. "Cool," he said. "Cass likes you. I'll give you some stuff when I leave. You can put her on ration. Feed her pot in between."

Coleman nodded. "She's a nice girl," he said.

"You can depend on Cass."

They had three malts and left. Broder's car was at the hotel entrance. Like Coleman, nothing flash but dependable. He took his keys to open the passenger door.

Coleman said, "I'll drive my own. You can see it from here. Battered but beautiful."

"Save yourself the bother," Broder said.

"No bother," Coleman said. "Cass might need a lift home. She'd have a shady nook somewhere."

"Ha!" Broder laughed. "You have it all mapped out." He nodded. "Cass has a cosy den."

"Yes," Coleman said.

Broder slapped him on the shoulder. "You know the trade," he said. "Follow my car."

They drove out of town, up the rise, past the last of detached outer houses, into the darkness. It was two miles to the hidden stillness of Cassland's bungalow. Coleman saw the beauty of steep rising ground and at its peak, black trees silhouetted against the pale night-time of the sky.

He took the gun from his waist and rested it in the pocket of the mackintosh.

Broder had stopped at the bungalow; it was walled, secluded. Light shone from windows and hallway. It was an innocent place. They drove to the gateway. From his car window Broder's hand was waving. Coleman went to him.

"You pick her up, Kearnsie. She'd like that."

Going to the door he'd leave his back exposed. But you gambled.

They'd shoot him in the house, Coleman thought. He stood on the doorstep, rang the bell. He heard footsteps. He could feel Broder's eyes on him.

Cassland arrived. She was sharp, even beautiful, now. An attractive girl. She was no druggie. But she had importance; she was no bit-player. She wore tailored amber slacks and a Chinese top, patterned, mandarin collar and sleeves. She was dressing for murder. She held out her hands and welcomed him, closed the door.

"Three minutes, Kearnsie," she said "I'll get you a drink.

123

Take a seat."

Coleman sat where he could see the entrance and exit of the room. She had left Broder in the car. Christ, he thought, she's the executioner! The gunshot would be a signal for Broder to arrive. Broder was the small boy; he worked for her. They would wrap him up and take him to float in the lough. His hand tightened on the butt of the gun; he released the safety catch. Silencers didn't matter here. He sat in the armchair, waiting, ready, hands in the pockets of the mackintosh.

He called out, "You look very special tonight."

She was laughing. "Got myself a fix, Kearnsie."

She entered, carrying a drink; a squat glass of plain malt. The other hand was out of view. She came close and leant over him. She would pick her spot. She was smiling. As she raised the gun, Coleman shot her through the face. The sound was deafening in the confines of the room. It faded.

He faced the entrance door now, heard a key in the lock in the outer passage. Then Broder was facing him, surprised. He saw Cassland's body: an open mouth, trickling blood. Coleman shot him through the chest, watched him crumple.

He stood for a moment, his face covered in a thin film of sweat. He pulled back Cassland's mandarin sleeves; her arms were smooth, unmarked. The needle prods had been a make-up job: a little cleansing cream had left her shining.

He had had enough, he knew; he would tell the kind academic man. The job was finished. That was the contract. Remove the killers. Suddenly, any more than the plotting and assassination of high politics, neither did he want the subterfuge, the chicanery, the amorality of boardrooms.

He had grown up in small places and would go back to obscurity, let quietness settle about him, contentment. The dirty water would flow away, time would cleanse him.

He turned away from the two murdered bodies, left the house lights burning as he had found them, moved out into the darkness.

He was suddenly halted, frozen in groping stillness,

crouched ready to kill again! Broder's car was being driven away! Who? As it passed, a face was turned towards him, the silent beautiful face from Cassland's and Broder's flat. In a moment the car was lost in darkness.

He was suddenly wrenched back from his reverie: the cold ashes in his grate, the ground-out cigarette stubs, the world of Belle Cannon, Rellighan, Sommerville. This town, his town.

The silent person, the face that had passed him, was Sommerville's housekeeper. Fourteen years ago, he thought, he had seen that face. Its strange beauty. Estel Machen!

He looked again at the cold fireplace, the dead cigarette ends.

It was a dirty world out there. But this was his home.

He remembered his own abasement, the pain, the screaming. Caution he had had always, but fear was something new. A bad feeling.

He tightened his coat, tilted his cap. Now this peace was threatened. He thought of Belle Cannon and Rellighan. Reality had distanced itself.

Jennifer Anderson's body was in the funeral home and soon would be removed to the church for prayers, the sprinkled ceremonial blessings and warnings to the living.

Finegan was clad in his Sunday best; his overcoat was mohair, expensive, but it sat awkwardly on his frame. The tanned battered skin of his face, his ropy neck, the crouching gait, would have been more in tune with oddments of unmatched farming clothes, rough woollens, a collarless shirt, laced unpolished boots. His lips were tight and characterised his hardened, long-crusted opinions. A dark grey felt hat, with turned-up brim all round, sat straight across his forehead.

Finegan wasn't dressed in sympathy or condolence; he was being careful. The town's pubs had agreed to mark this sad occasion by closing their doors for two hours of the afternoon and Finegan of course, a pillar of the town, its business and social committees, would show respect. At any rate, the afternoons were slow, were the doldrum period of trade. A few pounds wouldn't be missed and sharpened talk and thirst would fill the rest of the day, be a fair recompense.

It wasn't Sunday. It was a holiday weekend. Other licensed businesses, he knew, traded unperturbed behind window displays and drawn blinds. Bastard Christians. They damned drinking with the label of over-indulgence, even sinfulness.

Finegan walked the town's business streets, noted the closed doors of his competitors, listened for the sounds of secret trade. Damned two-facedness, hypocrisy. Selectively he tipped his hat to those who earned his respect.

He was a bitter man. Even with his wife, in their shared bed, in the procreation of their children, he felt he was in breach of the Lord's commandments. His wife, too, had committed herself to prayer for the salvation of their souls. Nothing else. Each one must, alone, seek his personal reward. The attainment of the Kingdom of Heaven was the purpose of life.

The town pavements were busy with shoppers, but young people, in groups, wandered about, talking, even smiling! In this pit of tragedy! Finegan was enraged. He felt they were disease-ridden, committing acts of what he called *impurity*, without a thought of God's hellfire and damnation. He despaired. They were poisoning each other, dying!

Soon now they would be gathering to file past the dead body, this latest corpse at Rellighan's funeral home, carrying rosary beads, perhaps even close to tears. Tonight they would be back to grabbing and groping, and strange cigarette smoking too; you could see their browned fingers, not their souls. Someone had mentioned the sniffing of deadly spirit in wood adhesives, nail cleaners, even paints. Their brains would be rotted.

It was an age of evil.

Finegan was parading his virtue for the town now. He avoided proximity with passing schoolchildren. He felt endangered, he was afraid. The town was in peril. He would avoid the funeral home and the funeral gathering too.

When this evening's death service at the church was completed, he would catch the sacristan, Simoney, to exchange a few words. The town must be cleansed. The righteous are bold, he told himself. It was time to act.

In the busy Square he suddenly stopped. He stood agape. Standing at his usual corner was the mentally disturbed Colleran – our village idiot, Finegan called him unforgivingly – smiling at people or at the sky or at nothing. He was in his twenties, showing the wear and tear of medication. Schoolchildren stopped and shook his hand, boys, girls. One long fair-haired slut handed him her lighted cigarette. She spoke to him. He smiled, laughed, occasionally muttered a few words. He had been standing there, every day, for all of two years.

Finegan wondered at the simplicity of it! They touched him, perhaps smoked the same cigarette, inhaled his madman's breath. He thanked God for a sudden moment of enlightenment, wisdom. He had been blind.

It would take careful planning, Finegan thought.

He crossed the Square and stood, at a safe distance, looking into Colleran's smiling face. He did a lot of smiling. Maybe he had plenty to smile about.

Finegan said to him, "Do you know who I am?"

Colleran was laughing silently at a vision, something a great distance away.

"I'm Finegan of Main Street Bar."

Suddenly Colleran said, "I drank beer once. At a football match." He was shaking with laughter.

"When was it?"

"I'm good at football. When I feel okay again I'll turn professional. Plenty of money." It was all smiling and laughter. "I might play in Europe . . ."

"When was it? When did you drink beer?"

Colleran was silent, looking out into another world where things might always be perfect, where Colleran might shimmer, dancing across crowded cheering stadia, the great invincible power-striker, Colleran.

"When, when?" Finegan was saying.

But Colleran, chin high, might be listening to commands. His eyes were thoughtful, unfocused. He was absent for moments now, absorbed with what might be shouting in his brain.

Suddenly he said, "I know poetry too. Wordsworth, Coleridge, Tennyson, Yeats, Kavanagh, Brooke, Owen, Goldsmith, Keats, Milton, Shelley, Dryden, Pope. All the poets are dead. I know Shakespeare's sonnets . . ."

"Beer, beer!" Finegan said. "Who gave you beer?"

"And history. Henry VII, Henry VIII, Edward VI, Lady Jane Grey, Mary I, Elizabeth I, James I, Charles I, Cromwell, Charles II, James II, William III, Mary II, Queen Anne, George I, George II, George III, George IV, William IV, Queen Victoria, Edward VII, George V . . ."

Finegan caught his wrist, held him away, whispered at him, "Shut up!" He looked about at the busy disinterested Square. School pupils were in the middle distance. He must hurry. Colleran's face was cringing in fear. Finegan released him.

"What about schoolgirls?" he asked. "And their legs bare or in stockings? And above that?"

Colleran was looking past him, smiling, laughing.

"Funny, is it?"

Only laughter, amusement, moments of listening. The school pupils were close. Finegan moved away . . .

Sommerville was in high spirits. He was watching. He had closed the door on Coleman, his hallucinations, his fears, and stood for moments in thought. Then he went to his surgery, from his window watched Coleman's progress towards the Square. He saw Finegan talking to the witless boy who stood at his habitual chosen place. Coleman might be seeing them too. But Coleman had a great deal of thoughts to worry him.

Estel Machen entered the surgery; she was smiling, looking at Sommerville with a special tenderness.

"My dear," she said.

"Inspector Coleman just left. A thoughtful Inspector Coleman. I was watching him through the window."

"He is well?"

Sommerville sat in his chair, looked towards the ceiling, filled the room with uproarious laughter. When he had finished he was a little breathless.

"I prescribed for him!"

"He is ill?"

"He died last night in the boathouse. He had been beaten and ripped asunder with knives. He awoke, miraculously unmarked, except by fear."

"I gave him a little punishment," she said.

Sommerville looked at her with admiration. He said, "I prescribed a mild sedative. Mentioned the nonsense of fears of instability, even unsoundness of mind."

"It would never do to have a mad policeman wandering about the streets of our town."

"I think you have already effected a cure."

Sommerville went to her and embraced her, ran his hands along the softness of her body. She was dressed in her long grey penitent's robe, thick lisle stockings, flat polished shoes, her starched tiara, bib and apron.

"I think you like seducing your servants," she said. "Your ancestors could command the attendance of growing girls in their beds."

Sommerville said, "I have what is most beautiful."

"Come," she said; she took him by the hand and led him through the hallway to the dining room. The warmth embraced him. The comfort and cleanliness glistened about them. The curtains were drawn, a fire burned in the grate. The table was set for two. A candelabrum showed the brightness of linen, the delph, the heavy cutlery. A bottle of sparkling wine, opened, rested in an ice-bucket. Sommerville held her chair while she seated herself, then sat facing her.

"We are celebrating," she said; she raised the dish covers from their plates and the aroma of food rose up about them. A dish of meat and spices and herbs. Sommerville's plate was overflowing; hers was a tiny portion. Sommerville gazed on it. It was heady, like a sudden breath of alcohol.

She poured wine.

Sommerville was already eating. "What is it?" he asked.

"You like red meat, don't you?"

"Yes."

"The rest is unimportant."

They raised glasses and Sommerville drank. He was absorbed with his food and drink. She tasted a little, drank a little. She added to his plate.

Sommerville laughed, smiled into her eyes. "I like the battles we have," he said. "No winners, losers, only sleep."

"Soon," she told him. "Then I must make my appearance in the church. It is funeral evening, the young body resting in darkness. Mr Simoney will be busy."

She paused, waited for absolute stillness, instructed him.

"You will drive to the sacristy at midnight. The gates will be open. I will be there alone. We will celebrate. We will set free the spirit of Jennifer Anderson."

"Yes."

His plate was clean, he finished the wine. She brought cognac, placed it before him, left only the candles burning. She set her stage. It was twilight, another world. She stood apart from him in dull working clothes.

She slowly began to disrobe. The tiara, the bib and apron; the flat shoes. She sat, pulled up the long dress to her thighs and peeled off the lisle stockings. The whiteness of her flesh in the half-light shone out towards him. She stood and let the gown drop away. She tossed her hair. She was a schoolboy in knee-length trousers and tunic shirt. Then suddenly she was naked, glabrous, beautiful. He watched her slip away from the room. Heard her footsteps on the stairway, and then in his bedroom.

130

He drank from the cognac bottle, undressed, flung his clothes about the room and followed her. He was a fleshy ludicrous figure in pursuit.

In the soft light of his bedroom, she lay there, supine, her arms raised in welcome. She held him in suspense for a long time. Then she enveloped him . . .

She stood and watched him lying there in a deep trance, open-mouthed, his breath grating in his throat, limp. He was an ageing vulgar piece of clay. She pulled the bedclothes across him, his sagging chest muscles, his bulge of abdomen.

She would tidy the house, shower, dress modestly, with dignity carry her memorial wreath to the church and then humbly place herself in the employ of Simoney.

There was no rush. Nude, she moved about her chores, feeling comfortable, refreshed.

It was nearing six-thirty. Coleman, before he left his empty house and the thoughts of almost fifteen years past, drank a measure of whiskey at the dull ashen grate in the gathering chill of the evening. He wondered when he might light a fire there again. The house was in stillness but sounds from the town drifted in to him. A little more sound than usual. The countryside shoppers would still be moving about, making the restless stirrings of the evening. There would be traffic to the funeral home too.

Atlantic Ireland could have moments of stillness and tranquillity, away from the chaos and bloody battles of the European mainland. Foreign people blended, were lost, in the wildness of the coast. They came and went. Some settled. Raging storms and sunny days passed them by: they sought obscurity, anonymity, in their hermetic lives. There were cranks and esoteric coteries, restless depressives, aspiring artists and artists manqué. Coleman had seen them all. If they could afford it and were peaceable, they could play their games. Who cared?

But Machen was evil and Sommerville was a conspiring

131

prisoner in his own house. They were beyond the range of Coleman.

Coming face to face with evil had brought fear.

Coleman stood, could only remember his own murder and his dying moments by the cove. The helplessness of pain. Hallucination? Invisible assassins? Reality, unreality, started in fear, ended in terror. He must step out to meet it, to find it. Somehow come to grips with it.

Changing his clothes to show deference at the funeral service mattered nothing now. He ignored it. There was a long night's work to be done. He let his leather coat lie open and set out along Main Street.

There were people in motion, but a certain quietness was gathering. The town should be out in respect and sorrow for the dead; but only scattered groups, a few cars, were moving. Rellighan had thought fear would be hovering and he was right. It was in the air, the town was colder.

Coleman rang at Belle Cannon's. He looked pale and angry, she thought. She closed the door.

"Good to see you in one piece," she said. "I worry a little about you, you know."

He said, "I sat before my empty grate and thought back over the years."

"We've had good years, Coleman."

"Yes."

"And before that?"

"Good years, always good years."

"Come upstairs," she said. "A few moments. Sit, unwind. You need a drink."

"I'm drinking too much."

The comfort of her lounge, its fabrics, colours and furnishings brought him only cold premonition. She would be here alone tonight and if punishment came . . .

She brought the drink and put it on the table. He held her shoulders as they stood facing each other for moments. Then he went back to the table and drank a little.

132

"You're worried, Coleman," she said.

"Yes."

"For me?"

"For the town," he evaded it.

Belle Cannon didn't ask him about his comings and goings: that was Coleman's business.

"We should go," she said. "The corpse. Seven-thirty from the funeral home to the church."

As they left, Coleman said, "You have a spring lock on your door. You should have a mortice too, a deadlock." He knew it was a thoughtless remark, vacuous, as if doors and locks or thick walls were barriers.

"Against invasion?"

Coleman felt a chill of pain in his body; he looked at Belle Cannon's face that always had for him its special beauty, gentle caring eyes.

He smiled. "Security," he said. "I'm brain-washed."

"I'll get one," she told him.

They walked across the Square into the quiet enclave where the funeral home, the convent, the parish church were within reassuring sight of each other. Two hundred mourners had gathered. A small crowd.

Belle Cannon said, "I see my pupils over there. They'll expect me. I'll go to them."

He nodded, watched her walk away; her schoolgirls gathered round her. In a little while he stirred, moved through the crowd and entered the funeral home.

Parents, relatives, a few friends, were touching the cold hands clasped in death, kissing the corpse in farewell, filing out. Four remained to shoulder the coffin. Coleman remained, stood beside it for a few moments.

The sleeping tranquil face, a little worn but still with its beauty, brought the reality of helplessness. He thought of Estel Machen for a moment: another beautiful face, a cherished teacher. Rellighan's beautiful woman. And then anger stirred when he thought of his own helpless death.

133

Rellighan was coming with the coffin lid, to screw it down. Coleman looked once more at the remains and, for an instant, saw the corpse of *Belle Cannon* lying there! He stood steady, held the catafalque. Christ!

Rellighan was saying, "Thank you for coming."

Coleman looked in the coffin again. The schoolgirl's body had returned. He nodded to Rellighan and went out into the cold refreshing air. Fear was Estel Machen's weapon. He looked and saw Belle Cannon surrounded by her girls.

The coffin was shouldered to the church where it would be close to God for the night. Its placing on the catafalque, the final adjustments were directed by Simoney, the church sacristan, this austere layman who might never have smiled, devoted to the house of God and all its objects of holiness. In these unrighteous times that shadowed even their own town, when vocations to the priesthood had dwindled to a few and God was forgotten, his work load had spread to encompass almost all the works of a deacon: he read lessons, performed the preliminary acts for the dead, silently supervised baptisms, dispensed communion.

The sacristy was his domain of vestments and sacred objects: thurible, monstrance, incense-boats, the tabernacle, its precious chalices, cruets and bottles of wine that, in transubstantiation, would become the blood of the Son of God. In his middle years, the last of his clan, beyond reproach and of comfortable means, he lived alone. People came to him for advice, brought presents or left donations in thanksgiving. He was tall, spare by nature or by acts of fasting and penance.

The coffin was placed to his satisfaction, the congregation settled in their pews, crowded here, scattered there. Simoney surveyed them, in black soutane, white surplice, he stood at the head of the coffin with his open book, looking out over Mass cards and wreaths piled on the lid. He bowed to God and to the ageing Canon seated in the shadows of the sanctuary. He began his eulogy of the dead girl, her purity, her virtues, God's need to have her in his Divine Presence.

Through our tears there should be joy that she had been chosen. "Let us pray . . ." He began to recite the five Sorrowful Mysteries of the Rosary.

Coleman looked about the old church that had given close on two hundred years' service to its parish – marriages, baptisms, deaths. He had seated himself on the rear seat of the nave. A comfortable half-light came through the stained glass windows (pray for the donors) and the clerestory faintly caught the blackening roof timbers. The polished pews, the confessionals, the graphic depiction of Christ's way to death, the stoups, the memorial tablets, the baptismal fount, the perpetual suspended tiny light of God's ever-presence in his house, these were sad, almost effete, reminders of great power abused, wasted, that might one day be restored with compassion. In the world's quantum leap the church was hardly awakening from sleep.

Simoney had begun to drone ". . . the first sorrowful mystery, the agony in the garden . . . our father who art in heaven . . . hail, full of grace, the lord is with thee . . . glory be to the father and to the son . . ."

Coleman had been drifting back across the years to the learning of catechism and gospels and prayers, first confessional, the wafer of the Host, the awful fear of mortal sin and burning in Hell for all of eternity. Simoney, this thin man, full of sound, was booming at them. His voice was thunderous. "How many grains of sand in all the sea shores of the world? Count them, one by one, and that is not even one grain of eternity . . ."

Rellighan sat at the most distant edge of the front seat, still as the great life-size statues in their niches, mercifully without their patient sanctity and the blue and red glare of their robes.

Sobs of grief came from the mourners. Simoney droned on ". . . may the perpetual light shine upon her and may her immortal soul rest in peace. . ."

A group of six formidable matrons, with voices diminished, dressed in blue, sang:

"Daily, daily, sing to Mary,
Sing our heart's devotion true,
. . ."

Suddenly Coleman caught the thick nauseating sweetness of last night's punishment. It was in the church now but the congregation unaware. With it came fear, a deadly chilliness in the air. He sat upright. Up the centre aisle, through the broad nave, the slim shape of Estel Machen moved at a slow balanced pace; she carried her extravagant floral tribute towards the coffin. The sweetness was intense, close to decay. Coleman watched Rellighan, saw him stiffen, turn his head for half a glance. Had Estel Machen chosen them for the special announcement of her presence? The congregation became aware of her. Simoney, Belle Cannon too. They saw Estel Machen move, a humble servant of God.

She reached the coffin and placed her tribute on it. A magnificent arrangement of delicate gentle colours. Simoney's face softened; he made a small motion of thanks. Heads, eyes, were raised in admiration; the beautiful face, the flowing hair, the pale hands. Schoolchildren were in tears, the congregation stirred. Coleman felt the coldness of the air.

Estel Machen returned down the centre aisle, sat for a moment in prayer, in the last seat, beside Coleman. She bowed her head in prayer. Simoney was caught in the emotional drama of accolade, on the example to his congregation of the selfless acts of our adopted expatriates. Coleman turned to look at Estel Machen: a perfection of bone structure and skin, magnificent Christ-like hair thrown back on her shoulders, lips so red she could have painted them. The eyes changed as she looked at Coleman, the smile vanished, she might be gazing from countless millennia, through him, to infinity. Coleman looked down at the pale hands and saw that they had changed. They were weapons now: below the beauty of tapering fingers, long nails that could slip through flesh. The sweetness suffocated again. Coleman held his breath, tightened every muscle, let his elbow shoot like a piston. Had he struck something? No body sat beside him. Had she slithered away out of range, fallen down towards the tiled ground? It was a soundless fall, unheard, unnoticed. He felt the tightening of fear again. Only Rellighan looked back. When Coleman stared about again, there was nothing. Then he saw Estel Machen, like a cloistered abbess, unmoved, untouched, passing along the side aisle to the sacristy. She had left him with the thought of ageless, immemorial eyes.

Simoney asked his mourners to stand. Children were of their parents, he told them, and their sins were the sins of their parents. A curse had fallen on the town. Evil.

Estel Machen listened to him from the sacristy.

He thundered at them, "Deliver us, O Lord, from death on that dreadful day; when heaven and earth shall quake; when thou shall come to judge the world by fire. I tremble, am sore afraid for the judgement and wrath to come. Eternal rest give unto her, O Lord, and let perpetual light shine upon her. In the name of the Father and of the Son and of the Holy Ghost, Amen."

A stillness was in the church, only the soft moan of the wind came from the estuary. The echoing words of the Lord wasted away into silence.

There was a sudden grating of wood, a flat resounding crash. People stood dumb, motionless.

The coffin lid and its tributes had fallen to the flagstones. Rellighan was on his feet, rushing to it. He lifted it, screwed it back.

Simoney had paled. He said, "There will be a Mass for the Dead tomorrow morning at eleven o'clock and the funeral will leave the church immediately afterwards." He turned to Rellighan with a withering glance. "The floral tributes, the cards, put them in place." It was a bitter whisper. "Take care, take care, Rellighan. Ask God to help you."

"Yes," Rellighan said; he could feel Simoney's anger striking out at him as he left. He met Coleman on the church steps. The wind was rising; people were hunched, hurrying to warmth of firesides. Away from death.

Coleman said, "She was beside me. A smell like sweet sickness. It clings to the skin."

"It was for us," Rellighan said.

"I saw the knives that did her cutting. Pale hands and polished nails." Coleman paused, tightened his fist. "I struck at her," he said.

"Flesh and blood? Did she feel pain, did she fall? Was she there?" Rellighan stared at Coleman. "What did you see in the funeral home?"

"A strange body in the coffin, for a moment."

Rellighan was far away, distant.

"Estel Machen sent the coffin lid toppling," he said. "Her flowers are to keep the body fresh. She likes to keep the dead fresh for her final rituals."

"Rituals?"

"The changing, the transubstantiation."

Coleman stood silent, confused. The changing. People were coming from the church now, dour, uncertain, angry. Facing for home and closed doors.

Belle Cannon came and joined them.

Coleman said, "This is Rellighan."

Rellighan didn't look at her; he nodded, raised a hand. "I know who you are," he said.

All three of them walked across the Square towards the funeral yard. Coleman saw Finegan, who had avoided the service, in quiet intense conversation with Simoney. Finegan and Simoney would be a dangerous liaison.

Belle Cannon asked, "Are we in danger?"

Rellighan said, "Yes, we are in danger." At the corner of the Square he took his leave; he said to Coleman, "Your car. Collect me in an hour."

Rellighan was already on his way to his store-rooms, the gloomy office, the waiting hearses, his salon of mortuary make-up. Walking, he was tall, straight, hardy. They watched

138

him out of sight. It was growing late, the coldness of arriving November in the wind.

It was a holiday weekend. There would be late night entertainment, drinking, singing; maybe brawling. People in celebration. Death had subdued it for a little while.

At Belle Cannon's door Coleman said, "I must collect my car. A call to Finegan's pub first, not very long. Finegan's is a listening post. I don't trust Finegan, he's one of God's soldiers. He was cheek by jowl with Simoney tonight. Today, on the Square young Colleran was his target."

"He's a harmless boy."

"Yes."

"You'll be back here?"

"Oh yes, I'll be back. There's work for you too."

She nodded.

Coleman parked outside Finegan's and sat for a few moments. The town was in fear, priming itself, but its targets were misplaced. Finegan's school-time coupling, kissing, groping, promiscuity, were exaggeration, over-coloured; a single carrier of disease, illness and death in few days. Would carriers increase, one, two, four, eight? They were in dread. Christ, Coleman thought, if you gave them the truth, that evil was surrounding them, they would move you away from their orbit. Your place was a madhouse cell, you were cracking, cracked, of unsound mind! He found comfort in the dripping street lights of the town.

He pushed open the door of Finegan's; the regular faces might never have left. The bar was noisy.

Finegan had closed again for the service; an additional public act of respect. He was behind his bar now.

He said to Coleman, "Rellighan is a botcher. Without staff to prop him up he's a botcher."

Voices everywhere.

"Trained in the U.S. of A."

"Not to screw down coffin lids."

"Not to screw anything."

"For parents to hear that lid clattering on the floor! Ah, the shock!"

Finegan said softly to Coleman, "That was an unforgivable mockery in the church."

"Was it?"

"I'd have Rellighan banished for desecration of the House of God and the corpse in its shelter."

"I was there," Coleman said. "You weren't."

"You saw it then?"

"I saw a coffin lid on the floor. I didn't see it falling."

Finegan said, "But Rellighan was there. It's Rellighan's job. Someone said he smelt of drink."

"Rellighan was there."

"And Simoney?"

"He was there."

"Simoney is a very angry man."

Coleman ignored it. "A half pint," he said.

"A *half* pint?"

"I have work to do."

"You're on leave."

"Driving."

The town had lost its rhythm, even the pubs were without laughter. Placid days, wet or fine, a job to do, as near to slap-dash as would pass muster, draw your pay, wipe the slate clean with God at intervals, kneel at Mass on Sundays, marriage, baptism, death: that was life. Teenagers discovering each other, copulating, naked beneath gym-slips to be ready for pleasure when it came. Finegan had considered it all, painted his own picture. He was ready to meet God at a moment's notice.

"The youth are without morals," he said. "Reduced to animals. Two of them poisoned and how many more?"

The conversation simmered and settled again. Coleman drank a little. He smoked. Six months ago the death of a schoolboy had momentarily shaken the town but left it with its peace of mind. Now the death of a girl and so many parallels with the first had thrown it into confusion. Shock and rain came and went. Time had paled one until another had risen suddenly to open old wounds. He looked about the angry vehement faces, listened to the clash of voices. They were adult or ageing, all of them. Morals, Finegan preached. A few were shocked, a few perhaps envious that they would never enjoy the licence of today. Fear had touched all of them.

If it were whispered, even with a smile, that Estel Machen, servant of the church, faithful custodian of Dr Herbert Sommerville, might be some timeless conjuration out of darkness, needing the unspoilt dead for her purposes, these spiky drunken warriors might run gibbering into the street.

A voice said, "Miss Machen moved like a saint through the church, I'm told, to lay flowers on the coffin."

"A custom of civilized people."

"A generous custom."

"She's a fine person," Finegan endorsed it.

Coleman was remembering flowers to keep a body fresh.

From the crowd: "I'll raise my glass to her."

"Her long life and health."

Coleman called for another drink and Finegan brought it, carefully placed it before him. Time and the fire were wasting. Finegan stoked it with coal. When he had finished, Coleman raised his glass and drained it.

"In three or four days, when things have settled," Finegan said, "there will be a special emergency meeting of the town council. We'll find this little poisoned bastard who is among us and we'll deal with him!"

"Any ideas?"

"Oh yes."

"It might be me," Coleman said, "or meningitis."

"It might," Finegan said, "but I'd be surprised."

"I wouldn't know," Coleman said.

"I keep my eyes open," Finegan told him.

Coleman raised a hand to the gathering and left; the northwest wind still blew and was cutting. Lights in windows were like some unreachable warmth.

141

He rang Belle Cannon's doorbell; she took his hand and led him upstairs. Hers was a world of reality and comfort, Coleman thought.

Beyond it, in Sommerville's house, in the church, in the cemetery, in Rellighan's mortuary, another world existed, took shape, had its own purpose.

Belle Cannon brought a bottle and a glass to him. They sat side by side on the sofa.

Coleman said, "I'll become addicted."

He poured a small drink and sat in silence. At the closing of Belle Cannon's door the town might have been cut loose, discarded; but phantom pain lived on in its absence. Days would be the same round of awakening, eating, working, illness and health, prayer and pleasure. There would be all the old sounds and movements. But was it a facade, a shadow-world? Coleman thought of his own disfigurement, the illusion of death; of a pale tranquil body in the church, the flowers on the coffin lid. The body, the flowers, the property of Estel Machen.

He could go down to the Square, climb on to the arm of the Celtic cross and shout to the town that it was being defiled, polluted. They would bring him down exhausted. Sommerville would send him into special care and recuperation for a little while. The end of Coleman: involuntary psychosis, hallucination, mild lunacy, but harmless of course. Coleman the law officer would be dead. That would bring pleasure to Machen and Sommerville.

Belle Cannon said, "We're quiet, aren't we?"

Coleman handed her the large glittering key. "The key of the church," he said. "I go with Rellighan now. An hour after I've gone, walk down there. When there's light in the sacristy and the church in darkness, then you enter. When the church is empty, you leave."

"Empty?"

"Of everything, living or dead."

"I'm no hero, Coleman," she said. "I'm afraid. But I'll do it."

"I'm afraid," he said.

"The coffin lid?" she asked.

"Call it an accident."

They stood and faced each other. "This morning you looked wan, Coleman. I worried for you, had no sleep."

"There's something you're not telling me."

"It must wait a little," he said. "It's better like that."

"Estel Machen touched the children's faces, their hair."

"A lot of children."

"She touched the two who died."

"It wouldn't prove anything."

She said suddenly, "Rellighan is strong, isn't he?"

Coleman looked at her, nodded; she had stood before him on the church steps tonight.

"What does Rellighan think?"

"Rellighan buries them. Doctors write certificates."

She took the glass from the table, handed it to Coleman. He drank.

She said, "You saw the Machen woman in the church tonight?"

"Yes. Flowers for the dead."

"She went to the sacristy."

"Yes."

"You fear her, Coleman, do you?"

"Yes," Coleman said.

"Everyone thought she was so fine, so generous. The children were in tears."

"And you?"

"Fear," she said; she looked at Coleman. "There was a moment of sweetness when she passed. Sickly sweetness. It didn't linger. A moment only."

Coleman stood at the window. Above the street lights it was pitch black night, only scattered bright rectangles of glass were markers of life. The sweetness. A sign for Belle Cannon.

"The girls," he said. "Did the sweetness reach the girls?"

143

Belle Cannon shook her head. "They didn't notice it. It wasn't mentioned," she said.

Coleman thought of Rellighan in his dumb soundless world, sensitive, aware of every intrusion. He thought of the clean windblown town, its waking and sleeping moments, the little sins that were indulged from day to day, sins of love and hate and greed. Little sins were part of living.

Sins weren't evil, Coleman thought.

"We are in danger?" Belle Cannon asked.

"Yes." Coleman looked at her. "And I must go," he said. "You understand that, don't you?"

"Yes."

"Rellighan and I, we have fear too."

"Of Estel Machen?"

"Yes. My being here with you wouldn't change anything. Not being here might." He held her for moments; she might suffer indignity, terror, abasement. He said, "We can't live, day in, day out, in fear."

She said, "I'll be in the church, Coleman."

Finegan's was a talking person's pub. Small towns are like that. You must know the geography; there is a place for everyone. The rough-scruff pub is for the man who can handle it: the town's messers and brawlers, the fighting men, the travelling people. They spend money but you earn it. The disco pub is for the youth – and the under-age and the border-lines – a thunderous world of noise and a school for budding bibblers.

Finegan's had a certain dignity. It had stood since the last days of Victoria's reign, when this island, shore to shore, had been her possession. Finegan's father and grandfather had stood behind the unaltered counter, imbued with propriety and good behaviour. Nothing in the pub had changed; polish and paint had preserved its character. Until the shortage of menial labour its floor had been scrubbed and only in recent years, and with misgivings, had modernity crept in with the laying of lino.

But Finegan thought it was the town's best pub, a man's pub, with a burning coal fire on winter days, bare tables and plastic ashtrays, hard wooden seats. His clientele was as good as you found in the mediocrity of a small place. And there were two, perhaps three, he could trust.

He looked at the clock. He knew the town and its movements. Simoney would have left the church and its corpse now, his hour of prayer before the altar complete. At peace with God. Simoney was a man of piety but he could put the fear of horned devils and hellfire into so many useless minds. That was good, Finegan thought; he served God and the town.

He quietly called one of his trusted drinkers to stand in his place for a while.

"Hold the fort," he told him. "I might be an hour, not more, probably less."

In the hallway he hung up his apron, donned the expensive overcoat and hat and gloves, stepped out into the sharpness of the night. Finegan didn't raise a hand to fellow citizens or acknowledge their salutations; he walked, head erect, through the streets, past the church and convent, to Simoney's detached house close by, sheltered by trees and dense shrubbery. The house was in darkness but Finegan confidently rang the bell and stood waiting. The hall light suddenly shone through the fanlight. Finegan arranged himself. Simoney opened the door.

"Christopher," Finegan said, as an equal citizen entitled to intimacy, "I hope I am not intruding. You are a busy man like myself. And not long from your day's toil."

Simoney returned the intimacy. "You're very welcome, Martin. Come in, won't you? God's work is never tiring."

Simoney didn't consider Finegan an equal but it was best to be charitable on these occasions. Simoney's family had been landed people. Once they might have been called gentry, but having reached some genetic peak, had been generations in decline. Simoney was the last of his line and, alone, inhabited the family town house in its walled privacy. His forbears had donated this enclave to the church for the greater glory of God and the salvation of their immortal souls. Simoney was of comfortable means. He looked at Finegan and saw a tradesman in a hardly reputable trade.

They walked through the hallway to Simoney's secluded study. It was well furnished and maintained but nothing was in excess. An air of comfortable humility. The heating was minimal. Cold, Finegan thought. Perhaps a penitent way of life.

"Take a chair."

Finegan sat. "I had a few words with you earlier. I come about town affairs."

"The town?"

"These deaths. These young people. Tomorrow two of them will be lying in our cemetery. In a space of six months."

"In the grace of God, let us pray."

Finegan hesitated. "I'd venture to say that children of today, are moving away from God."

"The church has its bad times and good times. It has a history of great strength."

Finegan was patient. "The town admires you, Christopher, for your great dedication and selfless life. But my work brings me daily in touch with the whisperings and calumny of the town. I am disturbed."

Simoney was nodding now, curious. "Is there something of importance that I should know?"

"There is little chastity left among our older schoolchildren. Trusted customers have told me, in confidence or course, that in dark places young girls raise their clothes and bare themselves and are penetrated. They laugh at virginity. And now people are talking about disease."

Simoney was cautious. "You're sure, Martin, are you?"

"When one or two talk it is gossip. When the town talks

we must listen. Take heed. Some of these lassies crossing the Square every day are bare beneath their skirts. Not a stitch to cover themselves. Sluts, I would call them. And the schoolboys are less than animals."

Simoney held up a hand for silence. He knelt, crossed himself and prayed for moments.

Then he sat and faced Finegan again. "Have you seen any of these things?"

Finegan was angry. "God has spared me that, but people come to me and I can trust them."

"You said *disease*."

"The town is saying it," Finegan corrected him.

"Calm, calm, Martin. I know you are a man of honour."

"Meningitis, a dying alcoholic doctor said six months ago. God give him peace. And now a locum, a stop-gap dabbler, says it again. Sign the certificate and send for Rellighan. Dig a hole and fill it in. It's easy."

"What disease?"

"I don't know."

"From where?"

"There's a poisoner in the town."

"A carrier?"

"A carrier, a poisoner, call it what you like."

"You know him?"

"Yes, and I'll deal with him."

Simoney was in doubt now, more cautious. "Isn't that Coleman's work?" he asked.

"Coleman would take too much time, Christopher. Time is something we don't have a lot of. Time is flying. Coleman's morals aren't much above the rest but he's an adult and he can sort out his problems with God."

"Why did you come to me?"

"For your blessing."

"I don't have the power to give blessings."

"You are the most respected man in our town. The people look towards you. I needed to talk to you, Christopher."

"Who is the person?"

"Colleran."

"That *simple* boy who wanders about?"

"Not simple. Mad, dangerous madness. My eldest son is a doctor in Chicago, you know that, don't you?"

"Yes, yes, you told me that."

"I telephoned him. What's a few pounds with a curse like this hanging over us?" Finegan took a scrap of paper from his pocket and studied it, broke the word into slow syllables. "Schizophrenia. That's what the madman has. Voices inside his brainbox are telling him what to do."

"There can be mild cases of schizophrenia, Martin."

"They can murder what's nearest and dearest to them, or themselves. They can molest and rape and kill women. And our schoolchildren stand talking to him every day, touching his hands, giving him cigarettes or smoking what he has had in his mouth. He should be confined: I said I would tell you, Christopher. But I will deal with it."

Finegan had left himself breathless. Simoney, weakening, in doubt, stood and patted him on the shoulder. "You are a good man, Martin. You have done well, I know."

"There is some evil in this town and Colleran is only the beginning of it. I must find it and destroy it!"

"Evil?"

"Yes, evil."

Simoney motioned to Finegan, invited him to kneel and pray with him. They faced each other.

Simoney prayed:

"Be mindful, O Lord, of thy covenant, and say to the destroying angel: Now hold thy hand, and let not the land be made desolate, and destroy not every living soul. Give ear, O gracious Lord. O God who desirest not the death but the repentance of sinners, mercifully look upon thy people that returneth unto thee; and whilst they are devoted to thee, do thou, in thy clemency, remove from them the scourge of thy wrath. Hear us, O Lord of our salvation: And delivering thy people from the terrors of thy wrath, do thou also, of thy bountiful mercy, grant them safety from danger. Amen"

Simoney said to Finegan, "Do what you must do in the name of *God*."

They sat again.

Finegan made the sign of the cross.

"Beyond these transgressions of chastity in the youth of our parish, is there another evil?" Simoney asked.

"The deaths of these children."

"Of disease."

"Of evil. Evil is the disease. People of the town can feel it growing."

Simoney brought a small brittle glass of pale sherry, handed it to Finegan. "I don't drink," he said, "but may God protect you from all evil."

Simoney sat, hands clasped, head bowed. He wasn't immersed in prayer; he was thinking of Finegan. Go back far enough and they were land-grabbers who bought for a song the land of evicted neighbours; stood watching while a foreign landlord, with military and police, rammed open doors and windows, and razed the stone and mortar walls. Terrible grief and suffering then. And blood wasn't spared in defending it either. Time had mellowed it, but *Finegan* wasn't a respected name. They had held their land and set up a shee-been in the town, once a place of no great repute, of drunkenness and market-day and fair-day brawls. Finegan's father was shrewd and had spawned shrewdness; he had rubbed shoulders with Parnell's politicians, improved his beer-house and legitimised it; he knew land rebels and terrorists. When the manhunts were on and the shooting came it was a safe house for some.

Finegan, in his very occasional cups, would tell selected company of his father who had lead men against the local British Force, left dead on the street accursed fighting-men of the oppressor. Old people of the town would say he had been a renegade, an informer. No, it wasn't a name that command-ed great respect.

Simoney said, "You have my prayers, for what they are worth, but my conscience and my commitment to the church wouldn't allow me knowingly to condone violence."

"Against evil?"

Simoney was silent.

Finegan said, "Your prayers are all I need. I didn't want your disapproval, Christopher. That was important. Your name will not be mentioned. Nor mine."

Finegan was thinking of the mixed blood of the Simoneys. It hadn't produced heroes. Simoneys had been great merchants in the town long before the Sommervilles, but they had mar-ried their Protestantism into native Catholic blood. It was the beginning of death. The seed had been poisoned, they became a barren stock. They had coastal steamers once, trade, grow-ing wealth, now their empty decaying store-houses, four, five storeys high, were a blight on the side of the cove. Simoney's father and mother were buried in the Catholic cemetery. His father had been an atheist. Bad blood, Finegan thought.

He said, "I've been giving Rellighan a lot of attention too. He isn't Irish, you know."

Simoney looked, listened. "Rellighan is an Irish name, I thought. An apt name for his profession. *Reilig* is the Gaelic for a grave, a cemetery."

"Maybe that's why he picked it. I wouldn't like to guess what his real name might be."

"He's been here a lifetime."

"All of fifty years and some to spare. I remember when he came."

"He's buried generations of our dead. Careless on rare occasions, but silent, dependable, in the past few days given a little to drink."

"He's a dago, a half-breed wop. No pure blood there. Dish water. He came from Boston in the war years. When Europe's guns had to be shouldered he was running for cover. He came with money too. We used to call him *Gipsy Rellighan.*"

Simoney thought about Rellighan. "Yes," he said, "he could well be a gipsy. The colouring, the eyes. But they have pure blood too."

"Not related to our tinkers, you know. Tinkers are Irish."

Simoney could feel the bitterness. "Of course, of course."

"I think it's time he retired. I don't want him handling my body after I've passed over to God."

"Yes."

For his parting shot, from the doorway, Finegan had held, "Rellighan's staff won't handle these young corrupted bodies."

Rellighan stood. The gas cylinder had petered out and the pungent smell of its emptiness drifted across to him. He was waiting for Coleman. A strange night. He switched off the valve of the gas fire and went back to sit at his table and stared at the elements empty of flame. He trusted Coleman.

In the mid-thirties, sixty years past, he was thinking, when he was thirteen years old, strong and hardy then, more than two hundred thousand high-stepping uniformed zealots were learning the trade of war in Europe.

A boy of thirteen, a gipsy, with a blood-related band, he was making the annual Spring journey from Sudetenland, through Bohemian forests, to Bavaria. Four generations of his family travelled, sixteen in all, with painted caravans, ponies, mules, all the tools of their trades.

They had crossed to Deggendorf and Ingolstadt when they were sequestered by Schultzstaffel, savagely beaten, interned, their property seized.

Camps of torture, experiment, extermination, had already begun in those early days, but were still haphazard, lacked the eventual expertise that was to come.

"Brownshirts," his father had said. "S.S."

The beating went on; he remembered the pleading, the screaming, the shame. It was two hours before they were locked in confinement. It was the stabling space of a country manor, secluded in grassland and trees, that had been purified, emptied of its residents, annexed by the state for official purposes. Daubed vertically on a gate pillar was 'Juden' and the paint had run on the stonework, and dried here and there in little congealed strings of black blood.

Now it was a medical clinic.

Gipsies, Romas, they spoke an Indic patois, but they knew the language, the jargon, of the countries they traversed. People came to view them, examine them, grasp and feel them like cattle, leave them perishing without food or drink.

Rellighan remembered a beautiful woman who arranged everything, so calm, efficient, detached, so beautiful. Her beauty shone. In a white medical coat, she might have stepped from some sterilised perfect world.

The women were stripped; uniformed men held them, clothes were torn from their bodies. The men, at gunpoint, were undressing. Rellighan could remember not his own nakedness but the wailing shame of his family. The clothing was taken away; they could feel the closeness of death. The older ones crowded together. He, the youngest, in poor light, climbed into the bare stable rafters and lay still.

He heard talk of altitude, oxygen, thin air, that meant nothing to him. But he remembered it. He saw a great metal vertical cylinder pushed in, its screw-wheel door open, long trails of cables and tubes stretching out into that other world of freedom that they had left. There were observation ports. Doctors, a lot of doctors, came to attend. He saw his family locked in this illuminated mobile prison and, over the head of an observer, he could see their fear, terror.

The beautiful woman of flowing hair said ". . . air will be pumped out so that oxygen and air pressure at the equivalent of 29400 feet altitude will be conducted on these test-persons of mixed age and sex and in good general condition. You will take notes independently for post mortem discussion immediately following..."

Words he had never forgotten.

Rellighan watched his people fight against the vacuum until their lungs ruptured. He watched them passing from sanity to raging madness, beat themselves against metal in an effort to relieve pressure. They tore at their heads and faces with fingers and nails in an attempt to maim themselves in their frenzy. They beat the walls with their hands and heads, seemed to scream in an effort to lessen pressure on eardrums. It took ten minutes to lose consciousness, a half an hour before death and autopsy...

He saw the steel death cell being hauled away out of sight to be hosed of body fluids and discharges and the precious dead bodies taken for dissection.

The stable doors had been left open. He waited until nightfall and, naked, slipped away like a ghost. His people had always survived fear, hatred. He stole clothing, money, food, took months to move into Belgium and Calais, to pass across depressed England and Ireland. In Ireland he became *Rellighan*, worked his passage – a deep sea galley boy – to Boston.

He didn't talk about the past. He had never shed a tear but he remembered pictures of screaming death. Horror had dried up emotion. He thought sometimes that perhaps he was barely human. He lived in a vacuum, unaware of friends or enemies. He remembered the face of the beautiful woman. She was not unlike Sommerville's beautiful woman; perhaps the same spirit clothed in another raiment of magnificent flesh. Always different, always beautiful...

Boston was a vast city where he could lose himself. He had turned fourteen. He had strength. A barman in a sheebeen, far from the city centre, a joker he supposed, had said, "You need a job, sonny, not beer." He wrote an address on a sheet of phone-pad and sent him on his way. "Meat packers," he said, "and the money will be fair."

Where the roads slope down to dockland he found it, a step or two off the main highway as if its privacy was important. Its public face was glass and gold lettering – dignity and reverence and fifty yards of a ten foot wall, tall and jagged-glassed along its coping. There were two gateways and wickets. The gold lettering said 'Franklin Funeral Services. Burials, Cremations, Embalming'. Meat packers.

A smile was rare on Rellighan's face but humour flickered for a moment. Always with death for companionship, he thought. A place here, he knew, whatever it might entail, would keep him out of sight. He would be a worker.

He entered the carpeted peace of the reception premises. A tall young man was clasping gentle hands, his face arranged, but he became aware of the incongruity of Rellighan. The light was soft and embracing and here stood a reasonably dressed schoolboy who had lost his way.

Rellighan said, "You have a vacancy, I think."

The young man said, "A position."

"A position."

"The second wicket gate. There's a bell," he was told; he was shushed out from the facade of quiet dignity, comfort and compassion.

A liveried chauffeur opened the wicket. His cap was back on his forehead and a cigarette jigged in his mouth as he spoke. He pointed to an office.

"Ask for Mr Felton, kid."

It was a small office and Mr Felton sat behind a desk. In dress and comportment he might have been a figure of great importance in a first class pullman, entrained for the city and his offices and staff.

Rellighan stood before him. "You have a position vacant, I think."

Mr Felton seemed pleased with him. "How old are you?"

"Fourteen."

"Good. Education isn't important."

"I can read and write."

"Excellent. And you want to be a mortician?"

Rellighan waited.

"An undertaker, a director of funerals?"

"To learn," Rellighan said carefully.

"Yes, yes, a lot to be learned. And it takes time. You aren't afraid of dead flesh? Bodies?"

Rellighan hadn't thought about it; he said, "No."

"A week's trial," Mr Felton said. "Come respectfully dressed as you are now. We supply working clothes. Report to the manager at 'arrivals'. You'll find it. Farther on. Part of our complex. He'll instruct you. Your wages . . ."

Rellighan spent a year and a half in 'arrivals' where body-bags were off-loaded. A strange sad place. The clean, the spent, the dirt-encrusted, old, young, some even beautiful, the john-does and wine bibblers from the river or forgotten back-rooms, the killers and self-killers.

The water-proofed gloved staff smoked and exhaled into the almost palpable air-mass of decay and fumigation. In a mix of loud babble and profanity Rellighan spoke only a lit-tle, crossed the threshold into another world. He found con-tentment. Each corpse, he knew, was still alive to be greeted kindly, welcomed, with dignity groomed and repaired. He washed, sometimes hosed them down, soaked disentangled hair and beards, arranged feet and folded hands, sunken cheeks and open mouths. He felt their presence, their close-ness and gratitude, at times burning anger. He saw the decay of men and women from youth to the ravages of old age. Rellighan was a corpse-washer. He was good, dedicated to perfection. His work passed from him to other theatres and finally to the caskets.

Rellighan too moved on to other theatres and, with the same silent correctness, was accepted. He hardly spoke. He became aware that there was beauty in death, aware that unseen persons watched him as he worked. He gave seven years to learning his trade. He was trusted.

Mr Felton came to him late one evening. Rellighan was

155

dressing a corpse, a male, no more than perhaps thirty-five years, with bad marks, mutilation. He had repaired the marks of beating and bullet holes. Rellighan didn't ask questions. There was work to be done, some trace of peacefulness to be restored; he did it.

"A nice job," Mr Felton said.

Rellighan nodded.

Mr Felton rolled in a casket of high quality. "The lining is special," he told Rellighan. "What's behind the lining, under the corpse, all around him, very special. A place of conceal-ment. I came to help you."

They lifted the body, arranged it in repose in the magnifi-cence of the casket.

"I lined the casket myself," Mr Felton said. "Tomorrow he will be buried. He will be six feet under, surrounded by all that luxurious satin. And half a million dollars."

"Yours?" Rellighan asked.

Mr Felton laughed, pointed a finger skywards. "Someone up there, a big wheel, a big gun. Very high. We do work like this from time to time. The grave is a place of silence. You are a silent man, Rellighan."

Rellighan waited.

"I'm promoting you. The casket will be in your care for a while. You can use a gun, can't you?"

Rellighan was waiting.

"They told me down at the range. You can put six rapid on the card anytime.,"

Rellighan broke his silence; he said, "I can do that. It pass-es the time."

"Worth money too."

"Shooting at targets?"

"Shooting for real maybe. A half a million dollars in your care. A responsibility."

"Shooting for the man high up?"

"That's it. Night work for a month. Get yourself out of sight in the cemetery, watch the grave."

"If people come?"

"You shoot. And tidiness is important. It pays well."

Rellighan said, "I know too much now, don't I?"

Felton laughed. "No turning back now. You could be a target card on the range."

"It's a good trick."

"Yes," Felton agreed; he slipped off his jacket. He wore a shoulder holster and a gun; he laid them before Rellighan. He brought spare clips and a silencer. "You start tomorrow night. Four weeks. Maybe nobody comes but, just like insurance, you get the premium."

Felton arranged his jacket and paused at the door, a pleasant face. "You're a good man, Rellighan. I wouldn't like to lose you." He pitched keys from the door and Rellighan caught them. "Your car is outside. Goes with the job. Attend the funeral tomorrow, see the grave. Leave your car outside the caretaker's house. Park it, leave it. The caretaker is *our* man. A month. A long time to keep your eyes peeled but you can do it, Rellighan. It's your job, you work out the details. No I.D. cards, nothing. Just a gun and money. See me when it's over."

Rellighan stood in the chill of the dressing-room and looked down at the peace he had bestowed on the hard face in the casket. He felt the bundles packed behind the sheen of lining. He felt he was being watched.

He wore the shoulder holster, carried the silencer and clips. When he went out to the car the night-watchman was at immediate attention; he opened the gate and Rellighan drove into the evening traffic. He was pondering it.

Rellighan lived only a mile from his work in what had once been a hilly suburban road but had been long passed by the urban spread and left spent and mouldering. A tide-mark. A few residents remained who let out apartments in what was now city dossland. Rellighan found space in a bordello where the madam and her sister, ageing in a make-up of pink bouffant and pancake filler, kept a paying guest or two to upgrade their premises. There was anonymity in a cathouse that suited Rellighan. He was strong then but already he had the gaunt distant stare that would grow old with him. The madam liked his silence, his respectability. It was the first home he ever had.

In his apartment he sat and considered his predicament for a long time. The doors had been closed on him, he was a conscript. He could be the hitman or the target. He was calm, matter-of-fact. The survivor was the winner. . .

When the funeral passed through the heavy gilded gates of the cemetery he was with it: moving in a sea of colour, gleaming carloads of flowers, tributes to this executed badman lying in his casket of satin-wrapped loot. Rellighan brought up the rear and parked his car behind the caretaker's house. It was a bright mid-afternoon but suddenly cold in the vagaries of Boston temperature. He saw the decorated grave on a hillock, stood at the fringes of a great crowd.

Mob funerals were big expensive moments, shows of power and strength of reigning monarchs of murder, vice and heist: glittering cars, a surfeit of flowers, big men, their women, clothes that were assessed in dollars, a dozen clergymen of rank in panegyric, an apologia for life's fitful fever.

Then close to these men of the cloth, the chief mourners, he saw *her*! The beautiful woman, the flowing hair. Always different, always beautiful. But to Rellighan, unmistakable. He bowed his head and remembered the tattered bleeding death of his family. When he had looked again she had vanished. That was *evil*, he knew then.

He went back to a local groggery and drank whiskey through the slow hours, late into the evening.

He slept well.

Entry to the cemetery had been arranged and was easy. In darkness he rang a bell of a side-wicket and the caretaker answered. Always respectful.

"Goodnight, sir."

"Goodnight."

Then he said, a reassurance, "Park behind the lodge. It will always be ready. It is in my care."

This was the tenth night. Rellighan had pulled his great-coat about him and stood two hours in watch, shrouded by monuments and evergreens. He could hear the highway traffic distantly, the muted shriek of a police car. The sound of metal alerted him! Then a man appeared. He seemed a giant, leaning on a table vault, peering into the darkness. He laid a pick and shovel on the grave and what might be a sack.

Felton's instructions had been, '. . . if people come you shoot'.

Not easy, Rellighan thought, to shoot without warning. The rules of a hard bloody game. To shoot even this great animal of strength. He took the gun from its holster, silenced it, waited for moments and stepped out into the open. There were ten paces between them. The sudden movement of the shadowy hulk deceived him. He was sharp as a cat. He flung himself prone and fired into the advancing darkness. The pickaxe cut the air above him. Three bullets had stopped him. Rellighan put a fourth in his head. He searched him: empty pockets except for ammunition clips. No marks of identity. But a shoulder holster, a gun and silencer and a huge hand gripped on the butt. Rellighan took the armoury, loosened the gripping fingers. He saw the caretaker arriving with his car. The planning was precise. Together they lifted the body.

In the morning he brought the car to Felton.

"Yes?"

"He came."

"Who?"

"A big man. Three hundred pounds, maybe more."

"Yes?"

"I shot him. He's out in the bay. His pick and shovel and sack are with the caretaker."

"Good."

"The back of your car needs cleaning."

"'I'll have it fixed. Your car now."

159

Rellighan said, "Fix me a berth, Mr Felton. It's time for me to go, I think."

"Go?"

"That's how I'd like it."

Felton sat and thought about it for a long time, smoked, looked at Rellighan.

"Yes, you're a good man, Rellighan. I could break the rules for you," he said. "I trust you. You can go. East or west?"

In a week Rellighan was on a freighter, sailing out of Massachusetts Bay, leaving Cape Cod behind, watching Nantucket and Martha's Vineyard come into view and then gradually fade from sight. In his suitcase he had ten thousand dollars, two hand guns and clips. These were the war years; they sailed to join a convoy. . .

He heard noise at his gateway, footsteps. It was dark; it would be Coleman. Rellighan sat in his habitual pose, motionless, in thought. The office was cold, bare, the dead gas fire freestanding at the centre point of the floor. Coleman's footsteps sounded in the yard. Rellighan had means, moneys, but possessions, comforts were of no importance.

Coleman greeted him.

"You brought the car?"

"Outside."

From beneath his chair Rellighan raised up two holstered hand guns, silencers and clips.

"Don't ask me where I got them, Coleman," he said. "But they're good, clean, maintained. I've had them a long time, a lot of years. Night glasses too."

"We'll need guns?" Coleman asked.

"Yes."

"When?"

"I don't know."

"You can use a gun, Rellighan? You've killed, have you?"

Rellighan nodded. "Have you?"

"Yes, I've killed."

Rellighan swept the holsters back beneath his chair. "We

leave the holsters. Load up, screw on a silencer, keep the gun at your hip-band. And bring clips."

"Where?"

Rellighan's newspaper was still on the table, the few small lines reporting animal savagery ringed by his pencil. Coleman looked down at the veined bony strength of the hand.

"A great saucer of rock that set there before our time and only a single road through it. But there are roads around it and tracks that lead into sheep tracks. I never forget roads or passes, north, south, east or west."

Coleman nodded.

Belle Cannon dressed against the cold blackness of the night that would lie heavily on the enclave of holy buildings, the sanctified ground, and inside the stony echoes of the church. She took a drink of whiskey that burned her and wondered at its offensiveness, then warmth came.

She closed her door and found the street lighted and busy. It was Halloween time. Tricks and treaters were abroad, the excited gangs behind eerie masks, knocking at doors; candles burned in the windows of the godly, party-goers moved in groups. She and Coleman should be with people too where there was food and talk and wine, nonsense-moments that might be remembered for a day or a lifetime.

There had been a lot of good times with Coleman. She thought of his danger now and her own.

She walked slowly across the Square into the quiet twilight acres of the convent and its high walls, past Rellighan's funeral home, empty, locked. The Canon's parochial house, the convent windows were in darkness. Religion had grown old, tired easily, was ready to drowse, to sleep. To the old people of the town there was a sanctity in these environs where open air Mass and public processions, displaying the Blessed Sacrament, had between wars marked it as a place apart. There were no shops, Simoney the only lay resident;

traffic and pedestrians avoided it except to fulfil diminishing obligations.

The church and its tall belfry spire loomed up, the great shining door, the black stretching curlicues of hinges. The rose-window was like a searching eye on the faithful.

Belle Cannon paused, then walked around the perimeter dwarf wall that enclosed a tiny burial plot, dressed with flowers and glittering marble chippings, that was the resting place of a hundred and fifty years of monumented incumbents, and some forgotten ones of earlier times. There was a sadness about it. The church was in darkness.

At the rear, light shone from the sacristy window.

She waited moments in the stillness, listened. Distant sounds came from the town's main streets. She gently fitted the key in its lock, gripped it and turned it slowly, slowly, to avoid sound. It was Simoney's well-oiled lock; it turned with ease. She pocketed the key again, stood inside the door, waited moments, soundlessly pushed it closed.

Two hours had passed since the funeral prayers and she had stood with Coleman and Rellighan on the sweep of the outside steps. Where were they now? The church was empty except for God and its schoolgirl corpse. The world was outside. She peered into the holy tenebrae, saw it shaping in adjustment, developing like a photoprint immersed in the dark-room pans.

The coffin and its nameplate shone distantly through the darkness. Gradually there was the noise of muted voices from the sacristy, a tone of softness, hushed respect. There was a confessional close at hand and she stepped in out of sight, sat there without penitence, only fear. The voices were distant. There was silence, then words again, and silence.

Suddenly there were footsteps. They came from the sacristy beyond the gleaming marble rails and the starched white communion cloth. Through the fretted screen of the confessional she saw Simoney at work, replenishing the supply of votive tapers at a candelabrum. Passing the tabernacle, he genuflected each time, then knelt on the stone floor for minutes as if in reparation for some hidden sin. It seemed a long time until he moved, head bowed, hands joined, into the sacristy.

She let peace and whispering return and then moved in Simoney's wake. Her eyes had grown accustomed to the darkness; so would the eyes of Simoney who lived in this underworld. She moved with great care, still tight in awakened fear, footstep by footstep, until the voices were distinct.

Simoney was a man of discipline who accepted the will of God in great humility. He felt he had been chosen. He could thunder at his congregation, fill them with dread. The protean Mr Simoney. He was tired.

In the sacristy he said, "A very long and wearing day. The funeral tomorrow will be a blessed ending."

"My dear, dear Mr Simoney." A woman's voice, honeyed, soft with sympathy. It was Sommerville's strange housekeeper companion, ice-cold Estel Machen. "You are a person of great patience. All's well that ends well."

"Impatience, Miss Machen. I hope the good Lord forgives me. I pray for the restraint you show."

"I am so imperfect," she said.

Belle Cannon moved back into the cover of the confessional, sat where the countless trivial sins had been whispered to a shadowy figure beyond the grille. " . . . bless me, father, for I have sinned . . . how many times? . . . ask God for strength against the temptation of the Devil . . ." The hand raised in absolution. "Absolvo te . . . Your sins are forgiven."

The sins of the town had been confessed and shriven, down two centuries, within the church's four walls, and penitents had stepped out happy into the light with a sheet clean, ready to be smirched and stained again.

In this precious enclave Simoney lived alone in an impressive detached house, constructed on secluded ground, a little distance from the church. He might have been a cloistered priest. He lived in monastic silence except for an attending daily help. A remote, almost forbidding man, at times a frenzied evangelist, the Lord's humble disciple. He played many parts, Belle Cannon thought. Perhaps with sincerity too?

The female voice again, "You counsel and give strength, I'm told, Mr Simoney?"

"People come to my home. I talk to them."

"With me?"

"Of course. If you are troubled."

"I have fears."

"This evil in the town?"

"Yes."

"Then you must come." He might be pausing, calculating. "Tomorrow, you know, will be a busy morning in the church too. A corpse on our hands, a service, the journey to the cemetery, the burial." He enumerated them, then he said, "Come in the afternoon, any time, later, when it's convenient for you."

"You give me great consolation."

"You are a good person," he told her. "Now I must pray for a little while in the church. In the darkness, the stillness, I feel very close to God."

They went out into the darkness. Simoney found his place at the communion rails; she knelt a little distance from him. The sanctuary lamp was a tiny flickering glow in a surrounding intimate firmament.

Simoney said aloud: "Dear God, thank you for giving us this day to save our souls. We offer you our hearts too. Assist us in our last agony. May we breathe forth our souls with you in peace."

He turned to Estel Machen. "Speak to God in privacy now your night prayers, your thanks to him."

In half an hour Estel Machen left in silence; the soft progress of her footsteps crept through the church, through the sacristy, there was the click of the spring lock as she opened and pushed the door shut. Simoney remained for a long time, raised his face towards the tabernacle, then covered it in penitence with his hands. He stood. He made a circuit of the church, pausing for moments before each Station of the Cross, fourteen pictures depicting Christ's journey from condemnation to crucifixion and death; and then, slowly, as an ageing man, he departed. The sacristy door closed behind him, the small noise travelled across the loneliness, the emptiness.

Time dragged now. Specks of night sounds from ageing walls and woodwork were clear precise instants; the sanctuary lamp was bright as a single star. Belle Cannon listened. The breastplate on the coffin caught a glint of the church's only light. An hour passed, more, doubts gathered about her.

Then small sounds began to reach her from the sacristy. Hushed voices too. All her cold and discomfort vanished. She stood still as an image. Only the lingering heavy smell of burnt wax pervaded. She looked at the shining panelled wood of the coffin and pictured Jennifer Anderson's still face, her clasped hands, the rosary beads twined about them.

Then the costumed figures appeared. They had been robing themselves for a ceremony.

They came in a slow processional walk. Estel Machen was the celebrant. She wore a long girdled white alb. Maniple, stole and chasuble were, even in the grey darkness, shimmering cloth of gold. The mitre was encrusted with semi-precious stones. Her final flourish of ritual was to expose the hallowed Roman pallium, so sacred to Simoney, on her shoulders. She walked a measured funereal pace, head erect, hands holding before her a large roll of gleaming linen: it had been prepared, laundered, ironed, folded with care.

Herbert Sommerville followed her.

Estel Machen had never left the church; she had remained in waiting to give admittance to Sommerville. Did she hide, had she been visible? She had escaped Simoney's scrutiny. And nothing in his church escaped Simoney's surveillance . . . ?

Sommerville wore a black cassock to his feet, a surplice fringed with lace, a biretta. He carried a brass vessel of holy water and a polished rod of aspersion.

It was an absurdist piece of fifties drama: straight faces over-elaborate costumes, a comic duo that might have scaled down and fled from Genet's balcony.

Estel Machen stood on the steps of the sanctuary, looked down on the coffin. Sommerville went about his appointed task. He laid aside the wreaths, cards and coffin lid. Everything calm, unhurried. The soft sleeping face of Jennifer Anderson might have had blood coursing beneath the skin. Estel Machen came down. She sprinkled holy water in parody about the catafalque. Sommerville spread the linen sheet on the floor. He lifted out the corpse and wrapped it.

Estel Machen carried the burden effortlessly, as if it were weightless, and went to the sacristy.

Belle Cannon watched, tasted illness inside her: she felt helplessness, shook. Her hands, her body, were trembling. She was filled with fear, breathing fast.

She heard the door opening for Estel Machen's exit to the churchyard, the snap of it closing on her return. She had left the body outside? Where? Sommerville screwed down the coffin lid, arranged the wreaths and cards with precision. He took off the surplice and with it dried the holy water on the wet floor. He moved away.

From the sacristy Belle Cannon, in her confessional, heard Estel Machen's voice greeting Sommerville. She would be smiling, she thought, perhaps caressing him.

Estel Machen said, "These are good days."

The body was outside, Belle Cannon would guess. In a gleaming white sheet? Black was the colour of night-time, stealth. A white sheet, a winding sheet? The rear door of the sacristy, the churchyard, a white shining cloth in the darkness? Belle Cannon was moving fast towards the church door. Circulation burned in her legs and arms. She ran, stumbled, pulled open the door, locked it behind her, stood in the clean air outside.

She moved in the shadows. The churchyard gates had been left open? She heard the starting purr of Sommerville's car, watched it pass into Demesne Street, drive out of sight towards the Square. It had been parked in the shadows behind the church. Only Sommerville, at the wheel, had been visible. Estel Machen and the stolen corpse were hidden.

She looked at her watch. It was long past midnight. The doctor's car would pass through the town unnoticed. Sommerville driving to a distant patient. A night call.

Belle Cannon walked back through the town to Main Street. A few were still on the move. There was noise of people and celebration. Halloween.

She opened her door and went upstairs to her lounge. It had been an evil dream. She drank whiskey and felt better. The thought of sleep brought a feeling of dread.

Sommerville was erratic in his driving. The roads were black, empty, but at every open stretch he sped and then was braking at sharp bends that loomed out of the darkness beyond the powerful probe of the headlight beams.

"Be calm!" Estel Machen soothed him. "An even pace. That's better, much better."

"With you," he said, "there is no danger, is there?" He felt the lightness of the steering. "Who is driving?" he asked.

She was sitting behind him on the rear seat. "We are driving," she said.

They had long left the fringes of the town and scattered country dwellings, the land bad or fertile, behind them. There were still twenty miles to travel.

Sommerville's hands were damp with sweat, cold on the steering wheel. He could feel a weight of dampness on his forehead; he dabbed at it.

"I need a drink," he told her.

"Of course, of course."

He reached in his pocket for a flask.

"No, no," she said gently. "Pull in for a few moments, rest. A drink is meant to be enjoyed."

Sommerville parked the car in the surrounding dark, the flat wind-scorched land. He unscrewed the flask and drank. The heat was restoring him; he drank again and lay back against the head rest of the seat. Behind him Estel Machen opened her door. In his rear mirror he could see her moving back, see her silhouetted against the boot of the car.

Estel Machen had made this trip before, alone, on the last day of April, carrying the body of James Anthony to his place of release, the seemingly limitless world of stone and sudden hills and plateaux. The thought of it was like a remembrance of prayer and sacrifice, of good works done. Body and blood. She remembered his pale body in the darkness.

Sommerville drank from his flask again and put it away. Alcohol brought warmth but no escape. He thought of drunkenness and its armour. They would release another body into this nether-world, this awful limbo. He felt moments of panic and fear. He felt revulsion.

Estel Machen said, "Don't be afraid."

She was back in her seat behind him. He hadn't heard her entry or the noise of the closing door. She had moved in silence. He turned and looked back at her. From the boot she had brought the body of Jennifer Anderson and sat, holding it, caressing it, in love with it. Sommerville turned away.

"Her body is in decay," he said.

"No."

"Dead."

"Beginning to live."

He was silent.

"We can drive now," she told him.

"Yes."

"When you were in your youth," she said, "soft but firm like this child, you were beautiful but empty. You are grow- ing stronger, like a warrior becoming skilled in battle. Fear will come and go and you will learn to enjoy it. You will need it. Tonight will become a great flood of pleasure."

"I feel unhappiness," he said.

She was smiling, a beautiful soothing face behind him; she stroked the dead girl's hair, arranged it. There was strength, reassurance in the sound: a cleansing, an absolution. Sommerville, a sad ageing man now, looked out into the white road that his headlights seemed to clear of darkness for moments before it spilt in again behind him in a torrent.

Estel Machen's voice coloured every sound. "Good and evil are only words, they rest against each other. Evil is the roadway to goodness. But goodness, when it is reached, can be evil in other guises. Without one the other does not exist. They need each other, they are bedfellows."

"Yes," he said.

She reached forward, touched his shoulder, the soft flesh at his jowl. "Indelible scriptures are overflowing," she said. "A prophet cried out, 'What, shall we receive good at the hand of God, and shall we not receive evil?' The Satan of Mr Simoney, the enemy of God? Satan is a son of God, obeying his commands! 'The evil one,' said Simoney. Carrying out God's commands? A strange thought. The man Luther threw an ink pot at him." Her voice was a sweet amused drowsiness. She pressed on Sommerville's shoulder and he could feel courage returning, even humour. "God made the tiger and the camel. We destroy one, cherish the other. Which? And who is God?"

Sommerville was laughing now.

She said, "Pope Pio Nono, Pius IX, had the evil eye, they say, and was dreaded by the people of Rome. But he was a good man, an evil man. He was a man."

Sommerville was silent.

She said:

"So runs my dream; but what am I?
An infant crying in the night,
An infant crying for the light,
And with no language but a cry."

In less than half an hour, over this convoluted desolate

road, they had reached the total bleakness of the vast limestone bowl, filled to the brim with darkness.

"Here," she said. "This is a special place. You will always remember it."

He looked out at the nothingness of everything.

He parked on the bend of the road. There were no grass fringes, hedges, wild growth. Beyond the road flatness stretched away, the beam of his lights fell on the sweep of timeless pavement, changeless as the first upheaval.

Estel Machen said, "In a little while now."

Jennifer Anderson was dressed in a long pale blue robe of purity. She was held in tenderness. Estel Machen might be her lover, clasping her, rubbing her lips on what must be the ice-cold flesh of her cheeks.

She looked out to where she had given freedom to the body of James Anthony in the April darkness of six months past. Sommerville knew it. That would have been the time of daylight traffic, bikers, hitch-hikers, walkers. James Anthony must be discovered in hours. He had never been seen. An empty coffin had been buried in the town cemetery and his flesh set free on these rocks. He had vanished. Not dead, Estel Machen had said; he had come to life in his home. This awful wilderness.

Fear was in Sommerville's mind.

There was movement behind him; the door was opened. Estel Machen, carrying the beautiful schoolgirl, walked along the beam of his headlights to a chosen flat rock. Her hair, her clothing caught in the wind, she was a beautiful wraith. She stood motionless there for minutes in the biting nighttime. She gazed into the darkness as if she had been searching for something and found it. Then she laid Jennifer Anderson on the stone bier and disrobed her. The white young body shone in the piercing light.

Sommerville felt overcome with shame.

Estel Machen walked back to him, a creature of desire and beauty. Her eyes were shining with an intensity of happiness.

He was in love with her.

She sat beside him in the passenger seat of the car, moved close to him, touched his hand.

"Drink in celebration now," she said.

Sommerville was in confusion; her hand had warmth and comfort. Drink, she had said. He found the flask and unscrewed it, drained the contents.

"You?" he asked.

"I'm celebrating with you," she said; she was looking out at Jennifer Anderson's naked body. "Go to it," she told him. "Stand and look at it for a little while. Find peace."

It was a command.

He left her there, stood out on the roadway, tightened his coat about him. It was an icy cutting wind, sweeping, scutching, along this sea of rock. He walked in the beam of light to the rock slab, to Jennifer Anderson. He looked at her young untouched beauty. Suddenly he was in tears. He knelt and wept aloud, unheard, in the noise of the wind. He looked about at the infinite stark desolation of this imprisonment of stone. It was a place of punishment. The cold had pierced him, he was trembling, perished, weakening, but tears still flowed.

Estel Machen, detached, without emotion, sat in the car and watched him. She saw the approach of the powerful, almost black-coated, animal. It sprang across the naked body and locked its jaws on Sommerville's throat. It pinned him down, tore at his flesh. In minutes he was a bleeding savaged mass, mutilated, ripped asunder.

The animal stood over the body of Jennifer Anderson. Blood dripped on her paleness. Estel Machen switched out the car lights; in the darkness, clearly, she could see animal and corpse, and the bloody remains of Sommerville.

In minutes the form of Jennifer Anderson had stirred, turned to lie prone for moments, then raised itself, crouched, almost on all fours. It followed the animal out, of sight into the dips and clefts.

On the narrow road Estel Machen reversed the car and drove away. Towards the town and Sommerville's home?

A mile distant, on a small drumlin rising to two hundred feet, Coleman laid down Rellighan's night-glasses. He sat in silence. Estel Machen's car passed below, driven at speed into the blackness, out of sight.

Rellighan said, "You saw it?"

Coleman nodded.

"You believe it? An illusion? A madman's story, more like it," Rellighan said. "But our town is still back there with its yellow lights, its church and Simoney's hellfire, looking for disease and sin."

"The animal?" Coleman asked.

"James Anthony."

"The body? Jennifer Anderson's body."

"Now there are two animals."

"And Sommerville is dead?"

"Yes," Rellighan said, "Sommerville is dead. We must go down there. We must go now. Check your gun, clips, silencer. Gunshots in this bowl of rock would crack like thunder."

"Who are we looking for?"

"*They* will be looking for us."

Coleman waited.

"The animals."

"Can they bleed, Rellighan?"

"Yes. And they can kill."

"What are they?"

"I don't know," Rellighan said; he moved behind his defences again. "They need flesh and blood to live. We hunted down people for it once, burnt, mutilated them. You only burn, mutilate the body evil has taken. A spirit moves on to other shapes."

Rellighan was silent. Coleman looked at the ridged yellowing face, the weathered skin, tight lips, a neck still strong after more than seven decades, the hair, not totally grey, blowing in the wind, the impenetrable grey eyes. His hands were steady, strong. Coleman locked at him with respect.

"We go down now?" he asked.

"These are killers," Rellighan said, "poisoned with evil too."

"Yes."

There were sheep and goat tracks winding through the great slabbed area of stone to tiny patches of grass-like sores on the smoothness of skin. Rellighan led the way, this seventy-odd-year-old, sure-footed as the animals he hunted. Coleman was close; they moved through the wind, quieter than its scraping sound. They moved in darkness.

They reached the tarmacadamed road: blackness in blackness. There was half a mile to be walked.

Rellighan said, "We walk in file, ten yards apart. And watch, listen. And softly. We have to be close to kill, to shatter skulls. Hackles at haunches, neck, shoulders are like armour. Don't waste bullets on it."

They walked. Five, seven minutes had passed before Rellighan halted, held up a hand.

"Remember," he said, "two animals."

"Soon?"

"Yes."

Rellighan was pointing at the ground a little distance from them. Sommerville was lying there. In the darkness his torn body glistened with blood; it flowed down a slope of rock into a deep crevice not more than an inch wide.

"They'll come for flesh and blood. Body and blood. They're moving already. They don't sit and wait like cats. They creep and spring, they strike with their jaws."

The blade of wind swept down at them across this other world of loneliness; sheets of wind sliding across a rink of stone, wailing against obstruction, driven past them into other curves and bluffs . . .

Suddenly Rellighan was shooting.

Coleman saw the two rising bodies curving towards them. They dropped short and gathered to spring again. Rellighan had hit them, halted them for an instant, hadn't pierced them. Coleman aimed at what was nearest to him, at point blank, pumped four, five bullets between its eyes, saw ruptured flesh and bone. Blood spattered him. He saw the shattered head and body, on its belly, still crawling towards him.

The other had sprung again. Rellighan was shooting; the jaws closed on his arm, took him to the ground. Coleman shot it through the throat. It released its grip. Rellighan held his gun against its head and sent in bullet after bullet until it dropped. Coleman pulled him to his feet. The crawling one had stopped and tumbled lifelessly among the rocks.

"Your arm?" he asked Rellighan.

"It'll be bruised," Rellighan said, "stiff, sore for a while. A week, maybe longer. Old muscles take time to heal. We all grow old except the beautiful people."

"Not bleeding?"

Rellighan turned and showed him the torn fabric. "Built for purpose, only a little style. A Crombie overcoat," he said. "A quarter of an inch thick. Forty-five years old. A thing of the past. I was a young man, when I bought it."

"Yes," Coleman said.

Rellighan took the flat half-bottle of whiskey from his pocket; he unscrewed the cap and held it out.

"No," Coleman said. "You drink first."

Rellighan drank.

Their voices were raised to be heard above the moaning of the wind. The cold was settling into them. They both drank, then drank again.

"There's a job to be done," Rellighan said.

He gave his instructions. With his feet Coleman forced open the long-snouted jaws and teeth. Rellighan, with two flakes of stone, held the tongues tight, dragged at them, sliced them off with a pocket knife.

"Something to carry them?" he asked.

174

Coleman gave him a handkerchief. He looked down at the almost black animals: five feet from nose to tail, three feet tall, a dense collar of protective hair at the neck, heavy tufts at the shoulders and haunches. In the gaping mouths the teeth were gleaming feather-edged knives.

"A poisonous gift," Rellighan said. "They are for Sommerville's beautiful woman." He knotted the handkerchief about them, looked into the pitch blackness of the sky. "Morning light is very close. We must be home in darkness."

Coleman stared at the grotesque dead remains of Sommerville. "What about him?"

"We leave everything. We never saw him. She will deal with it."

Coleman looked at his watch. "After midday today," he said to Rellighan, "you will be walking beside a funeral. Jennifer Anderson's empty coffin will be buried in the cemetery."

Rellighan was silent.

Coleman thought of Belle Cannon and her church vigil. He looked at Sommerville's body and the metamorphosed remains of James Anthony and Jennifer Anderson. Their transubstantiation. The body and blood of Sommerville.

He and Rellighan walked away. . .

Coleman saw the first yellow sodium gleam of the town lights distantly and leant on the throttle. The world was still dark but in an hour a grey livid edge would creep up from the eastern skyline.

The town would sleep late.

Coleman said, "Why did Belle Cannon sit with the dead tonight?"

"To watch."

"Watch?"

"Watch the corpse, where they might take it."

"You didn't know?"

"No."

"And we went out into a wilderness?"

"The newspaper, savaged livestock," Rellighan said; his mouth was tight.

Coleman watched the road with tired eyes; he smoked. "Today?" he asked Rellighan eventually.

"The church, the burial."

"And then?"

"There's a cross-roads village north of that stone world we left. A few shops, a church. Go there. Months ago children said something. The beautiful Mother of God, they say. Now people come to gawp and pray. Sommerville might have met Machen there. He was a curious man."

"Machen is a beautiful woman. A vision."

"Don't rack your brains with mysteries," Rellighan said. "Sommerville spent a night out of town. In the morning I saw him drive across the Square. There's a hotel on the coast up there."

"Early hours for a lazy man."

"Yes."

Coleman drove the last miles in silence. Dawn hadn't yet shown a crack of light. The town streets were empty, only discarded beer cans and food packaging showing the untidy marks of last night's celebrations. The town was sleeping away its hangover. Demesne Street was pristine. Coleman stopped at Sommerville's, watched Rellighan push through the letter-box the bloody mess of animal flesh.

Then he drove Rellighan to his yard.

"We need sleep," he said. "Even an hour."

Rellighan said, "I never sleep."

Coleman left him, drove across the Square towards Main Street and Belle Cannon's shop and flat.

Belle Cannon had stood in the churchyard and listened until the sound of Sommerville's car had faded. The cold night air braced, revived her. The awful fancy dress procession in the church, the touching, the caressing, the removal of Jennifer

176

Anderson from her rest, how her long hair had fallen loose when they lowered her to the sheet – minutes ago but it seemed a long time past, like a fairground peepshow automaton: a coin in the slot and the figures moved in their dumb show behind glass, completed their round and were suddenly still.

Belle Cannon walked into Main Street where there were lighted windows and a movement of people. She smiled and waved salutations and felt sickness in her body. She climbed the stairs to the sanctuary of her flat, put her phone on the coffee table and lay back, uneasy, unable to find rest even in this comfort. She looked across the colours and tones of wood and fabrics, the paintings scattered about, the good, the fair, the sentimental, the bad. The phone had been silent; she had taken no calls, made none. She lifted the receiver and listened: it was alive, the dialling sound was there.

She thought of the unscrewing of the coffin lid, the cold beautiful body that had been stolen! For what? Where had they taken it? To be stripped and violated, kept in some necrophiliac naked display until she had blackened and shrivelled and was no longer of use?

"Oh God!" she said aloud.

She stood, poured a measure of sherry and drank it. All about the town she could feel a hushed suppressed rhythm, a throbbing wound waiting to break and bleed. In a small town there could be surprise, gossip, laughter, scuffles, fisticuffs, all the day-to-day worries and crises. Not much more. This was a bad night. The town was laughing but it was in fear. It was in fear more than in mourning.

She missed Coleman. Coleman had buried his uneasiness and was out in search of something.

Something.

At moments, in fear, his absence seemed only a kind of impotent display of heroics. But she knew Coleman wasn't given to heroics, he played parts in low key, moved unobtrusively, with caution. She missed him.

Ten years ago, she remembered – she had been a junior teacher then – Coleman had arrived in town. He was twenty-four, a hard face, hair the wind could toss. Out of uniform, he dressed his age and fashion. He was smart. The girls liked him, made dreamy faces to each other when he passed.

Belle Cannon liked his style.

He came to the school one day and asked to see her. He had found her door keys with a name tag attached. He had come to deliver them. He held them out.

"You're a life-saver," she had said.

Coleman was unsure, felt a kind of warming glow on his face. "You're welcome," he said. "I thought I'd drop them in. You might have been worried."

He smiled, moved a bit, was ready to go. Belle Cannon wanted him there if only for a few long moments.

She said, "I hadn't missed them. The worry would have been later. I must be more careful."

"They were on the pavement."

"You're new to town," she said.

"Two months."

"I'm four."

He smiled his careful smile then. She knew she liked him. She knew Coleman liked her.

In love for ten years, she thought, and living alone. Coleman was right: you lived at opposite sides of the park, you gave love a chance. Meeting him, opening the door to him, there was always a freshness, an excitement. Almost ten years! She was thirty-one now. Coleman was thirty-four. She had her life, her own interests, her job, little ambitious plans. And sitting with Coleman, travelling with him, nights far away out of town together, food, friends, long walks on the estuary shore. And Coleman could make love. She smiled, and then was suddenly remembering the church again.

She missed Coleman tonight. He had been gone for hours, the phone had been silent for hours.

Sommerville, she thought, lived behind a cloak of great

decency in his fine family residence. Belle Cannon's customers talked, gossiped. The house had been refurbished by his father, a careful man who had money and loved it and wanted more. There had been a flourishing Protestant stock in the country-side then, on estates, in impressive houses hidden behind trees and shrubs, who drove motor cars even in the twenties and the thirties. They were moneyed people, socialised almost as a duty with each other, supported a church, a vicar. All that was gone now: some houses had been razed, some were peopled by suddenly enriched local farmers, some by aliens. The Protestant youth had fled from the violence of the twenties, or died in some war for their distant King safe in his own coun-try. The old order of the town rested apart in the Protestant cemetery or in corners of foreign fields.

Sommerville's father had *worked*, had practised medicine daily, made night calls, was present at births and deaths, the town recalled.

Monthly he sat and wrote his bills in copperplate hand, added little phrases of greeting or sympathy, an invitation to dinner even, and was paid for his attention, perhaps his skill. His wife had been a pious attractive woman, hardly a moth-er, whom he had brought from city life to *desolation*, as she liked to describe her dreary locus.

She had borne her cross and the distasteful intimacies – and Herbert Peregrine – with fortitude.

They had retired to live and die in Cheltenham, leaving the practice to an unmarried cold sybaritic offspring, a restless person, always estranged from them. They were proud of his brilliance, aware of his proclivities – Doctor Herbert Peregrine Sommerville, M.D., M.Ch., B.A.O., M.R.C.P.

Belle Cannon would like to see the house she had heard of so often: a museum of Victoriana, everything preserved and cherished as if time had stood still for a hundred years: heavy furniture, pictures, gilt- and leather-wrapped books, cabinets of china and crystal, screens and tapestries, old glass shades fitted on modern lighting . . .

She walked about her lounge again, took a book, opened it and closed it. Sommerville and Machen. What they had done was a chilling blasphemy, an outrage on any patch of ground, holy or unblessed. She threw the book on the sofa, settled for music, left a compact disc whispering to her across the room. She still wore the three-quarter length black skirt she had donned for the church service, pale transparent tights, but she had changed a blouse for a splashy red and white cotton top, hanging loose at the waist. She seemed to be wandering in shock from contemplation of the Sommerville house to the comfort of her books, her music.

The church was lodged in her thoughts, the waft of sweetness when Estel Machen had passed slowly, the perfection of poise, carrying her bouquet to the coffin in humble ostentation: the strange oppressive gloom that seemed to pervade with her sudden arrival and linger when she had gone. She was remembering again that Estel Machen had touched the faces, the hair, the shoulders of so many pupils. Did it matter? Had she touched the two dead ones? Coleman didn't squander time. It proved nothing, he had said. But she had seen the transfiguration of Estel Machen from beauty to rotting death-like ugliness, at an arm's length, before her eyes. A breathing death's-head. And then sometimes it could be an unreal picture blurring in memory.

The dead Jennifer Anderson, shapely, attractive, strong, missing now forever from the town, the school classroom. Estel Machen was more than beauty of face and body. Now her beauty was frightening. Even schoolchildren were in love with her.

Meningitis? Isolated cases? Allergy to drugs? In small towns tragedy was whispered, distorted. There was restlessness growing with passing hours.

Coleman had been uneasy, disturbed, as if trying hopelessly to come to grips with something unseen. Estel Machen was visible, tangible, generous with her talents and small means to all the worthy causes of the town. That was the picture she had created. But she was unreal, something evil beneath the sweetness. Even the sweetness was repulsive. Sommerville's house was her domain, a sealed fortress. She had replaced live-in staff with part-time, transformed dullness to perfection. And she was devoted to the service of the church that she could desecrate and outrage.

Belle Cannon tried to find comfort somewhere in the remembrance of good times but they too were receding. Even Coleman was caught in the tangle. The sound of laughter had vanished. Good times might never come again.

She sat and, suddenly, heard the sound of footsteps in her bedroom! She listened. Yes, distinct pacing footsteps. She was on her feet. It was a carpeted room but the footsteps were sharp and hard.

She stood for a long time but there was only silence. She was alone. Fear had gripped her. Alone, but the sound of someone in her home. Silence had settled.

She moved soundlessly to her landing and looked down the stairway to her front door. Emptiness.

She shrugged it off, walked noisily back to her lounge. She turned up the music a little louder. It had a soft soothing warmth.

Then the footsteps came again, now almost a rough stamping sound. She was cold with growing fear but she took up a weapon, a piece of cast brass, and moved towards the thudding noise. Suddenly, in an instant, there was silence and the room was empty, untouched. She searched the flat: shower, bathroom, wardrobe, even under her bed. Nothing.

She went back to her lounge and hopelessly tried to listen to the music but, somehow, it seemed to be fading, moving away from her. Now drowsiness enveloped her. The music was more distant, like a melody remembered. She had nodded, she thought, perhaps for a moment or two. Distant, distant music. She looked at a table clock, at her watch. The small hours had passed. She was shocked. She hadn't slept, of that she was certain. A feeling of drowsiness only. She

thought of her bed, of undressing and rolling into what
should be safety, softness, a beautiful warmth surrounding
her, and drifting away from danger. The footsteps? She had
brought her fear from the church, the sweetness of Estel
Machen, the crashing coffin lid. Coleman and Rellighan, on
the church steps, had been shrouded conspirators. Sleep was
impossible. In her bedroom she would be locked away, hidden, with some presence, vulnerable, stripped of all defence.

The music was scarcely audible now, even moments of
silence. She went to the console and raised the volume, waited for moments, listening to its strength, then went back to
stretch on the sofa. She listened.

Strangely, the streets outside were without sound: only the
wind grated against the houses. The music was fading again,
drifting away almost to nothingness. The lights had dimmed.
Fear was taking hold and she fought against it. The power
was failing. The lightning, the music?

In ten years she had seen power failures, black-outs. The
music was a whisper again, but it hadn't lost power, its tone
and speed were perfect. The light faded to a glimmer. The
room was suddenly cold: a total almost deathly coldness.

She tried to sit upright and found that weakness had taken
possession of her. Her limbs were weighted, leaden: her head
hung back, her mouth was open. A strange terrifying feeling
of losing whatever force kept her alive and in motion. The
creeping loss of bodily power held more terror than pain.

It was a bed, a hospital bed of shining metal where she had
been laid. She could see the pale green screen that had been
pulled around her to leave her in isolation. Figures stood by
to attend to her. She was laid flat, her arms folded. The figures spoke to each other; through her closed eyes she could
see them distinctly. They gazed down on her. On one side
Sommerville stood in surgeon's gown; on the other, facing
him, Estel Machen was the austere unemotional nurse. She
was a beautiful creature in this garb of mercy. Beside the bed
there was a stretcher-trolley.

Sommerville said, "The autopsy theatre. She's been dead a couple of hours."

He came round to join Estel Machen. They lifted her on to the mobile trolley and covered her. She wanted to scream, to run from this awful living nightmare. But speech was gone too. She wept in deep shaking movements but there were no tears. She was wheeled through corridors to a disposal lift, in the darkness of her cover, listened to the hum of descent to some hidden place. Then the final push to the theatre and exposure to light.

Sommerville and Machen were smiling now, standing beside a tray of gleaming steel.

Machen said, "You undress her, Dr Sommerville. A little pleasure will compensate for the dreary business of cutting flesh."

Belle Cannon suddenly realised she was fully dressed, without the strength to move or voice to shout her pain in mortal fear. In an agony of dread she wept.

Sommerville, with great care, unbuttoned her outer clothes, gently removed them, then her under garments, her tights. They looked down on her total nakedness. Sommerville caressed her body with his hands.

He took his scalpel and did his work: he made a long incision below the rib cage and two vertical incisions at her sides. He folded down the bleeding sheet of flesh. Then he cut and gashed her entrails.

The pain was an unbearable burning of flesh. She prayed, pleaded for death, but made not a sound.

Estel Machen, with an instrument, was clipping back the flap of stomach flesh. She cleaned the blood. They were carrying her away again, preparing her for burial.

Like Jennifer Anderson, she was lying in Rellighan's funeral home, clothed in a long blue gown, her face peaceful, her hair arranged, her body a crucible of white-hot corroding metal. Her hands were joined, beads entwined about them.

There was no dimension of time, she seemed to be drifting

from sea of pain to sea of pain. She heard Simoney's outraged voice echoing in the church, telling her of the damnation of her soul that was already burning in hell. He exhorted his parishioners to cast her soiled body from the cemetery of the town's dead, to bury her in a pit of unconsecrated ground.

She was in darkness, in some open cart or tumbril, jolting her way to burial. In her awful pain and fear she wept like a child. On the rough pot-holed road her body was tossed and shaken in its coffin.

It was the end. She was lowered into her isolated grave. She could hear Simoney's shouting voice.

"Deliver us, O Lord, from evil, Amen."

The earth thumped on her coffin, filled it with noise. She screamed and suddenly could hear herself. But it was too late. The earth was falling. She raised her weak hands for a moment and died.

Coleman drove his car from Rellighan's, through the Square, to Main Street and Belle Cannon's. They had delivered the dead animal flesh to Estel Machen's doorstep and Rellighan had gone to spend his sleeplessness in his office or his rambling house. Darkness was weakening.

Estel Machen had driven Sommerville's car. It was at his door. But Sommerville was dead?

Belle Cannon?

Coleman took Belle Cannon's key and silently opened the door. The hall and the stairway were in that last shadow of darkness before dawn. There was light on the landing. He stood and listened. Nothing stirred.

He quietly climbed the stairs, gripped the door handle, held it, tightened on it and turned it moment by moment until it opened. The room was warm. He pulled the curtains and let the first grey light flood in.

Belle Cannon was asleep on the sofa, her legs stretched out comfortably; a table lamp burned beside her, the telephone rested in its cradle. She wore a long black skirt, transparent hose, a red and white splashy shirt. He could see the regular movement of her breathing. Behind sleep and peacefulness she might be in a torment of pain, terror, shameful abasement, he knew. And then death. Coleman would let it run its cycle; he would wait for her to return, to awaken. Rellighan's church key was there.

He poured himself a stiff drink, sat in an easy chair out of view, and waited. He pocketed the key.

Today was the burial day. The day of an empty funeral: the services for the dead, Simoney's raging melodramatic warnings to the community, the silence of the church, the tears of grief that would be shed over an empty coffin.

He sat and drank and smoked.

Coleman was the last of a heavy brood his civil servant parent had procreated. His father, a widower in middle-age, a deeply religious man, had roused the house for daily Mass during his life-time, was a pillar of community excellence, a leader of processions and confraternities.

He seemed to have patronised his wife with useless consideration but she had outlived Coleman's birth only by months. The machinery of relentless reproduction had been hard on her. The great holy man of abstinence, pins, medals, scapulars, fittingly died in a church pew, alone, with only God for company. He had been caught in a downpour of rain and had run breathless yards to shelter. Coleman remembered the early years of growing up in the noise and bedlam of a crowded house, meals, chores, prayers. In his seventh year he had been taken in care by childless relatives. Good people. He supposed he had loved them. He thought of them with respect but had never visited their graves. Standing a few feet above mouldering bodies would have been a duty. Remembering their voices of instruction, laughter, sorrow, surprise, was living with them again.

The God of parents and their generation with memorised prayers and supplications had distracted them from evil: if you were good there was no evil. Coleman worked each day as he found it. He wondered if life wasn't a searching for good and meeting evil on the way. Evil might even be a religion, an incestuous selfish protection, saving, destroying souls.

The town's godliness smiled at Estel Machen, offered its blessing, received her services, her humble tokens of charity. Coleman thought of Rellighan, his creased pitted face, his silences. And his pale eyes. Rellighan was a lonely man in a lonely lifetime. But Coleman held him in regard, perhaps even affection...

The stealthy arrival of light, grey diluted darkness, marked the passage of time, the audible beat of a battery driven clock measured it. More than an hour had passed before the slight movement of Belle Cannon's fingers alerted Coleman. He watched. Her eyes remained closed, her hands, in fear, fumbled as if to disentangle themselves, searched along her stomach for the dreadful mutilation.

She had been punished, pushed beyond the barrier of pain, to death, Coleman knew. Eyes closed, hiding in darkness, she felt for wounds and blood. She opened her eyes, was confronted by morning first light, the familiarity of her room, her possessions, the colours and shapes she lived with.

She was untouched, resting on the sofa as she often did, her clothing undisturbed. She looked at her hands: no trace of blood or encircling rosary beads, no blue robe of death. She was on her feet, ready to loosen her skirt, examine flesh for reassurance, her body where Sommerville's scalpel had penetrated her. She remembered the stripping, the caressing of her naked body. She was in tears. The terror returned for an instant.

Coleman called her.

She swung round in fear, held out arms to ward him off, then gripped him, held him in her embrace.

"Don't go, Coleman!"

He felt her weight suspended in his arms and carried her to

the sofa. She was conscious, weak, still choking in the reality of mutilation and shame that had been present only moments ago. He brought brandy and put the glass in her hands. In a little while she sat erect and sipped it.

"You should have stayed, Coleman," she said. "You should have stayed with me."

Coleman looked at what remained in his glass and drank it back, sat on a low stool facing her.

He said, "I could have sat where I'm sitting now and watched you sleeping without movement, without a change in your breathing, and you would have suffered every cut and slash, every indignity and shame. If I had awakened you it might have been death, real death. I don't know . . . I don't understand."

She looked at him. "You too, Coleman?"

"Yes."

"Estel Machen and Sommerville? They were here!"

"I saw Sommerville. He was dead."

There were tears again. "I can't talk about it now."

"Maybe we should never talk about it?"

"Yes."

"You saw them, didn't you?" he asked. "In the church last night. They took Jennifer Anderson's body. You were there?"

Belle Cannon sat in silence. The church and the defilement of a human body awaiting burial, now was pushed away in her mind beyond her own awful shame and ravishment.

She said, "Yes, I was there. It was parodied, burlesqued like a little piece of meaningless comedy. She, in the ceremonial robes of the hierarchy, Sommerville her acolyte." Belle Cannon stood and went to the window and looked at Main Street that was in another place and time. "Oh God, Coleman," she said. "We had such a beautiful world. Is it gone forever?"

"They took the body in Sommerville's car?" he asked.

"Yes. They wrapped it in a linen sheet and carried it out. That's an empty coffin in the church."

He said, "The town must never know."

She looked and saw the pain and compassion in Coleman's eyes, his uneasiness.

"I understand," she said. "But an empty coffin?"

"When they raise it up it will seem tenanted. I am only blundering about."

"Tell me, Coleman, tell me."

"They took Jennifer Anderson's body," he said "up to that wilderness of rock flats miles from here. She stripped it, carried it out, left it lying there exposed. She sent Sommerville out to stand and look at it. Or his own curiosity took him. But Sommerville was weakening. He dragged his feet, walked like an old man. An animal was suddenly there. It tore him to pieces. I saw him dead. He should be out there, dead."

"And Jennifer Anderson?"

Coleman remembered the black night of just hours ago, his own fear, the courage of Rellighan; he said, "I went down from a hillock with Rellighan to the body of Sommerville. There are two animals now. Rellighan knew they would come; we waited. We shot them."

"Two animals?"

"James Anthony and Jennifer Anderson."

"Animals? James Anthony and Jennifer Anderson?"

Coleman looked out at the paling morning. "Yes, they're lying dead out there in that wilderness. And Sommerville's body torn to pieces."

Belle Cannon looked at her hands that had been dead and wrapped tight in a rosary beads. "What is it, Coleman?" she asked. "Not a dream?"

"Too real for dreams."

"Madness? You suffered too, Coleman."

He nodded.

"What is it?"

"I don't know, I don't know. If we can live another day with it, there might be an answer. No one must know," he said again. "You and I. And Rellighan."

"I love you, Coleman."

"That's what keeps me going."

They undressed and stood together in the shower, holding each other, letting the balm of warm water diminish the memory of wounds and blood, bring back some glimmer of the changeless humdrum world that should be out there.

Finegan thought himself a man of importance in the town where money was the yardstick. Bank officials saluted him; at a moment's notice he had access to the bank manager's office. His father, long since buried by Rellighan, had taught him the geography of the town and its surrounding desolation when small cabins still dotted it. Their dirt floors had once been the play-pens of teeming infant bodies. The fittest survived, illiterate, emigrated and were swallowed into a great permanent silence. Parents died, left a crumbling cabin on an acre, two acres of ground. Finegan, behind his bar, took note of deaths and passing years. With time he owned a great deal of land, and sometimes a reclaimable property, that he had gained for nothing or a pittance.

Finegan, in his seventies now, had lived through boom times, grazed cattle on a dozen plots, built homes in the windswept moorland that had some quaint quirky cachet for city dwellers and the newly rich. It was Finegan's philosophy that a high price enhanced a purchase; a low price would be unacceptable to them. He was a man of considerable bank balance. He was a county councillor, chairman of the urban committee, member of the town's board of trade. He tended his bar all of the time where gossip, hearsay and secret whisperings found a home.

And he attended church, was aware that religion was part of a public image; he had a seat labelled with a brass plate that proclaimed it the property of Martin and Stella Maris Finegan. A prominent seat.

It was an undoubted truth that Mrs Martin Finegan, before

or since her marriage, had never set foot in the licensed area of the family business. The living quarters, above the premises, were luxuriously over-furnished. Victoria Regina still lived in the parlour and various rooms that could soak most of the light from a summer's day.

Antique easy chairs of upholstery and polished wood, like sleeping beasts, faced each other across a fine lambswool rug before an open fire.

"Sit down, my dear, will you?"

It was a gentle command. Finegan, in carefully slippered feet, a gabardine trousers and a sleeved waistcoat, took his place. His wife was expensively dressed, severe, gold-spectacled, over-laden with jewellery. Her hands had never been soiled by house-work. She rang a fire-side bell for her middle-aged factotum.

"See that we are not disturbed, Christina."

"Yes, ma'am."

When the servant had gone she addressed her husband. "You are not attending this funeral today, I assume?"

"Of course not," Finegan said. His face was almost offended; he spoke in a kind of growl of authority.

"Of course not," she confirmed it. "Christina tells me the town is in a dangerous mood."

"Yes," he agreed.

"Rellighan's name has been mentioned. His staff, I'm told, are in revolt. These bodies. He's a silent unclean man, godless, I often think. Unclean in his mind, I'm sure. He has that half-caste look about him. He must never touch my body."

Finegan nodded; he said, "Drunken hands. He dropped the coffin lid on the church floor. An act of sacrilege. I thought there might have been an outcry."

"Well, in the circumstances, the congregation in attendance was hardly of account. From the Estate. You can't offend people like that. Substandard."

"Rellighan needs to be chastised," he said.

"You've arranged it?"

"I will."

"Very good, my dear."

"We have grandchildren," Finegan said. "Young growing boys and fine girls."

"At boarding school, thank God."

"In six weeks they'll be in this town for Christmas."

Mrs Finegan clasped her hands in shock.

"They must be protected!" she said.

"Coleman," Finegan told her, "He's not very bright. He talked about Dr Sommerville and his housekeeper."

"Dr Sommerville is the last of our gentry. His housekeeper is efficient and she knows her place. She does menial work in the church for which God will reward her."

"I reminded Coleman of the Sommerville importance to the town, now, and from the early decades of the last century. As you said, my dear, gentry."

"Good."

Finegan paced about. "I've given this matter a great deal of thought, I can tell you. In the bar, the opinions of the town are tossed about every day. I am always wide awake. I listen and discard. I have judgement."

"You have someone in mind?"

"Someone who stands at street corners or loiters about the Square for hours. Good looking, you'd call him, I suppose. The family are labouring class. They dress him, turn him out well. Clean, well-dressed, his hair in place. A smiler. Smiling always. But behind the smile?"

"Who?"

"That Colleran lunatic. I've kept an eye on him."

Mrs Martin Finegan was on her feet. "He's mad, he's mad," she said.

"Yes."

"Two years in the County Home for treatment . . ."

"To keep him out of harm's way, maybe," Finegan said. "You know what was our own son's advice from across the Atlantic? 'Dangerous,' he said. And he's a qualified man."

191

Colleran was a handsome boy, slight and gentle. In his school years and now, even in his illness, one could find the slow comfortable comprehension that schizophrenics sometimes develop, or discard. They smile and stare, are listening attentively to their own minds, for long, long moments unreachable. It is a malady without relief. He had led his class, was good in the games field, fancied by the girls. Then, in a month, he had entered his own uncharted world. There was no recovery. It might be a happy or frightening world of whispered encouragement or warnings or advice. He was scarcely eighteen then.

The County Hospital, the Psychiatric Unit, St Jude's Home – a single building – had stood for a hundred and fifty years. Recent times had re-christened it, bestowed on it humane titles to screen madness from our sane world. But it was still the lunatic asylum. Madmen had to be confined, locked away.

Colleran was drilled into the regimen of tablets and hypodermics – medication – that could create a zombie-like calmness in a couple of years. Illness wasn't cured but its manifestations were numbed. Then the convulsions of electric current might restore some normality.

He emerged with his madness unscathed and a constant craving for tobacco. Coleman always put a cigarette in his mouth, lighted it, and watched him draw in the soothing nicotine. He talked sometimes to Coleman, told long catalogues of memorised knowledge, history and battles, recited endless verse:

"Three ducks in a pond,
The green grass beyond
What a thing to remember for years,
To remember with tears."

He was in his twenties now, his wanderings a changeless pattern from dawn till dusk.

Finegan said to his wife, "Three times a day when these young school sluts with shortened skirts, sticking out their

192

thighs and tits, are passing, you find him taking stock of things, standing in the Square staring at flesh. Always smiling or looking into the far distance. They give him cigarettes . . ."

"The schoolgirls?"

"Schoolgirls! School books in plastic bags and their bloomers too!"

Mrs Martin Finegan made the sign of the cross.

"They wave to him, stop and talk to him, smile. And they touch him." Finegan said.

Mrs Martin Finegan whispered, "Does he touch them in special places?"

"Maybe he only needs to breathe on them. Grinning, talking to himself. Madness, is it?" Finegan paused. "*Possession* might be closer to it."

"God between us and all harm," she said.

Finegan crossed and patted her on the shoulder in reassurance. "I'll deal with it," he said.

"You look pale," she told him.

He studied his face anxiously in the mirror, poured himself a measure of whiskey, drank it back.

"There's illness everywhere in this town," he said.

Finegan went to the telephone and dialled a number; he said, "This is Martin Finegan. You can come now. Now, I said. Yes, it'll take a half an hour to get here. This time of day, winter or summer, he's always near the jetty. A quiet place. Windy and cold today, he'll be sheltering behind the boathouses. He could be dangerous, I don't know. I want a good job, remember. No half measures. Leave him where he can be found, in the open. Then move." Finegan paused a moment. "Wait," he said; two jobs for the price of one, he was thinking. "You pass Rellighan's on the way. Put his windows and doors in. A quick job, don't delay. Come and see me in the week."

He replaced the phone on its cradle.

Finegan had stockmen, labourers, on his land in a twenty mile radius. They were hard men, tough, greedy. They wouldn't leave a bad job behind them.

193

"Who?" his wife asked.

"There are men for every job. You don't need to know. The crinkle of banknotes is what matters." He smiled to her. "I'll drive down near to the jetty, pick a place where I can see the job done. I'll be back before opening time..."

Finegan drove down through the backways and parked his car in the solitude of the Simoney empty perishing warehouses and storage space. He could see the distant thin figure of Colleran, in shelter from cutting wind, sitting on a flat stone bollard. A cigarette was fixed in his mouth. A madman, a frozen image, dangerous, out there in God's precious world. He pulled hard on the butt-end of the cigarette and threw it away.

He watched Colleran hunched there, listening to his voices.

Finegan's men had arrived. The driver stayed at the wheel, a watchman. Three passengers moved across to Colleran. They laughed with him, handed him a pack of ten cigarettes. Colleran walked with them to a boathouse. It was a little while before they carried him out and dumped him on open ground.

He wouldn't walk straight for a long time.

Finegan moved. From the Square he could hear the hammering sledge at Rellighan's door, the shattering falling sound of glass. He drove back to his home. His wife took his coat and handed him a fresh work-apron. He smiled his success to her, went in to prepare his bar for opening.

Belle Cannon had driven Coleman to his home. He had changed clothes for the church service and burial.

Belle Cannon's paleness lingered, she was still disconcerted but, like Coleman, she was angry: their world, the world of Coleman and herself, had been reduced, degraded. Helplessness, emptiness, brought anger.

A half an hour before midday they were at Rellighan's. The street was littered with splintered wood and glass; a man worked with sheets of chipboard for patching, and swept scattered rubbish into piles.

On the street frontage had been parked the hearse and mourners' car. They were untouched. A fear of death and its ancillaries? At their appointed time, very soon now, they would move away to the church for the burial journey.

Coleman pushed open the wicket gate and they crossed the yard to Rellighan's office.

Rellighan, a black monument, was there, a weird catatonic figure with the seemingly vacant stare that might accompany Colleran's madness. Arms folded, he was standing. His faded eyes had their habitual unfocused disinterest in the world about him. But little escaped him.

Coleman opened the office door, saw the untouched newspaper on the desk. Rellighan, momentarily restless and perhaps bothered by the intrusion, waited for Coleman to bid him the time of day. Coleman, too, was uneasy; he moved about aimlessly, smoked. Belle Cannon took a seat by the window.

Rellighan took his place behind the table, looked carefully at her, ignored Coleman, spoke to her. "You were punished last night," he said.

There was a long pause before she nodded. "You know?"

"Yes. Are you afraid?"

"Yes."

"She wants you afraid."

"And you?" Coleman asked; he returned the gun, the silencer, the clips, the church key.

Rellighan didn't answer; before the first minutes of dawn, when he had left Coleman, he had come to sit in the imprisoned darkness of his office where he had suffered too: he had died in Ingolstad. With his family. They had found him hiding in the stable rafters; he had been herded with the rest, naked, into the great metal cylinder. He could feel the air growing thinner, the excruciating pain filling his body. He saw the blood streaming from his mother's mouth and wept for her. He remembered the face of the beautiful woman and the explosion of his own death.

"She wants my fear too," he said.

There was silence.

Coleman said, "Your windows and doors are smashed, hammered to pieces. A lot of damage."

Rellighan dismissed it. "A little while ago," he said. "I heard it. They'll mend."

Coleman nodded.

Rellighan picked up the gun, examined it, spun the chamber. He might be looking at it in admiration.

"It's empty," he was told.

Belle Cannon watched him wrap it and store it away: slow careful hands for something precious. Rellighan looked up at her.

Coleman told him, "She knows, she was in the church."

Rellighan stood, walked to the window, looked into the bright cleanliness of his yard. "Don't be afraid of guns." He glanced at her for a moment. "I was fourteen and I was a fugitive corpse-washer across the water. At twenty-one I had finished my time. Caskets can hide away more than corpses. You need a gun to watch graves."

Rellighan went back to his table, sat leaning back in his chair. Discussion of times past was closed.

Belle Cannon looked at the gaunt figure, could see the hardness of his frame. She looked at his hands and distant eyes, the worn face. Rellighan had probably killed. And Coleman? Last night, together, they had killed animals. She saw Rellighan, in darkness, guarding foreign graves fifty years past. The gun had been fresh and oiled.

Like Coleman, in silence, she listened to the sounds of the town, reality forcing its way to them.

Rellighan spoke softly, dragging old irrelevant thoughts up into the light, addressing no one; he was saying, reciting, "The Greeks called burial places cemeteries. A soft warm name. They set them apart from their cities and dwellings.

196

The dead never sleep in cities. We don't shut down our city graveyards when housing encircles them and moves on. We are busy. Putrid air rises up from decomposing bodies, diseased air. It needs wind and sky to dissipate them. When thousands of bodies are piled in little allotted spaces, air and water are contaminated. We dissolve into acids, water, salt."

Rellighan's voice tapered away. They sat in silence for minutes. Coleman lit another cigarette, exhaled smoke into the cold air. He said, "You've survived, Rellighan."

"My body is wasted. It has spent too long in graveyards, homes of the dead."

He stood up, put on his funeral hat and black overcoat. "Time for you to go," he told them.

Coleman and Belle Cannon left him there, a great shadowy hawk who had kept watch through nights, standing guard by buried caskets and whatever plunder they held.

"He's hard?" Belle Cannon asked.

"Not hard. He's seen hardship."

"You need him?"

"I like him."

They drove back across the Square to the church where the hearse and cars were parked. The funeral Mass had begun; the bereaved and friends made a small silent crowd scattered about the unused great spaces of the church. The Canon, aged and feeble, prayed on the altar. Simoney, in acolyte's robes, assisted him.

Estel Machen wouldn't be absent; somewhere, moving silently, Coleman thought, she was administering to the church's and Simoney's needs. Sommerville was dead. Estel Machen might be the celebrant of this death Mass and its empty coffin.

The Mass is a great sacrifice. The body and blood of dead and resurrected Christ are revivified with prayer, immense ceremony and conjuration on the altar, to feed wandering and weeping children in this vale of tears.

Life should be a strange and joyless regimen, a preparation

for everlasting peace, the sight of God, in the promised land. Coleman sat and watched the motions of the Canon, heard his weak whispering voice reading from the great missal on its brass stand. Simoney, head bowed in penitence, stood in waiting.

The congregation was in silence, the dying sibilant words reaching to four walls and lingering on fragrant aromatic incense that burned inside the sanctuary rails.

The coffin, on its catafalque, was piled with flowers and written pledges of future Masses to expiate the small sins of the deceased, to speed her journey to everlasting rest. Coleman looked at Simoney, in soutane and surplice, his face rigid in respect and devotion. Belle Cannon had gone to join her schoolgirls.

The Canon prayed. "O God, who art ever ready to have mercy and to spare, we humbly beseech thee on behalf of the soul of thy servant, lying here, whom thou hast this day called out of this world, that thou wouldst not deliver her into the hands of the enemy, nor forget her forever but command the holy angels to take her and lead her to the home of paradise, that forasmuch as in thee she shall put her hope and trust, may she not endure the pains of hell, but may come to the possession of eternal joys. Through our Lord . . ."

The Mass progressed through its parts: the ordinary, the proper, the asperges for the dead. An endless ritual. Coleman's mind wandered to Rellighan and guns, Sommerville and his saintly guardian, Simoney in the sacristy, the custodian of holiness. The Mass progressed, impinged and faded.

". . . For the Lord himself shall come down from heaven, with commandment, and the voice of an archangel, and with the trumpet of God; and the dead who are in Christ shall rise first. Then we who are alive, who are left, shall be taken up together with them in the clouds to meet Christ, into the air: and so we shall always be with the Lord . . . wherefore comfort ye one and other with these words . . ."

As the coffin, empty of its pale innocent remains, was shouldered from the church to the waiting hearse, the congregation fell in behind it. Simoney delivered the final fearsome prayer, "Deliver us, O Lord, from everlasting death on that dreadful day; when heaven and earth shall quake; when thou shall come to judge the world by fire."

It was only a few small steps, Coleman thought, to the unknown world of stolen corpses, spirits and risen dead and sacrificial offerings.

The risen dead.

Rellighan supervised the loading of the coffin, the arrangement of flowers. Beyond his reach, a beautiful wreath toppled from the coffin on to the coldness of the floor. Estel Machen's floral tribute. He stooped and picked it up.

Simoney was behind him. "You are drunk, Rellighan," he whispered. He leant close to him. "You smell of whiskey."

"Yes," Rellighan told him. "I smell of whiskey. I need whiskey to keep sober, Simoney."

The mourners' car was good, spotless, impressive; he ushered in the relatives, seated them, walked beside the hearse as it wound its way through the town. A few shops had closed in respect. At the cemetery he stood by the graveside, close to the mounds of earth covered in wreaths, listened to the Canon supported by Simoney reciting the De Profundis.

"Out of the depths have I cried unto thee, O Lord; Lord hear my voice . . . for with thee there is merciful forgiveness . . . from the morning watch even until night . . ."

The lowering of the coffin began, on soft nylon webbing. Except to the gravesiders, it passed out of view. It was dropped slowly, carefully, into its pit. Suddenly a wreath slithered from the piled earth, fell to rest beside the coffin on the floor of the grave.

"Leave it!" Simoney called.

The coffin lay with Estel Machen's tribute in the final darkness. The sweet smell of flowers was in the air. Coleman looked at the unloved face of Rellighan, at Belle Cannon with only a half dozen schoolgirls who had made the final journey to the graveside. The small crowd began to disperse.

Relatives stood about the grave to watch the earth being shovelled. They said their private prayers and shed tears. Rellighan waited to escort them to their cars.

Coleman and Belle Cannon stood at the open gates and looked back at the scene. The cemetery was on raised ground too. The wind was driving low cloud above them that filtered a little dusk into the poorness of daylight. The wind was cold, harsh against the flesh; the farthest stones and crosses were charcoaled dark grey against the sky. The mourners too were huddled, motionless, a petrified monument in memory of the dead.

Coleman sat in the car; Belle Cannon was driving. She put out a hand and gripped his.

She said, "I remember when funerals were someone else's time of mourning. I feel old. I died last night, Coleman."

"Yes."

"And you?"

"Yes, I died."

"And Rellighan?"

Rellighan doesn't talk very much."

Coleman looked at his watch: it was early afternoon but the light was older. Days were shortening, nights lengthening. He managed a smile for Belle Cannon. "We're going to the rock country," he said. "Push it a bit. Forty-five, fifty minutes. Take the road that passes through it."

"Is it important?"

"I think so."

Belle Cannon had the car in motion; she said, "You can smoke, Coleman. I never mind you smoking."

He smiled. "You're a friend," he said . . .

They had passed the last village and crossed the scarred acres of bogland to reach the winding tourist road, narrow, dangerous but deserted, smooth on a base of solid rock. Coleman looked for his rises and dips, the isolated spears of stone that were markers. The empty road wound a meandering way for miles, out of sight. Then he saw it.

"The bend," he said. "Pull in at the bend."

They stepped out, stood in the roadway, a desolate tape of mileage, a snail-trail in an empty bowl of limestone. It had taken forty minutes.

"Come," he said.

He took her hand; they walked a little distance across the almost sculptured floor of giant slabs.

Coleman said, "Sommerville's body lay here at our feet. He was savaged, ripped, torn, blood everywhere." He pointed to the sloping flat bier. "The naked body of Jennifer Anderson was there. She vanished into the blackness. Out there somewhere. Two animals came back. We shot them."

"They're dead?"

"We shattered their heads and brains."

"James Anthony and Jennifer Anderson?"

"Yes."

She gazed at the bleakness. "There's nothing out there now, is there, Coleman?"

"I don't think so. There's nothing *here*."

Coleman looked along the skyline of this cold unfriendly world, cracks, ravines, even caves. How old? Older than everything man-made. Our lives were only a flicker.

In the car he said, "We keep going. When we run out towards the coast we see soil and grass and foliage again. Houses and people. There's a cross-roads village. Stop at the church. We leave this dead world now."

It was five or six miles to the village: a few houses, shops, a church. Rusting cars were parked; two pedestrians had paused in the wind to talk.

Belle Cannon drove to the churchyard. A little grotto had been erected there of stone, shells cement. A statue was mounted. A box marked 'donations' was prominent. A woman was wiping away the blown dust.

Coleman said, "There was an apparition here?"

The woman joined her hands in praise. "God smiled on us," she said. "Sent his Mother to bless this ground." She pointed to a wheelchair and a few crutches. "Miracles!"

Coleman asked, "Was she very beautiful?"

"Shining with divine light. The eldest child described her in detail . . ."

When she had finished, Coleman put a fiver in her collection box and left. In the car he said to Belle Cannon, "An hour to the sea. And there's a hotel."

They moved away; she said, "That was description of Estel Machen, wasn't it?"

"It might be."

"How do you know all this, Coleman?"

"Rellighan."

The hotel was a clean comfortable place that, in days before computers and the mass network spread of telecommunication, had been a stopping place for *commercial travellers*, selling their goods to shops in isolated communities. It catered for the haphazard tourist now. The cleanliness, the comfort remained. Coleman's face was known.

The proprietor said, "An end of the year day, Inspector."

"Yes," Coleman acknowledged. "A small favour?"

"Yes?"

"A glance at your register for early April."

Coleman flicked through the pages. Sommerville's name was there. A single night. No women for days before or after . . .

They turned for home, following the coast road where, in the failing light, scattered windows began to shine.

"Sommerville spent a night there."

"Estel Machen?"

"No trace," Coleman said.

While Simoney attended the burial he had left the church in the care of Estel Machen.

202

When he returned now, the traces of her industry brought satisfaction to his face. She had anticipated every chore, left beauty glistening everywhere. She was a person of exemplary goodness. He would remember her in his prayers.

"Burials are always occasions of sadness," she said.

"It must be God's plan."

"I don't envy you listening to outbursts of grief on every occasion, seeing people in distress."

"I think of it as a work of mercy."

"It was an uneventful burial then?"

He glanced at her for a moment. "Yes, just another burial, may she rest in peace. One or two relatives a little hysterical. Oh," he suddenly remembered, "Your magnificent wreath fell into the open grave, lodged beside the coffin."

"What matter," she said. "People at burials are often distraught, moving about awkwardly, clumsy."

"Yes, clumsy. I instructed them to leave it there. What more loving tribute could lie beside a pupil. God might have had a hand in it."

"You are very close to God."

Simoney brushed it humbly aside. "The afternoon is almost spent," he said. "But I will wait to ring the Angelus bell at six. My prayers are a little late on funeral days."

"And I must take care of Dr Sommerville."

"An excellent person. He deserves your attention."

Estel Machen put on her outdoor coat and hat, paused at the door, stood there for moments. Simoney was puzzled, watched her, waited. She turned.

"I don't know if I should mention this to you," she said. "It sounds like idle gossip but there is a certain repugnance about it, you could say almost a nauseating ring."

Simoney was rigid. "Yes, yes?" he said.

"It was during your absence at the burial. Only two women in the church. They were whispering. In silence you know how whispers carry?"

"Yes."

203

"The young people who died in recent months. Rumours are abroad that their bodies were stolen for the most unthinkable outrages. Yes, even today's corpse. The town is outraged, they were saying, and in fear."

The blood had drained from Simoney's face; he sat on a hard polished chair. "Oh my God!" he said.

"I had to mention it, dear Mr Simoney."

"Of course, thank you, thank you. It must be investigated. But today's body only just buried . . ."

"It was an empty coffin, they said. And the first was an empty coffin too."

Simoney was in a fever of motion.

"I must rush! My prayers must wait. God will guide me. There are people to be seen, consulted. Where can I start? I must get to my home, telephone . . ."

"We had an appointment for this evening. Eight-thirty would have suited. But we can rearrange it."

"No, no, my dear Miss Machen. You must come. Your presence in my home will be a consolation. I am so deeply indebted to you. I had heard muttering and unrest. For days. But this awful act against God and nature . . ."

From the door Estel Machen said, "I'm so very sorry to bring you this news, Mr Simoney."

Coleman and Belle Cannon drove into town when the first deep greyness was colouring daylight. The town, the people, the bright shop windows were a celebration of welcome. Belle Cannon said, "This is a good place, Coleman. It's home."

"Our town," he said.

She drove down to Rellighan's and found him standing on the pavement outside his battered premises; she opened a door. Without salutation Rellighan bent his tall frame and took the rear seat. A calm expressionless face.

He said to Coleman, "You went back there?"

"There was nothing."

Rellighan nodded. "She's a good housekeeper," he said.

"We went to the cross-roads churchyard. There's a shrine

there now. The beautiful apparition? It might have been Machen."

"The hotel?" Rellighan asked.

"Sommerville's name is on the register."

"And Estel Machen?"

"NO."

There was silence for long moments: only the sound of a rising evening wind. Rellighan said, "We must visit the cemetery again."

"When?"

"Now."

"Why?"

"When you see important shopkeepers of the town gathering to meet at Simoney's. And relatives of dead schoolchildren. And ardent young town councillors. Something is wrong and someone is arranging it. I know this town."

Belle Cannon started the car and drove through the town streets, up the hill by the school and mouldering stone outcrops, and towards the cemetery. It was the last half hour between daylight and nighttime.

Rellighan said, "Drive beyond the cemetery gates and leave the car out of sight."

Coleman ground out a cigarette.

"This will do," Rellighan said.

Belle Cannon parked the car. They walked back to stand hidden behind vaults and monuments. The wind in graveyards must have a special coldness to preserve the dead. There was no escape from it; it spun around every stone tablet of remembrance, vaults and crosses and effigies. They waited.

The dimmed lights of approaching cars was the first movement. Then the pushing open of the gates. Twenty or more people were trooping in, Simoney the leader, Finegan in his wake. They took their places at the graves of James Anthony and Jennifer Anderson. They had picks and shovels.

Coleman stepped out to meet them.

Simoney said, "Stay out of this, Inspector."

"You're a law breaker," Coleman said.

"Not of God's law."

"I could stop you now," Coleman said.

"There would be no crimes like this if our town was in the hands of God-fearing people."

Finegan said, "Or madmen touching the flesh of our schoolchildren."

Rellighan held up a great claw-like hand; he said, "I buried them. Go on, dig for them now."

The pick pierced loose the older grave; the soft earth of today's burial came easily with a shovel. The young men worked. Simoney and Finegan stood in supervision. Only the male relatives of the dead were present. They seemed coerced, quiet in their anger. Rellighan, Belle Cannon and Coleman stood together.

In the fading light behind them the distant yellow glow of the town, the ring and scrape of metal tools, the audience of gravestones, it seemed a contrived frame that should be faced by an army of technicians, lights, cameras, shouts for silence before the commencement of drama.

It seemed to take a long time before there was the scrape of metal on wood; the coffins took shape, the glittering brass plate of today's burial, the older tarnished one.

Simoney ordered, "Uncover the coffin lids, clean them of earth, leave them." He was lowered down into Jennifer Anderson's grave. He made the sign of the cross . . .

Estel Machen's wreath had vanished.

Simoney unscrewed the lid and turned it back, with great reverence, like the cover of the holy bible.

Jennifer Anderson's body slept in peace.

"Close the coffin," Rellighan said.

Simoney was lifted out and lowered into the second grave. His uncertainty was showing. The lid was opened. The body of James Anthony lay there, blackened, shrinking, decomposing, the hair over-grown. Simoney's hands were shaking. He closed the coffin. They pulled him out. There was anger among the relatives, voices raised, a scuffle between peace-makers and belligerents.

"Quiet!" Rellighan said and waited. "Fill those graves carefully and with respect. Remember these are the premises of the dead. In fifty years I've laid an army of bodies here to rest. I don't need stones or inscriptions to tell me. I can walk to their graves even in darkness. The dead are close to us, always with us. Let them rest in peace."

Age had marked Rellighan's face but he stood tall with some ancient presidential authority. Coleman held his peace. Darkness had fallen. Belle Cannon felt a lightening; she was suddenly unburdened. She stood close to Coleman. With Rellighan they walked back to her car and drove the short journey back to town.

They went to Belle Cannon's flat; the town was stirring and alive. Halloween was still in the air. The colour of the town was soothing after a black and white world.

Belle Cannon said, "The bodies? I saw them take the body of Jennifer Anderson from the church. Sommerville was there."

Rellighan was quiet, thoughtful; he said, "Did we shatter only the animal forms that imprisoned spirits? The spirits of James Anthony and Jennifer Anderson out on the rockland last night. But they are free spirits now."

"You shot animals?"'

"James Anthony and Jennifer Anderson."

Coleman said, "Today on the rockland there was nothing."

"They were at rest. We saw them tonight."

"And Sommerville?"

There was silence: sounds from the street, people, traffic, the revving of tired batteries, a living world.

Belle Cannon said, "Take off your coats, throw them any-where. There's drink there, I'll bring food."

An hour later Coleman stood and wrapped up again; he said to Belle Cannon, "I'll leave you in Rellighan's care for a little while. I have calls to make. It might be over."

Rellighan might not have been listening.

She walked with Coleman to the hallway; she tightened his coat, tilted his cap.

"Someone took a load off my shoulders," she said "I feel lighter."

"Yes."

"And you?"

"I feel better," he said.

She kissed him and watched him, in cap and leather coat, stride away towards the Square.

At the appointed time Estel Machen dressed for her visitation of Mr Simoney, at his home. She had donned the flimsiest of underwear, a wrap-around gown with a tie-belt. Her beautiful hair had been drawn high and hidden beneath a peaked dress-cap. She wore a double-breasted loden coat, severe, smart, and high leather boots and a shoulder bag. She was all in black, even her hidden underwear and stockings. She smiled at her reflection in Sommerville's cheval mirror. Black was the colour of funerals and exhumations. She drew on black leather gloves.

Simoney would be in shame. His desecration of graves, his error. He had listened to her. He would be angry.

She walked her slow balanced step past houses, the church and convent, withdrawn, absent, unseeing. This devotion to God generated the kind of respectful fear that placed her beyond the detraction of the town.

The church was in darkness, darker now, as she passed, in the shortness of October's last day. Simoney's floor cleaners and menials would have gone, and he would have moved, head bowed in holiness, touching and moving precious objects, genuflecting, praying to his friend God, holding joined hands at his breast, crying out for forgiveness. He had erred.

Simoney's God was incarcerated in a tabernacle, peering through the keyhole at the faithful who came to visit, the half dozen people in shadowed corners, in meditation, in need of something, afraid of something.

And then there would be the tinkling of his keys, the locking-up. The days of open unguarded churches displaying semi-precious objects and poor-boxes were dead. God's house had to be secured against even his friends.

People would creep away into the night-time nodding their respect to Simoney, wishing him God's blessing from day to day. Some would stay to talk. Simoney would listen, nod. Yes, he would see them, they could bring their troubles to his house. Not today. Today it was the turn of another pilgrim.

She was at his house; she rang his bell. He opened the door on what might be an episcopal hallway: spotless well-worn carpet on polished woodblock, a hallstand with glove-drawer, mirror, drip trays, a chair on each side where pilgrims might rest before confrontation with the presence. Pontiffs and dignitaries, framed on the wall, scrutinised the weary and sad at heart.

Simoney was silent in a deep anger. In a moment she had convinced him of terrible evil in his parish and he had mustered good men to fight a battle. Was it possible to think that she had deceived him, exposed him to ridicule? He looked at her and was shocked at her painted face and lips, her apparel, the sweep of her hair. Everything.

He wore his mask of humility.

Simoney lived here, alone, in an odour of wax polish and sterility, awaiting his callers, hearing almost confessional secrets.

He touched only the fingers, the very tips, and prayed with the afflicted, told them they were better. They had implicit faith in him, they left donations. Simoney was careful.

No word was spoken. He led her along the hallway, in silence. Estel Machen stepped in front of him, halted him; she stood back a pace or two. Her face was infused with beauty. In a single movement she had flung back the coat and wrap-around gown and stood almost naked before him. She pulled his mouth against hers, rubbed her body against him in simulated passion.

In fear, he could feel his body in a grip of pain. He prayed for strength and deliverance.

Estel Machen was a whore, it exploded in his mind. A whore. She had been an image of devotion and faith, giving her services free to the church for all this time and, in moments, she had flaunted this awful suppurating passion. She was a servant of evil. The desecration in the cemetery had been of her making and for his humiliation.

He thought of the faith he had placed in her. Since the convent was in decline, that huge magnificent building peopled by diminishing aged survivors, she had entered their private world. Estel Machen had taken into her charge the care of the sacred linen of the Mass, the altar cloths and towels, restored them to life with her evil. He would burn everything she had touched.

And, of late, the vestments of the celebrant too! Her hands on these precious things! Oh God!

She was evil from the darkness beyond; he would drive her out. He had brought her here to comfort her, to salve her wounds but now he would inflict the punishment of the Lord!

In the hallway he stood and smiled at her, his eyes seemed to soften; said, "Miss Machen, you have two faces."

"Estel," she said. "Public and private."

"To the town, to the churchgoers, you are a dedicated untouchable celibate. In private . . ."

She smiled at him; the beauty of her face and eyes were death; he looked into himself, shut himself away from her. He could feel her wet lips slipping across his, her thighs and groin pushed hard against him. He could feel the trembling of his body.

He said, "You're hungry, aren't you?"

"Yes."

"We don't have to hurry, do we?"

"No."

He guided her to the library where there was a single window. There was no heating; he always prayed and ministered in penitent discomfort. He drew the curtains, switched on a corner table lamp. She went to him again to grind against him and kiss him in a silkiness of saliva. Where he should have been hard and stiff with passion, there was nothing: soft flaccid genitals.

Estel Machen had known that he was an emasculated religion-ridden freak; she had known it before she set eyes on him. The goodness, the peace of mind that humility gave him was his pride. She had ensnared him and he brought her here for healing and purification. Now punishment?

It was Estel Machen's plan, not his.

He said, "Let me change first. I'll only be moments."

Alone, she looked about his surgery of consultation and comforting, perhaps even healing. Distracted minds, in hopelessness, deficiency, perhaps in terror of the God that Simoney preached, would find a chill of response at the touch of his fingers, remembering his thundering orations against the useless clay of humanity in the church, hear his voice now softly pleading to God to free them from their infirmities. The power of healers of soul or body lay in the self-esteem beneath humility; they were inflated in confidence, had woven a web where they might sit and wait.

It was a large room without heat or carpet, a polished wooden floor, well-furnished in the careful low-key style of churchmen; everything was in harmony, the books, the lined curtains, the framed porcelain container of water where one dipped a finger and made the sign of the cross before venturing into a world of temptation and sin.

There was a cassette player. She set it in motion, waited until a gentle music whispered from it. It was perfect. Healing music, so soothing.

The door was opened. Simoney entered wearing a surplice and soutane. Some burning zeal seemed to flush his face. He had hard emotionless eyes for Estel Machen.

211

"Sit down," he said.

"You look so powerful, masterful," she told him.

"Sit."

She obeyed.

"I am a very strong man."

"Spiritually you are impregnable."

"You want me to submit, to drag me into your filthy body. Your filthy flesh."

"I want to love you."

"Oh God!" he said.

"A wave of pleasure," she told him.

There was a solid oak polished chair, without upholstery or cushions, beside him. He bent and gripped the base of a clawed front leg, raised the chair without effort, held it out from his body for perhaps fifteen seconds.

"Strong," 'he said, "In body and mind."

She nodded. "You are strong," she said.

"I could break your arms and legs," he told her.

He slowly lowered the chair., left it in its precise position. He looked across at her sitting figure.

"I believe you could."

He turned off the cassette. "The door is locked," he said. "For consultations and prayer and meditation no sound escapes from my room."

"Restful," she said.

"I'm going to punish you for your corruption. Punishment you will take to the grave with you."

"The grave?"

"Yes," he paused, clasping his hands, it might be in prayer. "I will destroy your already decaying beauty."

"Death?"

"You have exposed the shamelessness of your flesh and, Oh God, soiled me with it. And I will punish myself until the stain has vanished. Penance, penance! But first I will thrash you to death. That face, that body, will be nothing." He held up a heavy thorned club. "Killing you will be my act of reparation."

"Religions make terrifying destruction," she said. "Conversation with you is just a boring response to a litany."

"Your body will be found in the churchyard. You left me without respect in the cemetery today. I will leave you without respect."

"Another mysterious death."

"I will smash your body."

"Let me crawl to death?"

"Yes."

Estel Machen said, "You are beyond suspicion."

"Yes."

"Convenient."

"Stand up," he told her.

Estel Machen stood and gazed at him. He found himself motionless, without power, the blackthorn knobkerrie resting on both hands. Even to call for God's help was impossible. She turned on the whispering music of the cassette and meticulously began to finally undress: shoes, flimsy garments, stockings, underwear. He stood confronted by her nudity, unable to shift his gaze, unable to stir. She sat for half an hour, then moved before him, posturing, miming her love. She took the knobkerrie from his hands, unclothed him of his vestments, to the skin.

"You'll have to postpone your mutilation of me," she said.

She led him like a child to a chair and kissed him on lips. He slipped away into twilight.

It was dark outside. She dressed, took his keys and, with her usual unhurried dignity, retraced her steps across the churchyard to the sacristy door.

The sacristy, the holy dressing room where the celebrant of Mass clothed himself in sacred robes before, at the mensa of the altar, he created flesh and blood from a little cheap wine and a wafer of bread.

God's children of the parish may eat and drink, fortify themselves against the wiles of fallen angels.

Estel Machen laid out the vestments with care, as if to

honour her own sacrifice. She left them there, even, most precious, the pallium, that had been blessed and carried from Rome, a gesture of Papal beneficence. She had worn it.

She looked at the circular band of white wool, its six black crosses, which lay on the shoulders; pendants were weighted, fringed with black silk, and jewelled. A presentation from the Eternal City. Each pallium had been placed on the tomb of Peter in Rome, blessed, and distributed by the Vicar of Christ on Earth.

It was a reminder to Simoney that there were, beyond his allegiance, other powers, other sacrifices.

She left the keys in the door of the sacristy and crossed to the house of Dr H. P. Sommerville.

Coleman was tired, very tired, but he walked quickly through the town streets. The wind still pushed at him. There was brightness and colour. Belle Cannon would be asleep on her sofa five minutes after she had closed her front door. Rellighan, immobile, would be sitting in an easy chair. Rellighan didn't sleep.

Coleman believed it.

At nine o'clock the town was stirring for the last night of holiday carousal and festivity. It was a yellow wind-blown busy town. The time of all saints and all souls. The Celtic cross of the patriots, saints or sinners, was floodlit. Boys and girls sat on the iron balustrade.

Coleman crossed the Square into Demesne Street and saw Sommerville's car parked at his door. Across the broad sweep of street Estel Machen's car sat. When had she driven it last? Its nose was almost intruding on church ground.

He rang at Sommerville's door, waited, and rang again. The paint and brasswork shone.

Estel Machen opened the door. Her gaudery and nakedness of such a short time ago had been discarded like a stage costume. She was in her humble servile role.

Coleman stared at her.

She looked out and up at the darkness. "Really, Inspector, this is an outrageous time to call on Dr Sommerville. He's not available to anyone at this hour."

Coleman knew that she would give him admittance.

He said, "But he is at home?"

"Yes."

"Then I must see him."

"Impossible. He's had a very trying day and retired early. I will most certainly not invade his bedroom for some run of the mill police nonsense."

Coleman stared at her in silence for moments; he said, "Please tell him that Inspector Coleman is waiting. I can wait all night if necessary."

He knew that behind the offended motionless mask she might be smiling at his littleness.

She considered it. "Wait here," she said.

She moved along the hallway and up the carpeted stairway, out of sight. It had been a command. Coleman remembered Sommerville's torn throat and entrails, the blood, flesh, of only a few hours past, out on the desert of stone.

Estel Machen's voice sounded from the landing: no fear, shock, perhaps a trace of concern.

"Inspector Coleman?"

"Yes."

"Would you come upstairs?"

She met Coleman on the landing and led him to Sommerville's bedroom. It was a beautiful room, nothing out of place, it shone with care.

She said, "I'm afraid he's dead."

Sommerville might have been asleep, unmarked, unscathed, in total peace; his mouth was slightly open, his eyes not entirely closed. He was growing cold. He wore pale blue pyjamas with navy piping at collar and cuffs. He might be waking from an afternoon nap.

Coleman said his piece. "Was he feeling unwell today?"

"Dr Sommerville had a heart condition. Sometimes he rested in the afternoons."

She went to his bedside locker, took out two containers of medication.

"He has a private doctor, of course?" Coleman asked.

"Oh yes."

"Call him. Ask him to certify death and make funeral and burial arrangements. Dr Sommerville would hardly want local hands touching him in preparations."

"Certainly not."

Coleman went down the stairs and Estel Machen followed him to the front door.

"Good night," he said.

"Thank you for coming, Inspector. Otherwise I might not have discovered him until morning."

"Yes," Coleman said.

He heard the door shut and walked across through the church enclave. The sacristy was open, the key visible in its lock. It was in darkness. Vestments had been laid out with great care. The sanctuary lamp showed that God was in residence. No one else.

Coleman walked the short distance down to Simoney's and rang his doorbell. He rang a half dozen times. Then he walked round the back. The house seemed without life. With his foot he knocked in a kitchen window. The glass crashed and shattered. He moved through the darkness of the hallway. He found an open door and switched on lights.

Simoney sat in nakedness, sleeping, chin on chest, on a hard wooden chair. He had a great hairy frame. Coleman stood beside him and called his name. There was no flicker of response.

Simoney's clothes were scattered about the floor as if in a moment of breathless passion.

With his open palm Coleman slapped him hard across the cheek.

He stirred. Coleman struck again. When Simoney's

downcast eyes opened they saw at close quarters his thighs and genitals. He sprung up, stood straight as a ramrod. His eyes were in shock. He was breathless.

He cupped his hands over his despised vitals. "Oh God!" he shouted; he was in tears.

Coleman gathered his clothes, helped him into them, smoothed his hair.

"Shut up," Coleman told him. "I've listened to you shouting for ten years. You can *talk* now."

"My good name, my good name, Coleman. I could be a laughing stock. And the church in peril too. And my humiliation in the cemetery this evening . . ."

Coleman said, "The Machen woman, was it?"

"I don't remember much, my thoughts are scattered."

Coleman picked up the thorned knobkerrie. "You wouldn't have done her much damage with this."

"Where is she?"

"You could say she has left us now."

Simoney fell on his knees, raised his face to heaven. "Dear Gentle Saviour, forgive my misjudgements and omissions. I am sorry. I will do penance for them all my days. You tested me and, while didn't fail, I showed my weakness. I was found wanting. Give me strength to face the future. I was dragged down by the smiling face of womankind. Was I wrong to condone punishment to an idiot boy, of wandering mind? Was I in sin? . . ."

Coleman dragged him to his feet. "Who was punished?" he asked. "Raise your voice now, Simoney."

"The madman."

"Who?"

"Colleran."

"Who punished him?"

"I don't know. Finegan was in charge. He came here to my house to ask for permission."

"He came to shut your mouth. Where's Colleran?"

"The hospital."

217

Coleman stared at him. "Your sacristy door is open, Simoney. Vestments are on display."

Simoney was running, in surplice and soutane, on bare feet, across the churchyard. Coleman followed. He heard the dreadful angry wailing. "Her hands, immersed in filth, have touched these garments of God. They must be drenched in blessed water, anointed." Then he saw the pallium; he wept like an infant child.

Coleman let him settle. "Pray gently in future, Simoney," he said.

Simoney said, "I try, I try. Coleman, my good name, my nakedness. You must spare me. Please."

Coleman said, "I never saw you naked."

Simoney's voice, droning in lamentation, followed him as he walked from the church grounds towards the Square.

". . . In those days: All the captains of the warriors came near: and they said to Jeremias the prophet: Pray thou for us to the Lord thy God. And the word of the Lord came to Jeremias. And he called all the captains of the fighting men, and all the people from the least to the greatest. And he said to them: thus saith the Lord God of Israel, to whom you sent me to present your supplications before him . . ."

It was a kind of unhinged babbling foolishness. It faded. Coleman walked across the town to the hospital, walked along the polished corridors. It was a place of quietness.

He found a ward door and looked through the glass port. The door was locked. It was a geriatric ward of ten beds, half of them screened. Colleran's battered face was unmistakable, an arm was suspended in plaster. A walkman sat on his head and he was smiling.

A staff nurse approached Coleman.

"Colleran?" he asked.

"He's fine," she said.

"Good."

"Making progress."

"It's a geriatric ward," Coleman said. "A place for the incurables, the dying."

"A secure ward," she said. "Geriatrics, dementia cases. And a psychiatric ward too." She made a fluttering movement with her hand. "All a little deficient. Lucky we had a bed for him. We'll move him to the County Hospital when he's fit. Very soon."

"The Asylum?"

"The County Hospital."

"When he's fit? To walk?"

"Yes. He arrived in great pain. Bruises, abrasions, a fracture, mild hypothermia. The insane have an immense resistance to hardship. Heat, cold, hunger. They survive. Remarkable."

"Like stray dogs in wintertime?"

"Yes," she said very seriously. "It's a kind of mental retrogression to the animal state."

"You're a psychiatric nurse?" Coleman asked.

She smiled at Coleman; she thought he was handsome. "Well, I'm a general nurse," she said. "But I did a year in psychiatrics." She smiled again. "No smoking," she said.

"Ah," Coleman said with what seemed approval.

He raised a hand and took his leave. He would be seeing this locum tenens at the dispensary and talk to him about confinement. And he would see Finegan now. This town was Colleran's world too; he looked at it through innocent eyes.

Coleman walked back to the Square and, in Demesne Street, saw that Sommerville's door was open. There was a well-dressed tweedy man there.

Coleman said, "My name is Inspector Coleman."

"Dr Bryant," the tweedy man said. "Dr Sommerville's physician. A thrombosis, I'm afraid. Sad. Herbert Sommerville was a good fellow."

"Yes," said Coleman.

"The house is empty. The body has just been removed. And his housekeeper has left."

219

Coleman looked and saw that her car was gone.

"I can leave matters in your hands then?" he said.

"Of course. He was a personal friend."

Coleman looked back and saw the door was being locked. The end of a story, the end of a little dynasty. He walked to Finegan's pub. The cemetery, the digging, the tenanted graves, had chastened Finegan. The habitual drinking coterie was more silent too.

Finegan brought a glass of whiskey and put it before Coleman, leant close to him to whisper, "Have this one on me. We all did our duty, as we thought best, today."

Coleman said in the same confidential tone, "I'm holding you responsible for Colleran. I want him back, free to walk and talk, to stand and smoke. It's his town as much as yours. I'll be watching your progress." Coleman pushed the drink back. "And have a gang of men down to put Rellighan's house in shape. In the morning. You have a lot of gangs. Understood?"

Coleman waited.

"Yes," Finegan said.

"And Dr Sommerville is dead."

Coleman left him in silence, went out on to the sharpness of the street. Belle Cannon was at her door.

"I watched you from the Square," she said. "I waited."

They stood in the hallway together, not talking, remembering, listening to the wind rising up from the estuary.

"It's over," he told her.

"I'm glad you're back, Coleman."

They went upstairs; Rellighan said, "The loose ends are tied."

"Yes."

"And I know Sommerville is dead."

"How?"

"I don't know," Rellighan said. "He died in his own bed."

"Yes, he's gone now. They've taken the remains."

"And the woman is gone?"

Belle Cannon looked at the shape of Coleman, his back to her, looking down on the brightness of Main Street. There was a bottle and a glass on a table beside Rellighan. She brought a glass for Coleman.

J. M. O'NEILL

Open Cut

Hennessy lived in London: grafted, struggled and eked out his days in a London respectable people are careful never to see. A construction site world of 'kerbside sweat, open-cut trenches, timbered shafts'. A bleak, desolate world of whisky-dulled pain, casual brutality and corruption.

But Hennessy planned a change to his station in life. An abrupt and violent change.

"O'Neill's prose, like the winter wind is cutting and sharp." *British Book News*

"An uncannily exacting and accomplished novelist." *Observer*

"Exciting and dangerous, with a touch of the poet." *Sunday Times*

ISBN 0 86322 264 1

Paperback £6.99

Duffy Is Dead

A mournful, funny, warm comedy of Islington-to-Hackney Irish low-life, lovingly set among the streets, shops, pubs and people of London.

"A book written sparingly, with wit and without sentimentality, yet the effect can be like poetry . . . An exceptional novel." *Guardian*

"The atmosphere is indescribable but absolutely right: as if the world of Samuel Beckett had crossed with that of George V. Higgins." *Observer*

ISBN 0 86322 261 7

Paperback £6.99

J. M. O'NEILL

Bennett & Company

Winner of the 1999 Kerry Ingredients Book of the Year award

"O'Neill's world owes something to the sagas of Forsyte and Onedin, and his plotting has, at times, some of the pace and complexity of John Buchan, but the novel is, nonetheless, uniquely Irish with its sanctuary lamps, street-children, moving statues and bitter memories, and it is a contribution to an overdue examination of Irish conscience. The poor and the middle classes are indeed those of Frank McCourt and Kate O'Brien, but O'Neill's is a strictly modern and undeluded vision of the past. The writing is shockingly credible, and the straightforward, crisp narrative style may well engage a larger constituency of those who need to revise their national ethos, now stripped of half a century of self-delusion and dream visions. And the knowing reader suspects the author of revealing too early the corruption at the core of Edward Burke's own dysfunctional family, that too turns out to be part of J. M. O'Neill's gift as a storyteller." *Times Literary Supplement*

"He is an exceptional writer, and one we must take very seriously." *Sunday Independent*

ISBN 1 90201 106 6

Original paperback £7.99